Killer Body

Killer Body

Frank Catanzano

To order additional copies of this book, contact:
Xlibris Corporation
1-888-795-4274
www.Xlibris.com
Orders@Xlibris.com
102931

*To
Mary Diane
Juward Bill
are a good audience
musically
yours
Frankie*

ALSO BY FRANK CATANZANO

Drummer for the Mob

It Just Tastes Better

Acknowledgments

Killer Body took a little over two years to write. During that time, a number of people kindly pitched in to help me produce the very best story possible. Some of them are family, some are journalistic colleagues and others haven't a clue who in the hell I am but were willing to help anyway. To all, I offer my heartfelt thanks.

Let me begin by thanking my wife, Shelly. She has the patience of Job when it comes to me constantly making jokes, running my mouth, telling stories to complete strangers and generally acting like a goofball. She is my lover, best friend, confidant, biggest critic and most enthusiastic supporter. Without her, I probably would have been incarcerated years ago. Shelly was with me every step of the way, even adding her creative suggestions such as the name of Sandy's airline company, and how stylish women dress and present themselves in various circumstances. When it comes to what I know about how women think and what they wear I, like most men, am clueless. I don't know a sling back from a wing back.

Next, I owe a huge thank you to our daughter, Alexis, who teaches middle school in Raleigh, NC. The fact that she lives along a golf course made my editorial journeys stimulating. She read every word of the manuscript as it took shape, making suggestions and correcting my innate ability to screw up names and relationships from one chapter to the next. Alexis, you were a life saver.

And I can't forget our son, Jon, who is my unofficial publicist and supreme promoter. He was responsible for creating national buzz about my first novel, *Drummer for the Mob*, and single handedly making it a must-read among half the student population at the University of Tennessee.

A public relations client of mine, Corporate Investigations and its effervescent leader, Adrienne Taucher, provided solid background on FBI profiling, serial killers and the various ways the bureau investigates such crimes. I also would like to thank a fellow writer and client, Kevin Brown at Weirton Medical Center, for his encouragement and our discussions on giving 'voice' to our respective novels.

When it came to all things related to commercial aviation and the myriad duties performed by flight attendants, I am indebted to Marylu Zuk, a former flight attendant with American West Airlines. She was thorough and helped me accurately portray what flight attendants do to serve and protect passengers in the air. A 25-year veteran of USAir, senior flight attendant Jan Adams was also helpful, particularly when it came to understanding what a senior flight attendant actually does.

A note of appreciation to my brother, Robert. Always a supporter, he made thoughtful suggestions and his entertaining conversation and far left slant on life kept me thinking. I would also like to thank Pittsburgh author and fellow golfer, Karl Skutski, for his input and advice and Tara Hill Conroy for her editing skills. A final thank you to the folks at Xlibris, who stayed on top of me to get the book done in our lifetime. If I missed anyone, they will understand that I didn't omit them on purpose. Because, as is my standard response when I am questioned as to why I didn't do what I was supposed to do, "I forgot."

Frank Catanzano
July 18, 2011

To her shock, she realized she was being choked. She twisted around and saw the woman with a piece of yellow nylon rope in her hand. The rope was knotted; she was tightening it to cut off her air supply. The blonde's eyes were "penetrating, cold-blooded steel."

Katherine Ramsland
Addicted to Luxury: The Pampered Killer

Lizzie Borden took an axe
And gave her father forty whacks.
When she saw what she had done
She gave her mother forty-one.

Skipping-Rope Rhyme
1892

Chapter One

2008

Odyssey Airlines flight 243 from Michigan was setting up for its final approach on Runway 09L at Miami International Airport.

"Ladies and Gentlemen, this is Captain Ron Campbell from the flight deck," the resonant voice announced over the audio system. "We've been cleared for our final approach into Miami International. The temperature is a balmy 82 degrees with broken clouds and five miles visibility. We should have you on the ground in about 15 minutes. On behalf of the entire flight crew, I would like to thank you for choosing Odyssey Airlines today, and we hope to have the opportunity to serve you in the future."

The flaps generated a high-pitched whirring sound as they initiated their forward progress toward full extension. The Odyssey flight attendants began making their pre-landing check to ensure tray tables were stowed, seat backs were fully upright and an impatient passenger wasn't standing up in an attempt to get a three second head start on retrieving luggage from the overhead bins.

Senior flight attendant Sandy Garland carefully made her final check on the remaining 16 rows in the Boeing 757-200 and every pair of male eyes was glued to various spots on her voluptuous body. And a few pair of female eyes.

Sandy Garland was 28 years old and strikingly beautiful, with a mass of blonde hair that curled around a perfectly oval face, framing the palest blue, almost translucent, eyes. They expressed an acute level of intelligence that made many people uncomfortable, as she had a habit of staring, unblinking, as they spoke to her. They seemed to be peering down into the private recesses of their souls, where they stored their most intimate secrets. Sandy could quiet an unruly passenger just with her stare.

Sandy's workout regime kept her in peak condition, with a set of abdominal muscles that look like they were sculptured by Leonardo Da Vinci. They rippled beneath a pair of perfect breasts that were works of art, full and round, with tiny areolas that accentuated their fullness.

At five foot eleven inches, Sandy's most outstanding attributes were her legs. Years of studying martial arts and strenuous exercise created a pair of shapely legs of perfect proportion, with quads and glutes that looked like they were forged of cast high alloy steel. As physical appearances go, Sandy Garland, who could give a cadaver an erection, was flawless.

"Excuse me sir," she said to the corpulent passenger squeezed into 21A. "Please bring your seat forward." She noticed the seat belt extender pressing into his gargantuan belly.

"No problem," 21A replied, as he stared directly into her jutting breasts, which were tightly encased in the blue and white uniform of Odyssey Airlines. Sandy could sense the lascivious grinding of the internal gears of his id, as his subconscious replayed the scene he experienced as a child, when he accidentally saw his mother changing in the bathroom, door slightly ajar. It was the image of her pendulous breasts swaying as she struggled into a pair of slacks that was permanently branded into his mind, initiating a life-long fascination with women's breasts, or "jugs" as he referred to them. He would have gladly donated a left testicle just for a glimpse of Sandy's heavenly orbs. She knew it, too.

"May I take that empty cup?" Sandy asked, as she nodded toward the styrofoam cup perched on the vacant seat next to 21A. He could barely bring himself to tear his eyes from her chest.

"Uh, what, oh yeah," he mumbled as he grabbed the cup and dropped it into the plastic bag Sandy held open for him. His piggy eyes gravitated back to her chest. Smiling, she continued on.

A lanky, well-dressed executive type in 17C held up an empty bag of peanuts and his crumpled napkin. Smirking, his words leaking oil, he said, "Hey, babe, have any plans tonight in Miami? I know a fab Italian bistro where we could break bread and get to know each other."

Sandy paused for a moment as he discharged his refuse and looked down onto him with her translucent eyes, a smile fixed onto her face. Lanky executive grew uneasy as her stare lasted a tad too long, and while she was smiling, her whole demeanor assumed a menacing posture. Then she broke the spell.

"Thanks, but I have plans."

"Why don't you consider breaking them, and take me up on my offer," 17C said, undaunted by Sandy's apparent disinterest.

Ignoring him, Sandy, customer-service smile back in place, moved onto the next row of seats, collecting empty cups and reciting the mantra "please bring your seat to a fully upright position" as she continued her due diligence. The passenger in 17C stared intently at her perfectly round ass which was accented by her form-fitting skirt, a pornographic film starring Sandy and him taking shape in his mind.

As the aircraft began its descent into Miami, Sandy made a final pass through the cabin, stopping only a brief moment at 17C, surreptitiously handing the business executive a small folded piece of paper. None of the passengers, who were busily gathering up belongings or tending to fussy, whiny children, noticed the exchange.

As Sandy Garland buckled herself into the aft jump seat, she couldn't help but smile as 17C unfolded the note.

I'm staying at the Embassy Suites at the airport. Call my cell 201-466-4763 at 7 pm.

Gina

Roy Stellini couldn't believe his luck as he gazed at the note in his hand. This gorgeous woman would be his date tonight, setting up a perfect prelude to that boring sales meeting he was scheduled to attend tomorrow in a cloistered conference room in the Doubletree Grand on Biscayne Bay. As he began planning the evening's entertainment, with the denouement being a round of sweaty sex back in his room at the hotel, the beginnings of an erection began filling out his bikini briefs.

A sales associate for Wonderland Nutritional Products, Roy Stellini knew that his Tuesday morning sales meeting at the Doubletree would not be a pleasant one. Wonderland's owner, Jeff Strohman, a hulking former bodybuilder, was in a perpetual 'roid rage.' With sales trending downward, the fucking gorilla would be in one of his black moods and the meeting, which brought together the twenty regional sales associates from across the country, could get ugly. Thank God he'd at least have the pleasure of Gina's company tonight as well as the promise of exploring her absolutely exquisite body.

Stellini joined the line of disembarking passengers, who filed past members of the cabin crew, who perkily chanted "thank you" to each one. As he approached Sandy, he couldn't help but smirk as they locked eyes. As Sandy said, "Thanks and have a great day," Roy caught something cold and ominous in her blue eyes that rattled him momentarily, but he quickly shrugged off the feeling as he stepped into the humid air of the jetway leading to the terminal. She probably caught a ration of shit from a passenger and wasn't in the mood to flirt. Once the Stellini charm washed over his new friend, Gina, she'd be helpless to resist the Italian Stallion, the nickname he adopted for himself from Sylvester Stallone and one of his favorite movies, *Rocky*. Roy couldn't help but grin, as Rocky's slurred voice echoed in his mind. Yo, Gina, I'm gonna screw youse every which way from Friday. Fagedabodit!

At his hotel and unpacked, Stellini made a perfunctory phone call to his wife, Estelle, back in Grand Rapids to assure her that he arrived safely in Miami, and a "Yes dear, I'll be sure to be careful and no, dear, I won't let Strohman get to me." That juiced up, muscle head asshole, he thought.

Glancing at the clock, willing it to be 7 pm, Roy unlocked the service bar and poured himself a bourbon neat. This was going to be a 100mg Viagra night, he thought, as he washed the blue triangular tab down with a little help from his best friend, Jack Daniels. The Italian Stallion wanted to have a rod of steel tonight that would have the comely Gina screaming for mercy and for more.

Sandy Garland was in the middle of a set of push ups when her cell phone rang. She glanced at the clock. It was 7 pm and she knew that 17C was just dying to get into her panties. Wrapping a towel around her neck, Sandy grabbed her cell.

"Hello," she said carefully as if protecting herself against stalkers. She smiled at the thought of some dickhead actually stalking her.

"Gina, this is Roy, the passenger on the flight today. I had invited you to dinner this evening."

"Oh, hello, Roy, I remember you." You dumb fuck, I gave you my cell number of a phone she found left behind in the seat pocket on one of her flights. Of course, I remember you, she thought.

"Listen, Gina, I mentioned this great Italian place I know here in Miami," Roy said. "How about I pick you up at your hotel about 8:30?"

After a brief silence, Sandy responded, "That's fine Roy . . . uh?"

"Roy Stellini," he said. What the hell, no one in Miami knows who I am, he thought. And Estelle has no clue as to what her boy's going to be up to tonight.

"OK, Roy, after dinner I thought we'd go to a private club that I know that's in the area. You're going to love it. I'll be waiting outside the hotel since it's a lovely night."

"Hey, that's great," Roy said brightly. "See you at 8:30." Stellini hung up the phone, feeling as if he just won the lottery. I'm gonna bang this broad until her blue eyes are crossed, he thought. Then I'm gonna keep banging her until she sees straight. He laughed aloud at the old Stellini wit.

In the hotel gym, Sandy was completing her ten sets of one hundred pushups on her knuckles. She then began ten sets of one hundred crunches, which contributed largely to her sculpted abs. Her workouts at the dojo were legendary. No one in the Isshin-ryu School of Karate back in Pittsburgh could even approximate the intensity of her routines or the speed of her kicks and punches during kumite or sparring. Most referred to her as the 'freak.' Behind her back, of course. A sixth degree black belt, when Sandy was scheduled to lead a class, there were few recruits that day. Most couldn't endure the hundreds of painful reps of side kicks, front kicks, upper cuts and other strikes that Sandy would dictate as she pushed the small group of students to its absolute limits. Even the advanced belts suddenly had other matters to attend to when Sandy stepped in front of the class and bowed.

After her regular routine of punches and kicks, Sandy went back to her room and stepped into the shower to get ready for 17C, who was probably ejaculating in his pants at the thought of holding her body tonight. As she dried off, she stared into the mirror and liked what she saw: a perfect machine, tempered by thousands of hours of blood and sweat in the dojo and miles of running.

She was in peak performance. Few black belts, man or woman, lasted more than a minute or so during kumite with her. She was just too fast, too strong, and above all, too willing.

She walked toward the full length mirror on the bathroom door and held her own gaze for a few minutes, never blinking. Slowly pressing her naked body against the glass, her large breasts compacted, Sandy began to make love to herself. She moved in unison with her reflection, slowly at first and then faster and faster. Sandy suddenly shuddered violently, achieving a delicious orgasm. Now I'm ready for Mr. Smooth Talker, she thought.

Sandy was waiting outside the hotel when Stellini pulled up. He was surprised to see that she was wearing a jet black wig, but he liked it. It made her look a little like Melanie Griffith in *Something Wild*.

"Hey babe, how ya doing," he smarmed. "I like the look."

She smiled as she entered his rented Ford Focus. "Take me away, lover," Sandy replied. "After dinner, I have a special treat for you." Stellini nearly ejaculated as she pressed as close to him as the center console would allow.

*   *   *

As Roy was tossing down his third after-dinner Irish Mist, Sandy filled him in on upcoming events for the evening. "Are you familiar with 'swinging'?" she asked Roy, her expression sincere and informative, as if she were lecturing to an adult education class.

"I've talked to my wife about trying it a couple times, but she won't hear of it. She's a nun . . . none of this and none of that." He laughed at his own lame attempt at humor. Sandy merely smiled, thinking what a schmuk this guy was.

"There's a place called 'Brandy's Hideaway,' about five miles away, where adults who are into swapping partners meet on weekends," she said. "Let's go have some fun."

If an erection was a compass, Stellini's would have been pointing true north. He couldn't believe his good fortune in crossing paths with this gorgeous woman. She literally had a body to die for.

An hour later Sandy and Roy pulled into Brandy's expansive gravel parking lot. The private club was housed in a nondescript gray building with no windows. White lights were strung along the roof line and around the entrance, giving it some semblance of a festive aura. They approached the front desk, attended by an effete young man sporting gold earrings and a long seventies type shag.

"That'll be $50 for both of you, but that includes the buffet," he recited. "If you go into the orgy room or any of the common areas, you must be undressed. Remember, if someone turns you down, no means no." As he handed over locker keys, Roy noticed that Gina looked a little shy, keeping her gaze averted, which seemed out of character for her, but he had just met her.

As they were undressing, Gina suggested that they head immediately into the orgy room and just checkout who was in the club for the evening. She advised that there were usually some jerks and fatties they needed to avoid at all costs. As she counseled Stellini, he looked at Sandy, mesmerized by her naked, voluptuous body. She could have been reciting the Magna Carta for all he knew or cared.

It was very dark in the orgy room, which measured about forty feet by twenty five feet and was bare, except for mattresses that covered every inch of the floor. Euro industrial disco pounded from speakers built into the ceiling. Barely perceptible naked bodies were writhing together in two's, three's and other combinations; men with women, women with women and even two guys together. The various decibels of moans mixing with the chest thumping music made the scene seem surreal, as if it was a human enactment of Bosch's painting, "The Garden of Earthly Delights."

As they entered, Gina quickly became a magnet for both sexes, as they jockeyed for position to speak to her. She suddenly saw Anne Claridge, a woman with whom she once had a torrid relationship, but the bitch broke it off when she met some hooker who worked for a Miami escort service. Sandy promised herself that she'd get even with her no matter how long it took. And now, opportunity was knocking. Anne was a slender but curvy brunette with a deep tan and a perfect ass. Sandy approached her.

"Hey Anne, long time no see," she said, out of earshot of Stellini.

"Sandy, wow, you look great," Claridge replied. "Who's the guy?"

"Some dickless wonder who came onto me on the flight in. I'm just having some fun with him. Speaking of, why don't you and I get it on for old time's sake?"

"That would be great. Why don't we try and grab one of the private rooms?" Claridge suggested.

After a few moments, Gina walked back over to Stellini and told him that they and their new friend, Anne, were going to retire to a small private room for a threesome. Stellini pinched the inside of his elbow to determine whether he was dreaming as he slept back at the hotel, or possibly he had passed away and was in transit down to the nether regions. He wouldn't have been surprised if Lucifer himself showed up just as he was beginning to have sex with one of these beauties to tell him time's up. The devil would then assign him to spend eternity working in Hell's laundry or shoveling shit in his personal stables.

One of the unoccupied rooms they entered was much like the main room, mattresses covering the floor of the tiny but private space. Gina and Anne wasted little time as they began to slowly explore each other's bodies. Stellini stood watching, mouth agape and penis at attention. He looked like he was carrying the flag in the school parade.

In a few minutes, Gina looked over and seductively said, "Care to join us, Roy?" Not waiting for a second invitation, Stellini tried to slide in between the women. That's when something happened so quickly, that his mind couldn't process what was occurring until it was too late. With no wasted movement, Gina grabbed each side of Anne's head snapped her pretty long neck, the sickening crack muffled by the loud music and moans in the main room. Before Stellini could even react, Gina struck him with an open hand directly to his throat. Another crack, louder this time, as the force and speed of her blow crushed his larynx and the protective cartilage surrounding it. Wide eyed, unable to speak, Roy Stellini fell onto his back and slowly suffocated to death. Thoughts of not being able to attend the sales meeting in the morning were the final ones processed by his oxygen-starved brain.

Sandy, unnoticed by the growing throng of naked bodies crowding the orgy room, made her way back to the lockers, dressed and was out the door in less than five minutes. The cabbie dropped her off at her hotel, and she paid him without looking directly into his face. Although he would never be able to describe the woman with black hair who caught his cab at 3 am at Brandy's, it was a moot point. The cabbie was never identified or questioned.

Chapter Two

Detective John Gonzalez's cell chirped at 3:37 am. Oh shit, he thought as he grabbed the phone from his night stand and flipped it open. He had barely fallen asleep after a raucous night at South Beach.

"Gonzalez," he said in a hoarse whisper into the phone.

"Sarge," the voice replied. "We've got a double homicide at some private sex club over in North Bay," Detective Roland Wiggins said. "I'll pick you up in fifteen." The phone went dead.

John Gonzalez slowly began unfolding himself from the bed in which he had only flopped into a scant fifteen minutes earlier. A ten-year veteran of Miami Police Department's Homicide Division, Gonzalez had seen just about every type of murder and mayhem that can be inflicted by one human being upon another. He and his investigative team had been summoned to the bloody aftermaths of drive-bys, decapitations, assassinations, gangbang slaughters, torture and rape of children, bombings and just about every form of homicide some demented, anti-social human could conjure up in his or her twisted psyche.

A strikingly handsome man with the Latino light brown eyes and thick head of dark, curly hair, Gonzalez stood 6 feet 3 inches and had a chiseled body honed from hours in a nearby gym. There he held the bench press record of 465 pounds, and he routinely required two pairs of spotters to handle such weight during his bench press workout.

Never married, the 35-year-old detective was vain about his looks and physical conditioning, and it paid off. Gonzalez was popular with the ladies and seldom was seen without a beautiful woman on his arm. His sexual exploits were legion and legendary around the homicide unit.

Gonzalez led an investigative squad comprised of five detectives, who would bust ass around the clock on homicides, pounding the pavement to interview potential witnesses, tracking leads, following up on the background of the victims and all the myriad details necessary to solve a case. It wasn't glamorous, as portrayed on television, but it required an inordinate amount of grunt work,—and determination, mixed with a little luck to catch the bad guys. Gonzalez's team members were highly dedicated, both to their jobs and to Gonzalez. A natural leader, his men genuinely liked and respected him, and on his end, he would literally lay his life down for a brother detective. In turn, they were fiercely loyal to him.

Wiggins rapped on his apartment door and was admitted by a fatigued, over-served Gonzalez. "Sarge, you look like you were rode hard and put away wet," he said, with a grin.

"Screw you, Wiggins. I was out on assignment until early this morning," Gonzalez replied.

"Right, that assignment was probably 25 years old with a body that wouldn't quit. Don't bullshit a bullshitter." Both men laughed.

The early morning drive through Miami was quiet as the detectives sipped on coffee they picked up at a Starbucks on the way. "What do you have on this case so far?" asked Gonzalez.

"A man and a woman were discovered around 3 am this morning dead and naked in a private room at Brandy's Hideaway, an adult swing club over in Biscayne."

"Miami PD has worn a path to that place answering nuisance calls," Gonzalez said.

"The information I have on the scene," Wiggins continued, "was that the woman's neck was broken and the guy's larynx was crushed. Obviously, they didn't attack each other, so the early speculation is that there was a third party in the room having, as they call it, a ménage a trois. I don't know, jealous husband who ultimately couldn't stand to see his wife having sex with a stranger? They're checking the lockers to find identification."

"Has the crime scene been locked down?" Gonzalez asked.

"Yea, it's secure and a whole bunch of pissed off naked swingers are being questioned. Of course, we allowed them to get their clothes back on. In some cases, that was the best course of action, given their poor physical conditioning and eating habits, if you get my meaning."

"Yea, I'm sure that many of these cabrons look a whole hell of a lot better in the dark," Gonzalez replied.

Wiggins' unmarked pulled through Brandy's ornate gate onto a gravel drive. The parking lot was filled with Jags, Beemers, Corvettes and an occasional SUV, as well as police units and vehicles from the Medical Examiner's office. Emergency roof rack lights sprayed red and blue pulsating colors across the other vehicles. A blue-orange sky was just brightening over a still-sleeping Miami as investigators were descending upon at Brandy's. They didn't look like they were in the mood to party.

Stu Jenkins, a hulking Miami PD field operations officer, stood sentry at the entrance, checking credentials for those who wanted to be admitted. He brandished a long black flashlight, which he often used as a baton or what he called a 'persuader,' on the skulls of recalcitrant bad boys.

"Stu, what's up?" asked Wiggins as he and Gonzalez flashed their badges.

"Nothing good," Jenkins replied, grumpily. "My shift was just about over, and I had visions of a Bacardi and Coke and a warm bed dancing in my head. Then, bang, I get this fuckin' lock-down assignment at a sex club. Bunch of perverts crowded into the place. Christ, it looks like the bar scene from *Star Wars*." The detectives laughed.

"Look on the bright side," Gonzalez said with a smirk. "You could have been inside the place with your dick sticking out instead of that baton of yours when the PD showed up. You wife would have said, 'You got a lot of 's'plaining to do."

"You got that right," Jenkins replied. "Melissa would have been interested in the description of my 'under cover' assignment."

The club was buzzing with Miami Crime Scene Investigation officials, including Miami-Dade ME Patricia Solez, a petite, attractive woman known for her expertise and famous for her dark sense of humor. Gonzalez recalls one time walking into the pathology lab, only to find Solez eating a sandwich while she was performing an autopsy. As she hummed, she grabbed a Diet Coke that was balanced on the cadaver's chest. While she was a gifted pathologist, Solez didn't stand on ceremony, but her expertise kept her beyond reproach and her forensics were deadly accurate.

The CSI team was crowded carefully in the small room, taking photos, dusting for prints and performing the myriad tasks that will begin to paint a picture of what might have happened. After putting on shoe covers, Gonzalez and Wiggins stepped gingerly through the door. They were greeted with a man and a woman, both naked, sprawled nearly cheek to cheek, their eyes open and staring vacantly.

"Patty, what have you got so far?" Gonzalez asked, carefully bending down to get a closer look.

"I have one white female and one white male, very fucking dead," Solez deadpanned. The photographer laughed loudly once, sounding like a pig's snort.

"Talk about rough sex," Wiggins noted as he entered facts into his notebook.

"It looks like whoever killed these two did it about as efficiently as I have ever seen it done," Solez explained, pointing to the male. "He probably punched the man in the throat first. He knew exactly where to strike."

"Trained, as in Green Beret or Navy Seal?" Gonzalez asked.

"Possibly, or someone just brutally savaged them during a fit of rage," she replied. "Jealous husband might have followed her and watched her retreat to this private room with the dead guy there. Just slipped in and struck him in the throat as he was having sex with his wife or girlfriend and then grabbed her and snapped her neck like a piece of kindling. We'll get a clearer picture of what happened during autopsy. One thing is for sure, the guy who did this is quick and powerful."

"Why do you say that?" Wiggins asked.

"It isn't easy to crush a person's larynx with just your hand, given the protective cartilage surrounding it. And look at the woman's head. It's twisted nearly 180 degrees. Like I said, this dude is strong."

Gonzalez was gazing closely at a tiny black fiber caught under the woman's leg. Peering at it with his penlight, he extracted tweezers and picked it up carefully. "Looks like a black hair," he announced. "It's probably synthetic, from a wig. Give it to one of the lab techs for analysis. It's not the same shade as the dead woman's. It might have come from the killer."

Wiggins took the small plastic bag from Gonzalez. "Problem is, Sarge, that this place is wall-to-wall every night with naked bodies of all shapes, sizes, colors and sexual proclivities. Many of these pervs wear wigs. That hair could have gotten left there by a midget car salesman from Iowa."

"Or a gay swineherd from Tibet," Solez cheerfully added.

That retort elicited another loud snort from the photographer. Solez seemed pleased to have an appreciative audience, albeit the lone camera guy.

"Let's start questioning that motley bunch of sex fiends we have on ice," Gonzalez said. "Somebody must have seen something."

Gonzalez and Wiggins made their way over to the main lounge area, where a large gathering of people in various stages of undress was huddled, under the watchful eyes of Miami PD officers. One particular pair of eyes was laser intense as an officer stared at a woman's breasts as they struggled to break free from the tight red bustier she was wearing. The detectives' entrance snapped the police officers to attention and drew looks of contempt from the eclectic assemblage of swingers.

"How long yuse gonna keep us heh?" asked one skinny bespectacled guy in a nasally New Jersey accent. He was naked save for a pair of running shorts and a black toupee perched upon his pate, which resembled flattened crow along a roadside. Gonzalez couldn't help but think this guy couldn't have gotten laid in a women's prison with a handful of pardons. It takes all kinds, he mused.

"Long as it takes, partner," replied Wiggins. His response drew a collective groan from the group.

"Officer, there's no law against sex among consenting adults," opined a zaftig blonde with a colorful tattoo of Marilyn Monroe adorning her right forearm, accompanied by various other illustrations on her shoulder and back. A tattoo of a giraffe on one sagging breast might have at one time been a horse.

"'Madam, we are investigating a homicide," Gonzalez said, which elicited yet another rumble of nervous conversation among the group. "Our officers will be taking statements from each of you, so we would appreciate your complete cooperation and patience."

Miami homicide detectives had set up an interview post in one of the club's private rooms and were systematically ushering in members of the crowd to get their statements and to try and ascertain what they may have seen, no matter how trivial.

One voluptuous, nearly naked woman seemed to remember seeing a drop dead gorgeous brunette with a man who looked unfamiliar with the club and its sexual machinations. "She had a gorgeous body," the woman recalled. "I mean this babe was solid muscle with the curves in places where most of us don't have places. I didn't get a good look at the guy she was with. My eyes were elsewhere," she said with a grin.

No other interviewees remembered seeing anything out of the ordinary. For a sex club, that is. The women were too busy having orgasms, and the men were focused on keeping it up and sticking into unoccupied orifices. The detectives learned that swingers who frequented these clubs tended to remain discreet in their interactions with other participants for fear of running into a friend or acquaintance, which could put a crimp in their evening's entertainment.

"None of these fuzz-nuts saw nothing," detective Joe Handly reported to Gonzalez, open notebook poised for quick reference. "They were all too busy licking and screwing each other." Handly was a veteran of Miami PD's vice units; a Neanderthal who was a throwback to the period preceding 'political correctness,' when men were men, women were the weaker sex and gays were fags. But he was a great detective, with a book full of citations for bravery and righteous collars. He was untouchable, the department's answer to Dirty Harry.

"How could some guy sneak in here and kill two people with his bare hands and sneak out without anyone seeing him?" asked Gonzalez rhetorically, chewing on the tip of his pencil. His cell buzzed again.

"Gonzalez," he announced impatiently. His face assumed an expression of concentration, as he listened to the caller. "Jesus Christ, what the hell would a fuckin' vitamin salesman from Grand Rapids be doing at this club?" he asked. "You have an ID on the woman?" Again, Gonzalez listened intently, writing quickly in his pocket notebook. "Anne Claridge, an unmarried financial planner from Coconut Grove. OK, get to her place quick and you have vitamin man's room key at the Doubletree. Toss it before maid service gets there. I want to know what plans they both were making for this evening, who they may have spoken to, did they put anything on a calendar? A name, phone number, anything that can tie these two together. The smallest piece of information could be very helpful in an investigation."

Gonzalez snapped his cell shut and looked at Wiggins. "CSI found his pants in a locker here," he reported. "They got his room key, cell phone and a small slip of paper with a number of a phone that had recently been reported lost or stolen by its owner, one Reverend Horace Green, a minister at the First Baptist Church in Hackensack, New Jersey. Reverend Green was an unlikely candidate to be Anne Claridge's lover or a habitué of Brandy's. And did Claridge sign her name as Gina on the note?" he said, talking mainly to himself. "What the hell is going on?" Gonzalez asked in frustration.

"Sarge, we've got two dead bodies of people who didn't seem to know each other, which is common for these types of clubs," Wiggins said. "Somehow some guy slips in, tosses his clothes, figures out in what private cubicle his 'squeeze' is in playing hide the salami with Mr. Vitamin, kills them both with his bare hands without either of them making a peep and then disappears like this week's paycheck. Nobody knows nothing, nobody sees nothing. There's not much to go on with this one."

"Let's go check in with Solez and see what she's been able to learn," Gonzalez ordered. The two homicide detectives joined the exodus of weary swingers as they made their way from Brandy's in Miami's early morning heat and humidity, which already was clamping the city in its sweaty palms.

*   *   *

As the detectives entered the spacious Morgue Bureau beneath the Toxicology Lab at Miami PD headquarters on NW 2nd Avenue, the cool air was a welcome respite from the increasing heat. Solez was already hard at work at an autopsy station, accompanied by a forensic tech. She looked up at Gonzalez as he and Wiggins approached.

"Well if it ain't Toody and Muldoon," Solez said, referring to the old sitcom *Car 54, Where Are You?* Her assistant, Bobby Fong, guffawed. "You two taking a break from Dunkin' Doughnuts?" she asked.

"Funny, Solez," replied Gonzalez. And then in Spanish, "¿Usted tiene algo para nosotros o usted acaba jugar con ustedes?" Roughly translated: You have anything for us, or you just playing with yourself?

"No baloney slicing here, jefe," Solez said. With that she brought the oscillating saw to life and began expertly cutting into vitamin man's skull, as bits of bone and flesh sprayed onto her gloves and protective glasses. Once the skull cap was removed and the membrane connecting the brain to the spinal cord was severed with a scalpel, the ME removed the brain for examination.

"Well look here," she announced as she carefully extracted something from the layers of matter in the deceased man's brain. "Two tickets to Sunday's Dolphins game! And they're 50-yard line seats!" Solez and Fong laughed uproariously, then quickly settled back to business, when her wit failed to elicit any reaction from the fatigued Gonzalez and Wiggins.

"No evidence of trauma to the brain," she pronounced. "But this guy's larynx was completely crushed, which led to rapid asphyxiation." Solez pointed to the body, "You can see here that major injuries to the hyoid bone and epiglottal caused airway obstruction. In short, somebody popped this guy's throat perfectly, causing instant suffocation," she explained. "And that ain't easy to do because surrounding bony structures protect the larynx from injury. It takes a strong blow precisely to the weakest point to actually crush the cartilage," she said.

"This guy knew what he was doing," Gonzalez offered. "Maybe he was trained in martial arts or karate. Or he just got lucky."

"I don't think there was any luck involved," Solez replied. "The woman's neck was snapped by an expert, using the right combination of force and speed to rotate her head, completely severing her spinal cord, killing her instantly. And this is no small woman we're looking at here."

As the detectives were leaving the lab, Gonzalez said, "We got some spurned lover, trained in karate or who may have served in special forces. The guy could have followed the woman to the sex club, caught her in a private sex room and efficiently killed her and her lover, using only his hands."

"We can rule out Bruce Lee for sure," Wiggins deadpanned.

Gonzalez snapped open his phone as it rang. "Gonzalez." He listened intently for a minute. "You're certain? OK, I want to talk to her."

He looked at Wiggins as they reached the car. "Claridge was gay," he said. "We've located her significant other, a woman named Liz Tomkin, and she's identified the body. Yet another piece of information that makes no fuckin' sense. Why would she be at a sex club without Tomkin? Let's go and question her, and see what she has to say. More importantly, let's find out if Ms. Tomkin is a karate expert."

Chapter Three

A feeding frenzy erupted among the Miami media. The Herald's headline dubbed the killings "The Swinging Sex Club Murders" and reported the sordid details with enthusiasm. Its Spanish sister paper, *El Nuevo Herald*, quoted Detective John Gonzalez saying, "El Miami Homicid Oficina tiene un número de clientes potenciales y está trabajando diligentemente para encontrar al asesino." WFOR-TV's chief investigative reporter, Shelly McVeigh, announced details that the other media didn't have, including that, according to a reliable source in the Miami PD, the woman was a Miami resident and lover of Liz Tomkin, a professional escort who lived in the city's upscale Coconut Grove.

Gonzalez was furious at some of the details of the case that were revealed by the news media. "This is going to make our job more difficult," he announced to his team on Monday morning. "If I ever get my hands on this so-called 'reliable source' in our department, he . . . or she . . . is history.

"This McVeigh woman at Channel 4 is a pain in the ass, and I don't want her anywhere near me. And I don't want anyone on my team talking to her, period. Entiende usted? Now let's hit the streets and get to work. Brace your usual informants to find out if they've caught any rumble about the murders. Do they know a guy who has the skill and power to kill like that? Has anyone at Brandy's caused a problem in the past? Canvas the local karate schools and find out if someone there has the skill to kill like that. Wiggins and I have a date with Ms. Tomkin, and I'd like to get to her before McVeigh does, so vamos a pasar!" Gonzalez ordered.

Liz Tomkin lived in Miami's trendy Coconut Grove. The neighborhood, referred to by the locals as the Grove, is a veritable open-air food court, crowded with outdoor cafes and bistros offering up food of every nationality. Throngs of tourists promenade daily along its tree-lined streets, taking in the sights and scents of flowers of every variety and color, set against the backdrop of sailboats gently swaying in the bay.

Pelicans can be seen diving headfirst into the clear blue coastal waters to snatch unsuspecting fish. Local pickpockets, predators of the human variety, are not as easily spotted, dipping their fingers into a clueless visitor's pocket to relieve him of a wallet or money clip. It was just another day in paradise.

Tomkin lived in a high rise apartment on Southwest 27th Avenue with a panoramic view of Sailboat Bay. A criminal history background check on her revealed that she had a few prior arrests for prostitution but was never a street hooker; she normally worked out of high-priced escort services. No record of drug use indicated that she was probably a professional using her body as means to build a retirement fund and not as a vessel for heroin and crack cocaine, like most of the hookers in Miami.

Gonzalez and Wiggins took the elevator to the 15th floor and made their way to Apartment 15B. After a series of knocks, each growing slightly in intensity, a woman's voice called, "Who is it, please?"

"Miami police, Ms. Tomkin," replied Gonzalez. With those words, the door opened slightly, a chain lock still in place. Liz Tomkin peered suspiciously at the two detectives.

"Please show me your credentials." Both Gonzalez and Wiggins held their gold shields in front of them. The door's chain was unfastened.

"Come in," she said, as she wheeled and walked through the foyer, leading them into the apartment, which was exquisitely decorated in a stark white, minimalist style décor. A few expensive pieces of furniture accented the sparse landscape of the main room, which were set against the cool white and teal colors of the walls. Everything was form and function in the open, cheery room.

"You're here about Anne, right?' she asked as they entered the main room. "Please sit down. Can I get you some coffee?" Her demeanor was controlled, as it was when she was contacted to identify the body.

Liz Tomkin was an attractive blonde who wore her thick hair long, cut in soft layers to her shoulders. She was in her thirties, a petite, curvy woman who was unusually busty, most likely the work of a local plastic surgeon.

"No, thank you," said Gonzalez. "How long did Anne Claridge live here with you?"

"She and I have been . . . were roommates for a little over six years."

"Did you and Anne have a romantic relationship?" Gonzalez asked, to the point.

"We were lovers, yes. But officer . . . ?"

"Detective Gonzalez."

"We had our own lives apart from each other, as evidenced by her propensity to frequent sex clubs, which ultimately cost Anne her life. I warned her about those clubs, particularly Brandy's, which attracted a great many low lifes, STDs included."

"Did you ever accompany her to Brandy's?"

"God forbid I should ever go into a place like that," she said with sudden passion. "Look, I know that you gentlemen know what I do for a living, so let's cut through the bullshit. I trade sex for money, plain and simple. For a lot of money. That's how I can afford to live at this address. I'm not about to give it free to some hairy assed aluminum siding salesman from Peoria."

Her declaration was followed by a few moments of silence. "How did her visits to these clubs affect you?" Wiggins asked.

"If you're asking me whether I was jealous of her having sex with other women, the answer is absolutely no. She was promiscuous, yes. But then again, given what I do for a living, it would be disingenuous of me to pass judgment on her. Let's just say that I am not a candidate for the Mother Teresa award."

"Ms. Tomkin, have you ever studied karate, kung fu or any other martial art?" Wiggins asked.

"C'mon, detective, do I look like I waste time learning how to fight? I know what you're driving at, but I'll be candid; you two are sniffing up the wrong bush, pun intended. On the night of the murders, I was working. You can call my service and ask.

"Besides, a woman didn't kill Anne and that ass clown she was found with. No way."

"What makes you say that?" Gonzalez asked, his interest suddenly piqued.

"You read the autopsy report, as well as I. They were savagely murdered by someone using his bare hands; an extremely powerful person. Do you really think a woman, and I don't give a shit if she has five black belts, can do that?" She paused for a response.

"We agree with you to a point," Gonzalez replied. "You never know. Everyone's getting bigger and stronger, women included. Also, steroids have changed the way people build muscle and physical strength today. It's possible, though highly unlikely, a woman is the killer. But we have to pursue every avenue in a homicide, I am sure that you can appreciate that."

"What I would appreciate is one of you homicide boys catching whoever killed my Anne. While we're sitting here slinging shit, there's a killer running loose in Miami. And who knows, he might try it again."

Christ, I hope the hell not, Gonzalez thought. "Believe me, Ms. Tomkin, we have a team of detectives, police and forensic scientists working diligently to solve this case."

"Do you know anyone who might have wanted to harm Anne, or possibly held a grudge, such as a man who might have asked her out and was rejected, or someone at work who didn't like her?" Wiggins asked. "Anything at all that might come to mind?"

"Anne was a financial consultant at Raymond James, and was considered one of its leading advisors," Tomkin replied.

"She never mentioned any conflicts with co-workers or with any man who might have asked her out and was turned down. Trust me on this, Anne didn't give out vibes that she was available to men, so in my mind that's not an issue. She liked women, as do I. I just think she was in the wrong spot at the wrong time. And why she was hooked up with this clown from East Bumfuck, or wherever he lived, is beyond me."

Both detectives rose. "Ms. Tomkin, if anything comes to mind, please call us immediately," Gonzalez said, handing her a card.

Accepting the proffered business card, Liz Tomkin looked directly into his eyes. "Detective, Anne didn't deserve to die like that, her neck snapped by some bastard who didn't even know her. She was the only person in my life whom I truly loved. Catch this sick prick."

"We will do everything we can," Gonzalez responded, as she showed them to the door. "Without an apparent motive or a prior relationship, it's slow going. Everyone we have interviewed, like yourself, can't provide much information or has an airtight alibi. We're confident we'll get a break in this case."

*   *   *

Close to 4 pm Liz Tomkin's service called her private number. "Yes?" she said softly into her BlackBerry. She recognized her service's phone number in the caller ID.

"You have a date at seven," the voice on the other end instructed. "It's a woman, and she's paid a premium for the pleasure of your company this evening. Meet her at the Capital Grille on Brickell, in the bar. She has dark hair, is tall, and her name is Cindy."

Tomkin abruptly terminated the call. At least for this evening's work she'll be with another woman, a happenstance she would like to see repeated more often, she thought. Having to pretend that she is even remotely interested in some overweight traveling salesman who pays top dollar for sex while his wife is back in

Pleasantville, or wherever, tending to home and hearth makes her want to puke.

At a few minutes past seven, Liz Tomkin entered the lounge and immediately spotted a tall brunette seated in a plush black leather chair at the long mahogany bar. The Capital Grille was an expensive and exclusive steak house where members of "the old boy's network" came to swirl sherry in crystal snifters, smoke pricey Cuban cigars and discuss the vagaries of the stock market. The restaurant had a reputation for being a secure, safe haven for cheating spouses, where everyone minded his and her own business. The tuxedoed bartenders 'heard and saw no evil,' and the more generous the tip, the less they saw and heard.

"Cindy?" Tomkin said as she approached the woman seated with her back to her. The leather seat slowly turned, and Sandy Garland, a wide smile displaying even rows of white teeth, extended her hand.

"Hi," she responded demurely, taking Tomkin's hand. "It's lovely to meet you. I suggest that we grab a cab and retreat to a private club to which I belong. We can get to know each other over a bottle of 2003 Iron Horse Chardonnay, my favorite. I have taken the liberty of ordering ahead."

"I like a woman who takes charge," Tomkin whispered. She couldn't believe how sexual this stunning, tall woman was. "I'm all yours tonight," she said, smiling, as the two women were leaving the bar.

As the bartender was clearing Sandy's martini glass, he was delighted to see a hundred dollar tip under the cocktail napkin. I have no idea who would have left a gratuity like this, he smiled to himself, as he surreptitiously pocketed the bill.

Chapter Four

"What?" Gonzalez said irritability into his cell. It was nearly 2 am, and he was just drifting off into a much-needed sleep. Lying at his side, snoring softly, was the lady he met in Churchill's Pub, a regular haunt for Miami police. Blonde and buxom, just as he liked, she came onto him aggressively as he sat with a few other detectives after a long day of getting nowhere tracking thin to vaporous leads on the murders. There was something about a man with cuffs and a handgun that turned some women on, and the fact that Gonzalez had rugged, Latin good looks was a definite plus. He drew women to him like corner dope dealers attracted addicts.

"Liz Tomkin was found murdered in an alley near a lesbian bar called the Café Bohemio over on Southwest 22," Wiggins reported. "Her neck was snapped. What the fuck is going on? Did our killer do this? And, if so, why?" Wiggins rapid-fire rhetorical questions rattled around in Gonzalez's weary brain.

"Give me twenty minutes. I'll meet you downstairs. Is the scene locked down?"

"Affirmative. I have some blues questioning the women in the club, but so far no one has seen bupkis. It's like we're tracking a fucking ghost. And what would a guy be doing anywhere near this club? He'd stand out like a rapper at a Clan rally," Wiggins whined. Then the phone went dead.

Gonzalez slowly extricated himself from the warm bed. As he dressed, his bedmate opened her eyes. "Where you going? It's the middle of the night," she asked, glancing at the clock on the dresser.

"Gotta get to work on a case," he responded. "Go back to sleep. If you're here when I get back, we'll have a bite to eat. Help yourself in the kitchen. If you need to leave, just make sure that the door's locked."

She watched him closely as he slid his handgun, a Glock .40 into his shoulder holster. God, was he gorgeous, she thought. "I'll hang out until around 7 am, and if you're not back I gotta leave."

"That's fine. I'll call the apartment when I'm on my way." Of course, he knew that he'd probably not see her until their paths crossed again back at Churchill's.

Wiggins' unmarked black Ford slid to the curb just as Gonzalez was exiting the building. "Hey," Gonzalez said tersely as he folded his large frame into the front passenger seat. "What do we have so far?"

"One of the women in the club stepped into the alley for a smoke and saw what looked at first glance like someone had dumped a pile of clothes near a dumpster. As she walked closer, she saw that the pile of clothes was the body of Liz Tomkin. She immediately called Metro-Dade on her cell, who patched the call to our squad."

As Wiggins guided the Ford in front of the Bohemio, he saw that the ME, Pat Solez, and her team were already there, working behind yellow police tape that was guarded by a Miami officer. Gonzalez and Wiggins flashed their shields and bent down under the tape.

Patricia Solez looked up as the detectives approached. "Christ, everything was going so good, too," Solez announced to her team. "The cavalry has arrived. We can all stand down now."

"Give me your initial, yet astute, observations," Gonzalez ordered, ignoring her jibes.

Liz Tomkin, looking nothing like the attractive woman they interviewed earlier in the day, was sprawled in full evening wear, her legs obscenely akimbo, skirt up displaying a thin black thong. The only clue that she was dead was that her head was spun completely around like the kid in *The Exorcist*.

"Somebody applied an amazing amount of force to this person to completely crush her cervical spine and twist her head around like this," Solez said. "I've never seen such damage to a person's vertebrae and the occipital, not even blunt trauma from car accidents. This guy must have been full of rage to exert the strength it takes to do this."

"Let's talk to some of the ladies in the bar," Gonzalez said to Wiggins. "Someone must have seen something." Together the two detectives opened the bright red door of the Café Bohemio and walked into the confines of a smallish lounge, populated with women of varying shapes and sizes, some with colorful tattoos on their arms and necks and others with metal adornments in their noses and tongues. A few were attractive, model caliber even, and they were accompanied by masculine, powerful looking bull dykes, who wrapped their arms protectively around their mates. It was a grim, humorless looking group that wasn't taking kindly to the interruption.

Miami PD officers were scattered through the room, which was cathedral quiet, as the women watched Gonzalez's every move. "Ladies, I am Detective John Gonzalez, and my partner here is Detective Roland Wiggins. We are investigating the murder of the woman discovered in the alley this morning," he said, holding aloft a color file photo of her. "Did any of you see her in the Café during the evening, and if so, was she with anyone?"

Silence for a few beats, then one of the women spoke up. "We don't recognize her and am sure that she wasn't in here tonight, Detective." The others shook their heads affirmatively. "Most of us have been here since early evening and know for certain she never was in here."

"Maybe one of you have saw her on the street outside or approaching the café." Again, unanimous head shakes, reminding Gonzalez of a bobblehead convention. Many of them weren't looking at the photo.

Frustrated at the apparent lack of interest, "Well, ladies, thank you. Now the officers are going to be interviewing each and every one of you, so please make yourselves comfortable." A collective groan arose, drowning out Gonzalez's final words.

"Just a minute there, jefe," announced one of the more formidable looking Hispanic women. More than six feet tall, her arms decorated with colorful sleeves of tattoos, she walked up to within inches of Gonzalez, staring directly into his eyes. He could detect the strong odor of alcohol on her breath.

"All of us have told you and the other puercos we never saw this putan," she spat defiantly, spittle spraying Gonzalez. "You have no right to keep us here. It's late and we're leaving." With that, she motioned for her partner to join her, as well as the others.

"Miss," Gonzalez said firmly, "two more steps and I'll charge you with impeding a homicide investigation, which is a felony in the state of Florida. That means that we will be arresting and handcuffing you and any others who attempt to leave these premises before the officers have had a chance to question them."

Without warning, she threw a punch at Gonzalez, who deftly moved his head a fraction of a second before it made contact with his jaw. He swiftly grabbed her hand, bending it painfully back at the wrist and then lifting her arm behind and high above her. She screamed in pain, as she was immobilized within a fraction of a second.

"What the fuck, usted hijo de una ramera. Patearé su asno," she yelled in pain, as Gonzalez grabbed handcuffs from his waist. Then, all hell broke loose. Every dyke in the café came to her sister's aid and swarmed the two detectives. One of the officers called for back up on his radio and then waded into the fray. Fists flew until one of the Miami blues pointed and fired his Taser at a burly combatant, who let loose a blood curdling scream as nearly 1,000 volts slammed into her stomach, rendering her incapacitated. That instantly quelled the melee, as the women began to back up. The police began handcuffing those who took part in the resistance, as the front door swung open with additional police.

"Ah, shit," said Gonzalez, as he led the handcuffed Latino woman out to a waiting paddy wagon. "The paperwork on this mess is going to be a bitch," he said to Wiggins, who was wrestling with a woman three inches taller and about fifty pounds heavier.

"I'll be happy to handle the paper back at our nice quiet station," panted Wiggins, "that is, if we make it alive."

Chapter Five

Pittsburgh
2002

The stocky, heavily muscled man in the starched white gi secured with a black belt, with a perfectly formed knot stylishly centered against the stark background of the uniform, circled his opponent cautiously. Attentive students surrounded the perimeter of the dojo, watching the combatant's every move as they engaged in kumite, the ancient Japanese form of controlled hand-to-hand sparring. This form of feudal Isshin-Ryu style fighting tested the participant's speed, skill and ability to score points when a light blow was delivered, unblocked, to the opponent's body or within a few inches of the face or head. The Isshin-Ryu style was designed for close-in fighting, consisting of short, lethal punches, front and side kicks and leg sweeps.

Sometimes overzealous students used full force to the body and the face, particularly the thugs who were studying karate merely to inflict pain on others on the streets. These sadists had no interest in learning the beauty and gracefulness of a martial art like Isshin-Ryu. They just wanted to hurt people. Like Joey Calderon, who has found himself in a match with Sandy Garland. Calderon was a member of the Brookline Blades, a notorious Hispanic Pittsburgh street gang with a reputation for selling drugs and murdering those who got in its way. He has been studying karate for more than five years and attained the rank of shodan, or first degree, a few months previously. And Joey let everybody know that in his words, he was a "trained killer."

Though unusual for a man to fight a woman at the black belt level, it wasn't unheard of, particularly when the woman is Sandy Garland, who towered over the 5 ft. 7 in. Calderon. No other student in the Isshin-Ryu dojo, man or woman, wanted to match up against Garland. She was too quick, perfectly balanced and unrelenting in her attacking style of sparring. There was also something about Sandy's temperament that frightened other members of the dojo. She was reckless in her fighting style, more than willing to accept a blow in order to deliver a match-ending strike to a vital area. The fact that Sandy exhibited no fear was even more unsettling to her fellow students.

Dojo sensei Master Bill Deardon skirted the fighters, watching closely for any points scored. Calderon moved first, a slight feint to his left, followed by a lighting fast leg sweep, throwing Sandy temporarily off balance. Then he delivered a full force blow to her jaw, knocking her on her back. Deardon yelled "yame" to stop the match.

"Sandy, you alright?" the sensei asked as he bent over her. Calderon was laughing, as he preened for the onlookers. Trying to shake the cobwebs from her brain, Sandy rose slowly to her feet, aided by the sensei.

"Calderon, you are disqualified for contact to the face," Deardon announced. "I've told you before that I won't tolerate this behavior. You better start controlling your techniques or the next move is out of this school permanently."

"Sensei, I'm okay. Let the match continue," Sandy said. "It looked worse than it was. Really, his chicken-shit technique had nothing on it."

Sandy smiled as Calderon replied menacingly, "I'll show you chicken shit, you puta." The sensei reset the fighters, had them bow to each other, which they did grudgingly and cautioned them both to follow the rules of kumite.

"Yame," Deardon announced in Japanese, sweeping his hands between the fighters to restart the match. The hematoma on Sandy's jaw was already turning a yellow mustard color and beginning to ache. Calderon, with growing confidence, decided to push an offensive attack, rather than wait for Sandy to strike first. He didn't want to give her the opportunity to launch a counter-strike and was aware of her speed and tenacity. He was going to deliver the first blow. It turned out to be a serious mistake.

Calderon attempted a short front kick to Sandy's midsection, that was to be followed quickly by a shuto-strike or knife-hand, to her collar bone. He was preparing to deliver the blow full force, despite Sensei Deardon's admonitions. His thrusts were short and deadly, but Sandy's counter was even faster. She blocked the kick deftly, redirecting its force, while parrying the knife-hand in midflight and locking Calderon in an arm bar at the elbow as his arm was extended. She then used her strength and height advantage to lift Calderon's straightened arm up, using powerful leverage. Calderon's elbow snapped with a sickening "crack," as his tendons and ligaments gave way.

Calderon screamed as he fell to his knees, clutching his dangling, dislocated elbow. "Yo le mataré, usted ramera," he spat. Garland regarded him as if she was looking at a cockroach she just squished. Sensei Deardon and other senior instructors quickly helped Calderon stabilize his dangling arm, as an ambulance was summoned.

Sandy was heading to the shower as Deardon caught up to her. "Sandy, it's clear that you applied that bar as retaliation for his blow to your jaw."

"Sensei, that's not accurate. The blow to my jaw didn't have enough force behind it to break an egg," she said. "However, that shuto the little prick was planning on delivering to my shoulder did have speed behind it. It was just a natural reflex on my part to protect myself by applying the bar."

"But why didn't you stop at that point?" sensei asked. "Why apply upward force knowing that the leverage you had would break the elbow? Calderon will be out of commission for months."

"I would have stopped if he hadn't called me a 'puta,'" she said matter of factly, continuing on her way to the locker room.

Deardon was waiting for Sandy as she emerged from the locker room. "C'mon into my office for a coffee," he said. "I'd like a few words with you."

After they were seated in the tiny confines of his cluttered office, the school's sensei came immediately to the point. "Sandy, I'm worried about you. Every one of our students is reluctant to take part in a class you lead, and no one wants to spar you, except for a gangbanger like Calderon. And that includes my other black belts. You seem to be fighting demons in addition to other students," he said, concern creasing his forehead.

Sandy sat calmly, cradling her Styrofoam coffee cup, her pale blue eyes looking straight into Deardon's. A distinguished man, with thinning grey hair always perfectly coiffed, Sensei Bill Deardon was one of Okinawa's rising stars in the ranks of top Isshin-Ryu karateka. Master Tatsuo Shimabuko himself had plotted Deardon's pathway to become one of his leading instructors in the United States. He exemplified not only leadership, but a savvy business acumen to keep students and dollars coming into the Academy. Of course, a monthly percentage of student fees made its way over to the Okinawa Isshin-Ryu World Headquarters, to the delight of the Master. That's why he loved America.

Weighing her words carefully, Sandy responded, "Sensei, I've been a student of yours for nearly six years. During that time, I have done everything in my power to follow the way of Isshin, the 'one heart method'." I have never done anything to discredit this school that I love above all else, and have only defended myself from thugs like Calderon when I have been presented with no other option."

An uncomfortable silence hung in the office. Deardon cleared his throat. "Sandy, I know you are by far our most highly dedicated student, and the countless hours you train are unmatched by any one else in the school. However, I'm sensing an anger within you that seems to be worsening over time and am fearful that it may get someone killed."

Sandy smiled, setting her empty cup on his desk. "I can assure you that is one thing you will never have to worry about," she said pleasantly as she rose from the desk chair. "Among those countless hours of training that you mentioned I spend an equal number of hours in disciplining myself to never use my skills unless defending myself from harm. And even then I would be careful to use only the force necessary to protect myself. Thanks for the coffee, sensei."

As Deardon watched Sandy Garland walk toward the front doors of the dojo, he couldn't help but wonder . . . was Calderon's painfully crushed dislocated elbow an example of Sandy's self discipline?

Chapter Six

1986
Pittsburgh

Sandy Garland's first grade teacher, Susan Chima, was growing concerned about Sandy's behavior. In addition to her precipitous weight gain, the other children were bullying her mercilessly, making her life a living hell. At recess, the most enthusiastic group of taunters would chant, "Garland, Garland, the gargantuan glob!" She spent most of those periods in tears, cowering near a teacher.

Sandy and her family lived in Pittsburgh's East End, where fast food joints had sprouted like weeds on every corner, providing the basic staples for the Garland family, because they could only afford this cheap, nutritionally unsound food. Her father, Henry, was a security guard at the Westinghouse Research and Technology Center, the research division of the gigantic Westinghouse Corporation, one of the city's shining corporate stars for more than a century. Like many companies during the tumultuous 90s, it would eventually be broken into many disparate parts and sold off to diverse companies around the world in order to maximize shareholder return.

Besides being a world-class under achiever who spent his working career toiling in minimum wage jobs, Henry Garland was also an alcoholic who grew nastier the more alcohol he consumed. No one was exempt from his wrath as he drank, particularly Sandy, who he referred to as the "Pittsburgh Porker." Sandy's mother, Gloria, dare not confront Henry over his treatment of Sandy for fear of physical reprisal. He would often strike her, and because of his minimal training in security, he knew where to hit to exact maximum pain, leaving no external evidence.

Gloria, fearful of Henry's temper, would privately console Sandy, offering what little solace she could muster in her quiet, timid manner. Sandy was both terrorized at school and continually insulted by her drunken father, causing her grades to plummet and her personality changes. The once social, happy little girl was becoming sullen and withdrawn.

Susan Chima called Gloria to set a personal meeting with the Garlands to discuss Sandy. "I am concerned about Sandy. She is becoming more withdrawn every day. We need to address the constant bullying she is facing. Her weight seems to be a contributing factor in this situation. I am fearful that if these problems are not resolved, she may she may develop irreversible changes to her personality. I strongly recommend that we sit down and explore ways in which we can help Sandy establish a sensible program that combines exercise and proper nutrition," she said to Gloria. "It's important that we support her both in this area, as well as confront the constant bullying she is encountering during school. She's at an extremely vulnerable age."

"Ms. Chima, this is merely a phase Sandy's going through. I know that there are days when she's very reluctant to go to school, but for the most part Sandy ignores the other kids' remarks. Both her father and I are very supportive and will help guide her through these 'choppy waters'." In reality, Gloria Garland was scared to death of her alcoholic husband getting involved with the school administration, much less having his foul mouth and breath unleashed on Sandy's teacher.

"At the very least, Mrs. Garland, I would like to recommend a psychologist that we refer children to who can counsel Sandy and help her come to grips with some of the problems she has been facing each day. Again, I am concerned that if left unchecked, these issues could adversely affect her development as a child into adolescence and possibly even into adulthood."

"I appreciate your concern, but that won't be necessary, thank you, Ms. Chima," Gloria said. "We are confident that working together, as a family, we can solve the situation. Last month we bought her a beautiful red Cocker Spaniel that she named 'Tiny.' Sandy truly loves and dotes on that dog, and Tiny seems to take her mind off her problems." Gloria hung up, hoping that her lies to Sandy's teacher would not ultimately cause her daughter further harm.

Sandy continued to have problems at school, which were exacerbated by her father's constant caustic remarks. She was continuing to gain weight and was having difficulty sleeping. Gloria sensed a growing paranoia that Sandy was developing, in that she seemed to be distrustful of everyone and devoted her complete attention to her dog. Even her interactions with the dog seemed mean-spirited. Sandy would play games with the Cocker that often resulted in the animal being bound and gagged as she would fantasize a sort of kidnapping and rescue scenario, during which she would become the heroine, rescuing the dog before it ran out of air.

Over Thanksgiving vacation Tiny disappeared. Sandy was inconsolable as she and Gloria searched the neighborhood for the Cocker Spaniel. They posted printed photos and descriptions of Tiny on utility poles in the area and contacted their neighbors on whether they had seen her. Heart broken, Sandy was barely communicating and seemed to be withdrawing.

Christmas approached and the dog hadn't been found. Gloria was doing her best to decorate the house for the holidays, without any help from Henry. She decided to try to hang some wreathes stored in the basement. When she descended into the dank, silent cellar, a place she avoided because of the dirt and grime that had accumulated over the years, she noticed a foul odor coming from its most remote recesses.

Gloria carefully began moving boxes to find the ones marked 'Christmas Stuff' in red ink. As she worked her way deeper into the haphazard collection of boxes and containers, the smell became more pronounced. That's when she discovered Tiny's decaying body completely bound with rope and a rag stuffed into the small dog's mouth. Its muzzle had been completely wrapped in black electrical tape.

Gloria's screams brought Henry staggering down the stairs, nearly breaking his neck in the process. "What the hell's going on? Jesus Christ, you see a spider or what?" That's when Henry saw Tiny's putrefying body. "Holy shit, Gloria, who in the hell would have done something like that?"

That's when Gloria Garland decided to call Susan Chima and get the name of the psychologist.

*   *   *

Gloria Garland was apprehensive as she and Sandy entered the first floor elevators that led up to Dr. Marilyn Stone's offices on the sixth floor. Dr. Stone was a John Hopkins University trained child psychologist, highly recommended by Susan Chima. She was often quoted in the local media covering child abuse cases and even appeared on national news shows after a seven year old child shot his sleeping mother in the head point blank with a .357 Magnum, because she refused to let him attend a movie he wanted to see. The media dove on the story like a flock of vultures, offering up scores of opinions from so-called experts on why a young child would commit such a brutal crime. Dr. Stone was a voice of reason during the tempest of media speculation, earning her interviews with everyone from Mike Wallace on CBS to NBC's Bob Dotson.

Dr. Stone's waiting room was cheerfully decorated in colorful primitive paintings depicting children in various stages of play with other children and pets. Her diplomas also were displayed prominently, contributing a level of comfort to parents that she was qualified to treat their children.

The door to the inner office opened, and Dr. Stone, an attractive blond in her early forties entered the waiting area. "I am Dr. Stone, and you must be Sandy," she said, gazing pleasantly at the six year old little girl."

"Hello, I am Sandy's mother, Gloria," she said, extending her hand to Dr. Stone. After introductions and some banter about the weather, Dr. Stone led Sandy into her office for her initial hour's consultation. Gloria came prepared with a novel to pass the time in the waiting room.

Dr. Stone led Sandy into her office and motioned for her to have a seat on a nearby couch. After preparing herself with notebook and pen, she began interviewing the young girl. "Tell me a little about yourself, Sandy. What is your school like, how are the teachers, what do you like about school and what do you dislike about it? I know those are lots of questions; let's start with what do you like about school?"

"Nothing," Sandy responded. Silence.

"OK, what teachers do you like?"

"None of them," Sandy said. Silence.

"And what exactly don't you like about school?"

"The kids there pick on me every day."

"What kinds of things do they do?"

"They call me bad names and push me. They say that I am a fat glob."

"Have these children been reported to the principal?"

"No, my Daddy tells me that I have to protect myself and not tattle on the other kids."

"What about your mom?"

"She's afraid of Daddy, because he gets mean when he's drunk and hits her."

Dr. Stone looked up from her notes for a moment. "Does your father drink a lot?"

"Everyday he smells stinky like he's been drinking."

"How does that make you feel?"

"Like killing him," Sandy said matter of factly.

"You don't mean that, right Sandy?"

"No I mean it. I would like to take a knife and chop off his head. Especially when he calls me names like the other kids do, and comes into my room to say goodnight."

"When your father says goodnight to you, does he ever touch you in your private places?"

Silence. Dr. Stone cleared her throat. "Sandy, has your father ever touched you where you didn't want to be touched?"

Sandy spoke slowly. "No, he hasn't. He just calls me names. I don't like that."

Dr. Stone changed the subject. "I understand that you had a wonderful dog that you named Tiny. Tell me a little about him."

Sandy brightened. "We used to play the best games, and I would always be the one to rescue him from trouble. He ran away."

"Why do you think he ran away?" Dr. Stone asked.

"I don't know. My father probably left the door open when he was drunk."

After the hour was up, Dr. Stone led Sandy back into the waiting room and asked if she could speak to Gloria for a moment alone in her office. She offered Sandy some illustrated children's books to occupy her.

Dr. Stone came right to the point. "Mrs. Garland, I have only spent one hour with Sandy, but I suspect she may be suffering from early-onset bipolar disorder. Of course, I can't offer a more definitive diagnosis and treatment plan until I have the opportunity to work with her further."

"What's does that mean?" Dr. Stone. "What is early onset bipolar whatever?"

"It's a disorder that can produce a range of anxieties in children, causing them to overeat, suffer from mood swings ranging from severe depression to joy and elation and to have sleep disruptions. In the brief time I spent with her today, I get the sense that Sandy has a low sense of self esteem, exacerbated by the constant bullying she encounters daily at school and from her father at home. She seems to exhibit a lack of accountability, shifting the blame on others. Sandy also seems to have anger issues that could eventually lead to violent behavior."

"Oh my," Gloria could only respond, beginning to tear.

"Mrs. Garland, Sandy mentioned that she doesn't like it when her father comes to her room to say goodnight." Are you aware of these visits, and do you think he might be behaving inappropriately with Sandy?"

Gloria rose instantly from her chair. "Dr. Stone, her father . . . my husband . . . is a hard working man who may drink a little to relieve his stress, but he would never . . . ever . . . touch Sandy in an inappropriate manner." Having said that, Gloria Garland abruptly left the office, gathered up Sandy in the waiting room and left the office of Dr. Marilyn Stone, never to return.

Chapter Seven

Philadelphia
2009

Sandy Garland's flight into Philadelphia arrived on time at 4 pm into the city's International Airport. She and the Odyssey crew grabbed a shuttle to the nearby Hilton, where a few of her fellow flight attendants planned to get together for dinner around 7 pm. As usual, Sandy declined, planning to get in her daily workout at the hotel gym, followed by a solitary meal in Philadelphia's Center City area. She abhorred the variety of small talk and gossip her colleagues dished during these excruciatingly boring dinners together. She much preferred her own company and the unanticipated adventures the evening might bring.

Following check in, Sandy unpacked, changed into her tracksuit and headed to the fitness center on the third floor. After two early morning routes into Charlotte and then Philadelphia, she was more than ready for some stretching and lifting. The hotel gym was empty, as most hotel guests spent late afternoon hours lifting martinis at the bar and not iron in the gym.

Sandy was in her comfort zone. Running on the treadmill, lifting free weights and countless hours spent perfecting the intricate fighting techniques of the fourteen Isshin-Ryu katas had become an important part of her lifestyle and were as integral to her well-being as attending church was for Christians. When she performed a kata, or form, the casual observer would perceive someone dancing around throwing random punches and kicks in the air. In actuality, Sandy was honing her speed, balance, power and stamina. A properly executed kata required hundreds of hours of practice, and once a student learned its complex techniques, the pursuit of perfection was a life-long journey.

Soaked in sweat, Sandy had completed her weight lifting routine and was dedicating time to Kusanku Kata, the longest and most difficult Isshin-Ryu kata, consisting of flying reverse kicks that tested the student's agility and speed. She performed this kata literally thousands of times in tournaments and alone in hotel rooms, and still was not satisfied with her execution.

As she crouched in a defensive position, in preparation for a counter front kick, she noticed a man watching her in the gym's mirror. She hadn't seen him enter the small gym and immediately stopped her kata work, self conscious that another person outside her dojo saw her practicing. Sweating profusely, she began stretching slowly. That's when he made his move.

"Hi, I couldn't help but notice what you were doing," he said. "Karate, right?"

Sandy just nodded her head and continued stretching, hoping that he would just give up and go away. But it was not to be.

"I'm Kent Renale," he said. "I saw you in the hotel lobby and figured that a woman in the shape you are would most likely be in the gym. I hope you don't mind my boldness, but I did want to introduce myself to you. I'm here in Philadelphia for a trade show. I am a chemical engineer for a plastics company in San Diego."

"That's nice," Sandy responded, offering scant encouragement to continue the conversation.

"Your name is?" he persisted.

"Look, I don't mean to be rude, but my time in this gym is limited, and I can't afford small talk. I hope you have a great stay here in Philadelphia and do really well at your plastics show."

Taken aback by her apparent disinterest in a good looking guy like him, Kent said, "Look, lady, I was just trying to make pleasant conversation. But if you're one of those women who have a chip on their shoulders, thinking your ass is golden, then that's cool. Just forget I even said anything."

He started toward the door, when Sandy Garland spoke. "Okay, let's start over. My name is Jen, Jen Thomas, and I am a sales consultant for Revlon. I am just about done with my daily exercise program," she said to his back as he was leaving the room.

Renale stopped and turned around, smiling. "Hi, Jen Thomas. Pleased to make your acquaintance. Listen, would you be interested in joining me for dinner this evening?"

"You look like a married man to me, Kent," she responded, nodding toward the gold wedding band on his left hand.

"Oh, no, I'm not married. Well, I am. That is, I am in the process of getting a divorce."

Lying bastard, Sandy thought.

"I'll tell you what, Kent. I have to attend to some business in the city this evening. How about I meet you around 8 pm at the restaurant of your choice?"

"Terrific," Renale said. "Since you are interested in karate, let's meet at Morimoto on Chestnut, a great restaurant I try to visit when I'm in Philadelphia. They have about the best Japanese food I've ever eaten."

Grabbing her towel, Sandy said, "See you there at 8 pm" Asshole, she thought.

After a long shower, Sandy put on a classic, form-fitting little black dress that accented all her curves. She slipped on a new pair of black dress stilettos, Beverly Feldman designer shoes that displayed her tanned, muscled legs perfectly. The final touch was her black wig, her Remy model with 100 percent human hair. The effect was absolutely sexy, she thought, turning her perfectly round ass toward the mirror.

Sandy grabbed a cab and, eyes averted, told the driver, "Take me to the corner of Rhawn and Craig."

"Any particular location there, 'mam?" the cabbie asked, slightly turning his heavily bearded countenance toward the back seat.

"No, just let me off at the corner"

"That's a pretty tough area for a pretty young lady like yourself to be strolling around alone," he persisted.

"I'll be fine," Sandy said with finality. The driver got the hint to shut his mouth.

As he glided the yellow cab toward the curb at Rhawn Street, he said, "That will be twelve fifty." Without a response, Sandy handed over fifteen dollars and got out of the cab. She waited until the cab was out of sight, and then she turned in the direction of Club KamaSutra, a highly selective, secretive sex club. Only members of a chosen group even knew the address, let alone how to access the key code on the club's nondescript grey metal door. Sandy got the information from a female partner in a Phoenix swingers' club shortly before she met her untimely demise.

As she began walking toward the address written on a slip of paper in her hand, she noticed two young men eyeing her from across the deserted street. They were wearing the uniform of the streets—pants drooping below their asses, high top sneakers, handkerchiefs protruding from their back pockets, displaying their gang colors. Each wore a baseball cap sideways. Although they were trying to act tough, they should have had "punk" silk screened on their ratty T-shirts.

As they crossed to Sandy's side of the street, walking cockily toward her, she purposefully led them away from the KamaSutra's location and into an alleyway. She could hear the men chattering in Spanish and laughing, as they began to close the distance between them.

Suddenly, Sandy stopped midway down the alley and turned. 'What do you two faggots want?" she demanded. Those words and her demeanor stopped them in their tracks.

"Wow, chickata, you called Carlos and me 'faggots'," the first punk said, with facetious amazement in his voice. He looked at his companions and said, "Esta perra se va a follar duro."

"Usted dos payasos tendría que haber dicks hacer eso", Sandy shot back in Spanish.

His wide smile revealed gold teeth. "You know, puta, that's not nice."

There goes the 'puta' again, Sandy thought. "Well, then, gentlemen, what can I do for you two upstanding citizens? I am late for an appointment."

"Well, ramera, mi amiga, Carlos and I would like a blowjob and this seems like the perfect location for you to get down on your knees. With unanticipated speed, he snapped open a switchblade and began to wave it menacingly.

To their surprise, Sandy didn't run but walked slowly toward them. "Okay, boys, but you have to give me a moment to get my bifocals on, because my eyesight is not so good anymore and trying to see your little dicks in this light will be a problem."

The boys looked quizzically at each other, trying to determine if this bitch was loco. Carlos made the first move, as ill-considered as it was, lunging at Sandy in an attempt to knock her off her feet. With very little effort and a quickness that caught the two boys completely off guard, Sandy struck Carlos in the temple with a bottom fist strike, knocking him unconscious.

The other awkwardly swept the knife at Sandy's midsection in an effort to eviscerate her. She parried the knife sweep with a powerful forearm rising block, knocking the knife from his hand. In the split second that his arm was suspended in mid-air, Sandy delivered a devastating sidekick, the heel of her shoe tearing into his exposed ribs, shattering two. He howled in agony as he fell to his knees. Sandy calmly retrieved his knife, walked up behind him and slit his throat from ear to ear, with a speed and precision that even impressed her. The boy died in a fountain of blood, as his miserable young life sprayed down across his T-shirt and baggy pants.

Sandy walked slowly over to Carlos and stared down at him. As his eyes began to slowly open and awareness of his surroundings gradually returned, Sandy knelt down and whispered in his ear,

"You know, you really shouldn't have called me a 'puta'." She drove the blade into his brain.

After wiping the knife and dropping it in her pocketbook, Sandy strode from the alley as if she was just coming from the theatre and glanced at her watch. I had better keep my date with the "I am married, but actually not married" Kent Renale, she thought, as she hailed a passing cab.

*   *   *

Sandy walked into Morimoto's a little after 8:30 p.m. and found Kent Renale waiting anxiously at a small table in the rear of the restaurant. "I was beginning to get worried that you might not show," he said, standing to pull out her chair.

"C'mon, Kent, you know I couldn't resist your dinner invitation and, most of all, your charm," she responded. Something in her pale blue eyes caught his attention. It was almost like there was a vacant room behind them, as in the old saying, "the lights were on, but no one was home." Her expression troubled him, but he quickly ignored his feeling, anticipating future delights.

"Jen, tell me a little about your self," he nervously asked as they were settled and perusing the menu. Oh, Christ, Sandy thought, he's trying to pretend he's actually interested in me. This fucktard is amazing.

"Well, let's see, I grew up in Pittsburgh and attended a school where my classmates made my life a living hell. I was taunted daily for being overweight, bullied by a group of mean little bitches who picked on me mercilessly. My home life was worse. My alcoholic father not only verbally abused me, but he abused me sexually. The little maggot would steal into my room late at night, lift my pajamas and try to have sex with me. Most of the time, the pathetic asshole couldn't get it up. Other times, he could."

A deafening silence enveloped the table like a heavy fog. Finally, the waiter broke it, asking for their drink orders. "Why sake, of course," Sandy requested brightly. Ken Renale sat staring at her in stunned silence. After the waiter asked him for a second time, he was jolted back to reality and said, "A vodka and tonic please, with lime." He continued to stare at Sandy in a state of shock.

"Jen, I don't know what to say!"

Sandy laughed loudly and said, "I was just fooling around. Do I look like I was overweight and bullied?"

Kent relaxed, laughing tentatively. "You had me going there for a minute, I must admit."

I'm going to get you going, you prick, Sandy thought. "Let's order, I've worked up an appetite," she said, thinking about her exploits in the alley.

After dinner, Sandy boldly suggested they retreat to Kent's room at the Hilton. Renale thought he surely misheard her idea. "You want to join me in my room?" he asked incredulously.

"Am I speaking Japanese?" Sandy said with a sexy smile.

"Let's go," Kent immediately responded, as he withdrew his billfold and summoned the waiter.

During the cab ride to the Hilton, Sandy kept her face buried in Renale's shoulder. Within minutes, they were in his room. "Let's get naked and make passionate love. I'll be back in a second," she said over her shoulder as she entered Kent's bathroom.

Renale sat completely naked, waiting patiently, on the edge of he bed as Sandy emerged from the bathroom, hand behind her back. Her body was absolutely amazing, as he stared hard as her gorgeous, full breasts.

"Let's get started," Sandy said, as she revealed the knife that belonged to the punk in the alley. Renale had only a fraction of a second to process this information before Sandy Garland, or Jen Thomas, plunged the sharp switchblade directly into his forehead. Death was instantaneous, but not before Kent Renale thought about his wife and two daughters back in perpetually sunny San Diego. Then there was blackness.

Chapter Eight

Miami

Gonzalez addressed his team at 8 am on a damp, dreary south Florida Monday, which perfectly matched the detectives' collective moods. "We've got el cero on these cases, and I have the mayor and city commissioners on my ass to close them out," he announced. "Whoever killed these people covered his tracks as efficiently as I have ever seen." The sergeant looked tired and puffy eyed, no doubt having put in another late night at South Beach. The "Swinging Sex Murders" investigation, so dubbed by the ever-creative Miami media, was at a dead end, and Gonzalez's homicide unit was frustrated.

"The lover of Anne Claridge, our latest murder victim, was Liz Tomkin. She was otherwise occupied at the time of the murders, plying her trade from a high-priced escort service. Her alibi is now a moot point, in that Liz is currently deceased," he said as he drew a line through her photo on the board. She was brutally assaulted outside of a lesbian bar on Bayshore Drive. Her neck was snapped, much like the murders at Brandy's.

"We know this much," he continued, gesturing to the photos and maps behind him. "The unsub is powerful and trained in hand-to-hand combat or jujitsu. He was able to quietly and quickly kill two people in a busy club and make his escape without anyone noticing. Of course, the fact that there was a noisy, sexual extravaganza taking place in every room was of immense help to him. And the nice ladies at the Bohemio Club," a few snickers, "saw nothing out of the ordinary."

"In short, no one saw nada and the only person of interest we have so far is a guy named Joe Badiali, who was seen with Tomkin earlier in the day," he said, gesturing to a photo mounted on the board. Our boy, Joey, has an 'airtight' alibi, in more ways than one." Gonzalez's last remark elicited a ripple of laughter from the assembled detectives. "He was an identified as a vocal participant in a gay orgy at the Club Ram over in Sobe. Plus, Joe Badiali is 5 ft. 4 in. and overweight, hardly fitting our killer's profile. He's in the clear," Gonzalez stated emphatically. "But I put a surveillance team on him just in case.

"The only shred of tangible evidence we have is a black hair that is not human, found under Anne Claridge's body at the crime scene. But with all the traffic of people through the club, that could have come from a wig worn by any one of a thousand sexual adventurers. There was no semen on either female vic, no fingerprints, no skin under the nails, nothing. This guy waltzed into a crowded sex club, dispatched two human beings like he was fuckin' Bruce Lee and disappeared like a mist. The question is did the same guy murder Liz Tomkin in the alley beside Café Bohemio, and if so, why?

"Russo, I want you and Keller to canvass area karate schools and boxing clubs, and identify students who might exhibit the skills and demeanor to hurt or kill someone like our unsub. You come up with a candidate, brace him to see where he was on the night of the killings. Cutrazulla, you and Simmons visit area wig shops with the sample to see if you can get a match on the fiber and color. It's a long shot, but better than sitting on our asses. Wiggins and I will be running down the families of our three victims to determine if they had enemies, jilted or jealous lovers or any of a thousand variables that could get someone pissed enough to snap their necks."

As the team dispersed, Gonzalez sat in a vacant chair next to Wiggins. "Wigs, I have a bad feeling about this. These are related homicides, I just sense it. I think we might have a psycho just getting warmed up here in sunny Miami, killing for perverted reasons known only to him. I am going to have our people check with NCIC to determine if similar killings have occurred in the state or region, or anywhere else for that matter, that might give us a lead."

The National Crime Information Center is a massive criminal database maintained in Clarksburg, West Virginia by the FBI that provides law enforcement officials around the country 24/7 access to information compiled about crimes and criminals that can help them track felons, terrorists, missing persons, sexual predators and others who come into contact with the criminal justice system at some point.

Gonzalez walked over to the division's IT department and knocked on the manager's office door. Kathy Henderson looked up from her computer screen.

"Hey, Sergeant Gonzalez, to what do we owe the pleasure of your handsome countenance here in 'geek city'?" she asked with a coquettish grin. "Surely there can't be anything we have that could be of interest to Miami's preeminent homicide 'dick'," Henderson asked, with an emphasis on the final word.

"Cut the comedy, Henderson," Gonzalez said with a bit of irritation creeping into his voice. "Listen, I need you to do an NCIC information link search. Input query strings in the following files to see if something pops. Search recent violent crimes and acts, sexual predators, acts of terrorism, gang violence and related homicides. I know these queries are weak, but we got to get some traction somewhere. Buzz me when and if you get some matches or miracles, whichever comes first." Without even waiting for a witty response, Gonzalez wheeled and left the room. Who pissed in his cornflakes? Henderson mused.

*   *   *

It was 7 am Saturday morning and Gonzalez and his team were reporting on what they had each learned. The tension in the room was palpable, the tone having been set by Sergeant Gonzalez who was catching an inordinate amount of flack over the sex club killings and the probably related murder of Liz Tomkin. The consensus among the mayor and city council members was that, because of the sexual aspects of the killings and the surroundings in which they took place, Miami was taking a public relations broadside. News media from across the country, which included CNN, Nightline, 20-20 and other national news outlets, not to mention every blog and Twitter controlled by people who had time on their hands and opinions on everything, were weighing in on the cases. What made the subject even more attractive were the lurid details of a sex club and lesbian bar that served as private playgrounds for people who got turned on by indiscriminate sex and alternative lifestyles.

"OK, let's start with team Russo and Keller. What do you have for us?" asked Gonzalez, as he prepared to take notes.

"Sarge, not much," Russo began, after hesitatingly clearing his throat. "We hit more than twenty schools of martial arts in the area, and received the same bullshit from most of the owners. They maintain that their students are devoted to the art of their particular style and couldn't even suggest one who might have the personality and skill to commit the murders. Obviously this is a crock, because these schools have to have one or two who play outside the rules."

"We did get one potential hit at the Korean Academy of Taekwondo over in Carol City," Keller said. "The owner, surprisingly named Mr. Kim, told us that he has an African-American kid ready to take his black belt exam but has a lousy attitude and a hair trigger temper. He is always causing trouble during sparring exercises at the facility, which he referred to as 'the dojang'," Keller reported as he added squinting at his notes. We ran a background check on the kid, named Latrelle Watts. His record consists of misdemeanors and a marijuana bust, nothing that would rise to the seriousness of murder, and there was nothing that would hint at a tendency toward violence."

"We went to see Mr. Watts, who resides in the scenic Liberty City section," Russo continued. "It was around 1 pm and our persistent knocking shook him from his beauty sleep. Believe me, there was nothing beautiful about this guy. He looked like a Mike Tyson opponent after a ten-round beat down. This kid's nose has been broken more than a politician's promises."

"OK, Russo, we get the picture," Gonzalez said. "Save the standup and get to the point."

"Yea well, Latrelle has a pretty airtight alibi for the night the murders took place. The stupid mook was in the slammer for a DUI. He was observed driving erratically on I-95 around 9 pm and was transported to Baptist Health South to have blood drawn and from there was escorted to Miami-Dade lockup. He was released the following morning. He definitely ain't our guy." Russo slammed his notebook closed putting a final coda on Latrelle Watts.

Gonzalez looked over at Cutrazulla and Simmons. "OK, you guys are up."

"We took that hair fiber to more than a dozen wig shops in the city and came up empty, Simmons said. "It's an expensive synthetic black hair that is called mono fibre synthetic, considered to be a superior quality alternative to other fibers. Because of its length, it was definitely part of a woman or transvestite's wig but that's as far as we could go with it. There are hundreds, maybe thousands, of these wigs sitting on the heads of women and some men in the city of Miami as we speak. And that hair could have been lying there for days."

"We also haven't too much to add at this point," Gonzalez admitted. "Estelle Stellini flew into Miami to identify her husband, Roy's body. She wasn't too broken up over the murder. It seems Roy fancied himself a stud and as a frequent traveler for his sales job, was a known womanizer. Estelle told us that he had no known enemies, even among cuckolded husbands that she was aware of. She indicated that he was a prick but a careful prick."

Gonzalez stood up, stretching his muscular back. "God, we could use a break in this case. If these are purely random murders, we're going to need to get lucky. Fast." Just as the team was filing from the room, his cell rang.

"Gonzalez."

"Hey, guy, you in a better mood?" Kathy Henderson asked cautiously. "I might have something to cheer you up."

"Kathy, I could use anything at this point. What do you have?"

"There were some interesting matches on NCIC. A couple of days ago there were a couple of murders in Philadelphia that might get your attention. A chemical engineer attending a conference named Kent Renale was found murdered in his hotel room at the Hilton near the airport, a switchblade jammed into his forehead. He was naked but looked like he never had the chance to get it on with his companion, who Philly police assume was a hooker."

"You get anything on the knife?"

"It was nearly wiped clean. I say nearly, because they found one print on the very end of the handle. It was identified as belonging to one Heraldo Ruiz, a member of a south Philly gang called the Latin Kings. It seems that Mr. Ruiz and his colleague, Carlos Sandovol, were dispatched by an unsub in an alley in Philly's center city section the same day as Renale's body was discovered dead in his room at the Hilton. Ruiz's throat was cut ear to ear, and his ribs were crushed by blunt force, probably a kick. Sandavol died of a blunt trauma, a knife wound, into his brain. The Philadelphia medical examiner's office reported that the knife that killed Ruiz and Sandavol was also used on Renale."

"So we have a couple of murders in the City of Brotherly Love that have a connection to each other, possibly committed by a person who is trained or is just a fast, mean sonofabitch," Gonzalez thought aloud. "Any check on Kent, what was his name?"

"Renale," Henderson responded.

"Was he gay or what they call bi-curious now-a-days?"

"Don't know that yet," Henderson said. "But here's the kicker, no pun intended. Both Renale and our vic Stellini had something in common." Silence on the cell.

"Are you going to share?" Gonzaelz asked, impatiently.

"They both flew into their respective cities on Odyssey Airlines."

Chapter Nine

Edgewood
1995

Sandy was entering Edgewood High School, a small suburban school located seven miles from downtown Pittsburgh. The tiny Borough of Edgewood was an exclusively white enclave surrounded by people of color, making their own escape from the encroaching ghetto, which was insidiously creeping forward, devouring property inch by inch. The community of four thousand people knew each other intimately, where no secret was safe and everyone's business was fodder for gossip. No one was familiar with Sandy Garland's background, but eventually rumors about her and her dysfunctional family would begin to spread.

When Sandy was seven the family moved to Edgewood from nearby Squirrel Hill, in an attempt to give her a fresh start and respite from the merciless bullying that she was experiencing. As she grew taller her weight began to normalize and she began to exercise. By the time she was ready for high school, Sandy had become a tall, attractive young lady, albeit a very troubled one. The years of taunting by her classmates and abuse by her alcoholic father had exacted a price.

While Henry was oblivious to the interpersonal dynamics of his family, his alcoholism providing a psychological 'firewall,'

Gloria Garland was extremely concerned about Sandy's mental health. Her grades had improved, and she seemed to have become outwardly immune to any caustic remark leveled at her by a mean-spirited classmate. And the school was loaded with snotty, mean-spirited kids. But Gloria sensed that something was missing in Sandy's soul. She couldn't articulate it, but the girl was different, and she sensed something was wrong.

When she transferred to Edgewood Sandy seemed to take to her new surroundings. On the surface all was normal as she went about her daily routine of school and homework, but she kept to herself and rarely socialized. Some of her classmates attempted to befriend Sandy but to no avail. She fast developed a reputation as a loner. That is, until she met Tom Stanion, the captain of the high school football team. Stanion was a tall, good looking athlete who was desired by most of the school's female student body and envied by every male. He was being recruited by most of the Division I universities and the consensus among the sports pundits was that he was a can't-miss All-American candidate and eventual pro. Sandy was for the first time attracted to a boy, and unfortunately he had to be one of Edgewood's most arrogant and snottiest of all.

Tom Stanion was a member of a well-to-do family that lived in the wealthiest area of the small town, His father, Doug, was a cardiac specialist at nearby Columbia Hospital, and gossip had it that fixing hearts wasn't the only specialty of the good doctor. He also specialized in 'breaking' them. He romanced the most comely of the hospital staff, of which Tom's mother, Sue, had full knowledge. She had her own specialty, which consisted of a series of lesbian relationships with other bored, married women.

The Stanions indulged Tom's every whim, and as he grew and matured, so did his ego and sense of entitlement. While his teammates depended on his athletic abilities to lead them to a conference championship, they couldn't abide his abrasive personality. He was not a likeable young man, and Tom Stanion could care less. The girls whom he dated were merely sexual objects, and when he tired of them, they were discarded like yesterday's newspapers. Tom Stanion was a misogynist in the making. Sandy Garland was not aware of his reputation and with no confidants, she wouldn't know until it was too late,

Sandy was in the school cafeteria when Stanion and his tray suddenly appeared.

"Mind if I sit here?" he asked, all dimples and white teeth.

"Sure, go ahead," Sandy replied.

"I'm Tom Stanion," he stated proffering his hand.

"I know who you are. You are on the football team."

"Yep, I'm the captain. And you are . . . ."

"Sandy Garland."

"And . . . .?" Stanion's question hung in the air.

"And what?"

"Tell me a little about yourself."

"There's nothing to tell. I transferred here from Schenley over in Squirrel Hill."

"Why did you come to this little backwater town? Schenley's a larger school."

"My family thought I'd do better in a smaller environment."

"Yea? Well, this is a smaller environment alright. Everybody's so far up everyone's ass in this burg you can taste hair spray."

"That's good to know. I'll try to keep my business to myself," Sandy said.

"What are you doing Saturday evening?" Stanion asked. "I mean after we kick the shit out of Verona High School."

"Nothing, why?" Sandy asked coyly.

"There's a recreation hall dance at the club tonight. Maybe we can get together and hang out." The Edgewood Community Club and its swimming pool were a temporary refuge in a morally bereft neighborhood, where housewives came to display their tits and asses, and to dump off their kids for the lifeguards to babysit. The adults worked on their skin cancer, and the children performed 'cannonball' dives, splashing and annoying the hell out them. They were all just living the dream.

"I don't think so," Sandy responded. "I have some work to do at home."

"C'mon," Stanion said. "It'll be fun. Plus, I can introduce you to some of the guys on the team."

Sandy was clearly torn. "I don't know . . . well I guess it will be okay."

"Great, meet me at the club around 7:30. See you there or be square," Stanion said with a smirk.

*   *   *

Sandy walked into the Edgewood Community Club around 7:40 that evening and looked around for Tom Stanion. He was nowhere to be seen, and Sandy began to get a little anxious. She suddenly spotted him walking through the club's French doors, an attractive blonde on his arms. Sandy started to walk toward the exit.

"Sandy, hey Sandy," Stanion shouted across the dance floor. "Where you goin'?"

"Where *you* going?" she shot back. "Looks like you're otherwise occupied."

Stanion began laughing and the blonde looked amused. "Hell, this is Janet Simpson, the school's head cheerleader. We're old friends. I asked her to hang out with us tonight." It was obvious that the two of them had been smoking some weed.

Sandy was taken by surprise but played along. "OK, what's up?"

"To celebrate our lopsided victory over Verona, I thought we'd go for a little late swim over in the club's pool."

"Is it open tonight?" Sandy asked. Stanion and Janet both laughed.

"It will be in a few minutes. And don't worry about security. The head guy's a sports nut and loves the team."

"I didn't bring a suit," she said.

"What suits? We don't need no stinkin' suits," he said, imitating a line from an old movie that he saw on cable. It went way over Sandy's head.

"I don't think . . ."

"Don't worry about it," Stanion urged, flashing his smile.

"We swim there all the time," head cheerleader Janet added. "And no suits required."

Sandy hesitated. "OK, I guess . . ."

"Alright," Stanion whooped, clapping his hands as if he was breaking a huddle. "Let's get ready to rumble."

The three of them left the dance and made their way down a staircase and through an underground hallway that led to the pool. The music from the dance slowly receded and gave way to the silence of the pool, save for the gurgling of its chlorination system. Moonlight illuminated the gently rippling water in the deserted pool. Stanion produced a joint from his breast pocket.

"A hit for my ladies?" he asked gallantly, offering the small, rolled cigarette to Janet, who gladly accepted. After a deep inhalation, she passed it to Sandy who tentatively took it

"OK, sports fans, let's get wet," Stanion urged as he began removing his clothes. Janet followed his lead. Sandy was uncertain what to do.

"C'mon girl," Janet cajoled. "Time to go swimming."

Still unsure what to do, Sandy began to tentatively remove her clothes. Both Stanion and Janet were already in the water, watching her every move.

"C'mon, Sandy," Stanion said, exasperation beginning to edge into his voice.

"Okay, okay," she said, finally removing her bra and panties and quickly jumping into the pool.

Stanion and Janet moved toward her, their arms surrounding her, encircling her. They began pressing their bodies against her's. Janet's hands reached for Sandy's breasts and nether region, groping and fondling. Stanion pressed his engorged penis against her buttocks, sliding it back and forth across her cheeks. Sandy's head was spinning from the marijuana, and she was having difficulty comprehending what was happening.

Instinctively, she lashed out at Janet and Stanion, trying to push them away. The two of them kept her locked in tightly in their arms, as Janet penetrated her with her finger. Sandy gasped and renewed her struggle, to no avail. Suddenly, Stanion and Janet began to laugh, releasing her. Sandy awkwardly splashed her way to the side of the pool.

"What's the matter, little girl, don't you want it?" Stanion taunted. Janet was pressing against him, lasciviously stroking him beneath the water, while she stared at Sandy.

"Why would you do something like that?" Sandy cried, as she struggled to pull her pants over her wet legs. "I thought you were interested in me."

"I am interested in you, sweet cheeks," Stanion said, still laughing. "I am interested in *screwing* you."

"Me, too," Janet added, enthusiastically.

Tears stinging her eyes, Sandy gathered the rest of her clothes and began to frantically look for the exit. The sounds of their laughter receded as she ran from the club.

Sandy Garland was devastated that Tom Stanion, the school's premier athlete and most sought after male would treat her like a piece of meat, unworthy of any human consideration. She knew the rumors of the incident would spread like wildfire among the students, and she was embarrassed. Not to mention angry.

*   *   *

Edgewood's football team won the conference title in November but was unexpectedly defeated in the state championship game in Hershey, Pennsylvania. Tom Stanion accepted a full scholarship to the University of Tennessee, an unusual decision for an athlete courted by the likes of Coach Joe Paterno at Penn State and the persuasive Jackie Sherrill at the University of Pittsburgh. But the Vol's hostesses who were assigned to escort the potential scholarship athletes had a major influence on Tom's decision, who was impressed with their Southern hospitality and other attributes.

To celebrate his scholarship, Stanion invited a few members of the team and their girls for the weekend at his family's chalet in Ligonier, a quant little town east of Pittsburgh. The Stanion family weekend getaway home was a 4,000 square foot structure with floor-to-ceiling windows that afforded a breathtaking vista of Pennsylvania's Laurel Mountain range. Heavily wooded with evergreens and hardwoods, its slopes made for excellent skiing during winter.

The unusually moderate temperatures this particular late fall provided perfect conditions for shooting the white water at the Ohiopyle Falls along the Youghiogheny River, which boasted a series of treacherous rapids that claimed its share of lives over the years. Stanion and his group were loading up his parent's Range Rover when Jerry Borstrom, the team's short, compact nose guard, announced that the vodka and orange juice had been left back in the cabin. They had been drinking heavily all morning and were planning to continue the festivities on the water.

"I'll get it," Tom yelled. "Don't start without me," he called over his shoulder as he made his wobbly way up the long path to the chalet. As he staggered into the house's massive great room, he stopped momentarily to admire the expanse of pine and glass, the walls of which were decorated with the heads of exotic animals that the elder Stanion had slaughtered on reserves. Dr. Stanion and his band of wealthy white hunters paid handsomely to kill beautiful beasts that were trapped and defenseless. Tom admired his father's way with wildlife and women, and it was what he aspired to emulate.

Tom spotted the bottles of vodka and mixers sitting outside on the deck, which was perched over a 200-foot canyon, a sheer drop that gave the Stanion's chalet a uniqueness and vertigo-inducing quality that the architect thought was the piece de la resistance to his award-winning structure built into the side of a mountain. The railings around the deck were steel-reinforced and bolted together more securely than the Golden Gate Bridge in San Francisco, and the Stanion home and its distinctive amenities were the subject of articles in the local newspapers and a number of architectural magazines.

As Tom pushed the vacuum-sealed door leading onto the deck, he noticed that a couple of the bottles were spilled and lying up against the railing. Sliding in the alcohol pooled on the deck flooring, he grabbed onto the railing and looked curiously over into the abyss. That's when he caught a figure moving out of the corner of his eye.

"Hi, Tom," Sandy Garland said, as she pushed him with a suddenness that caught him completely by surprise, throwing his already unsteady frame over the railing. As Tom Stanion plunged the 200 feet into the rock strewn canyon, his last thoughts were of Sandy's perfectly formed breasts that he and Janet stared at in the dim light of the pool last month and the fact that in a few months he had to report to football orientation at Tennessee. Of course, he never would.

*　　*　　*

Tom Stanion's death was ruled an accident due to his alcohol consumption and the high probability of him slipping on vodka that that had been spilled onto the deck as he hurriedly gathered up the bottles to run out to meet his inebriated friends. Sandy Garland managed to enter the house, shove him over the railing and ,make her quiet escape from the chalet's side entrance without anyone seeing her. That included her parents, who hadn't noticed that the family car was missing for an afternoon, while they visited friends down the block.

As were many of her classmates, Sandy was shocked and saddened to learn of Tom Stanion's death. She even gave her smirking, heartfelt condolences to Janet Simpson.

Chapter Ten

"I want the passenger manifests and names of the flight crews of the Odyssey flights into Miami and Philadelphia on those dates," Gonzalez ordered, as he addressed his team. "I want to know if there are any matches of passengers on those planes who might have come into contact with our vics. If you get one, we're going to dig into his background to determine if he's had any military or martial arts training, his sexual history, where he went to school, the whole nine. This is the first decent break we've had in weeks."

"Sarge, we checked the rosters of both flight crews and got matches on three flight attendants, Raleigh-based Kirsten Brooks and Elizabeth Charles; Sandy Garland, out of Pittsburgh; and a first officer, a guy named Dennis Allison, who's based in Raleigh," Detective Simmons reported.

"Initial conversations with Odyssey haven't turned up anything hinkey. All of them are long-time employees, have clean work records and never any problems to speak of. But here's something interesting. Allison flew helicopter gunships in Nam during the late 60s and we're contacting the Army to get his record. Garland, according to my contact at Odyssey, is drop-dead gorgeous but a very quiet and aloof person. We're checking with the Pittsburgh PD to see if she has had any charges in the past, but human resources at Odyssey reports that she's a capable, experienced flight attendant who often serves as lead on her flights. A senior attendant, she just does her job and doesn't socialize with her colleagues and takes part in few of their activities. Likewise with Brooks and Charles. Both are good employees and upstanding citizens."

"I don't figure a woman for these murders, but we'll take a look at those three," Gonzalez said. "Let's keep digging. I want to know when this pilot, Dennis Allison, and the flight attendants are scheduled back in Miami, so that we can have a face to face. Russo, handle that through Odyssey, and let's not telegraph that we want to talk to them until they're in the city. We'll let the airlines set the meetings at their hotel. Wiggins and I will conduct the interviews."

"Let me guess, Sarge," Cutrazulla asked with a grin. "You're taking Sandy Garland." Ensuing laughter from the assembled detectives.

"Well, mis amigos, somebody's gotta take on the grunt work, and as your leader I wouldn't ask you to do a job I wouldn't do," Gonzalez said, amid more laughter. "Vayamos."

*   *   *

As the Odyssey flight crew was checking into the Miami Embassy Suites, Sandy's cell phone rang. It was a human resources administrator with Odyssey informing her that a Detective Gonzalez from Miami Homicide would be contacting her for an interview.

"What's this all about?" Sandy asked, nonplussed.

"Routine inquiry regarding a couple of homicides in Miami a few weeks back," the voice said. "The detectives are just checking our personnel and passengers who were on certain flights. Detective Gonzalez said that he would be contacting you at the hotel to arrange an informal interview. There's no reason to be concerned."

"Oh, I'm not concerned at all. It's just that I am preparing to go out. Do you have any idea when this policeman will be calling me?"

As those words left her mouth, her hotel room phone rang. Sandy concluded her call with the Odyssey HR administrator and grabbed the beige handset cradled on her night stand.

"Hello," she said cautiously.

"Is this Miss Sandy Garland, a flight attendant for Odyssey Airlines?" Gonzalez asked.

"Yes, it is. Who is this, please?"

"This is Detective John Gonzalez, Miami PD," pause, "Homicide Division."

"Yes, Odyssey alerted me that you might be calling. What can I do for you, detective?"

"We are conducting an investigation into three murders here in the Miami area in the last month and cooperating with police in Philadelphia where a murder with similar, shall I say, attributes occurred."

"Detective . . . ?"

"Gonzalez."

"Detective Gonzalez, I haven't killed anyone . . . within the last month at least," Sandy added with a chuckle.

"I'm sure that you haven't," Gonzalez responded. "We are interviewing flight crew and passengers who happened to be on specific Odyssey flights with two of the victims. Strictly a routine interview, I can assure you. As senior attendant, you might have noticed or remember something that may just help us piece together the last few hours of their lives."

"And who were the victims and what flights were they on?"

"Miss Garland, I would rather discuss this in person at your hotel. The interview won't take long. When would be a good time?"

"Now is as good a time as any," Sandy said. "I have an appointment later this evening, so the sooner the better."

"I am already here," Gonzalez said. "I'm down at the front desk. I'll meet you in the lobby, and we'll go into a private conference room here at the hotel."

This guy is sure of himself, she thought. "I'll be down in ten minutes, Detective."

When Sandy Garland approached the hotel's front desk fifteen minutes later, John Gonzalez was, for once, speechless. She was gorgeous, with the lightest blue eyes he had ever seen.

Nearly as tall as him in heels, this woman was one fine el bebé. She had the shapely legs of an athlete but was stacked like a stripper. She extended her hand.

"I'm Sandy Garland."

And I have an erection, Gonzalez thought. "Good afternoon, Miss Garland, as you probably have surmised, I'm John Gonzalez," he said, taking her hand in his.

"Yes, I surmised as much," she responded, smiling. "Where is this conference room? I don't have a lot of time."

"Right down that hall, he said, gesturing with his forefinger. "Room 202."

"Lead the way, Detective."

"Please, call me John. May I call you Sandy?"

"Please do, John," she said, as they made their way down the hall. What the fuck is this, she thought, be nice to a policeman week? Her smile never faltered as they assumed seats opposite each other in conference room 202. Gonzalez, business-like now, took a small notebook from his jacket pocket.

"To begin, may I have your full name, age and place of residence."

"Sandy Michele Garland, age 28, and I live in Pittsburgh, Pennsylvania."

"Where in Pittsburgh?" Gonzalez asked.

"Little town called Edgewood, not far from the city."

"How long have you resided there?"

"I have lived at the same address since I was seven years old. My folks passed away when I was in high school, and I just continued living in the house. It's convenient to the city, and while it's a small town, it's really a quaint little 'oasis' on the fringe of the city." And the residents are assholes who talk behind my back, saying terrible things about me, she thought darkly. She rescued her smile as it began to fade.

"Something wrong?" Gonzalez asked.

"No, just had a fleeting memory of my parents," she said. Especially my prick of a father she thought, who in his drunken stupors would come into my room and stick his penis into me. I know mom knew what he was up to, the dumb shit. Too bad they had to meet their untimely demise. Her smile grew brighter as she recalled more pleasant times.

"I see," Gonzalez said consulting his notebook. "You were on Flight 243 from Michigan into Miami back on October 3rd. Is that correct?"

"Yes, I am routinely assigned to that flight. It's nice to have a few hours here enjoying your great weather before routing north."

"Did you notice a tall, thin man in seat 17C?"

"John, do you know how many Odyssey passengers I encounter during any one day? I have absolutely no recollection of a man in 17C. Why, did he do something to draw attention to himself?"

"Not really, but his wife in Grand Rapids told us that he thought he was pretty smooth with the ladies. It wouldn't be a stretch of the imagination to hear that he might have come onto you or one of the other cabin crew members."

"What happened to this guy?" she asked.

"I'm not at liberty to provide details of the investigation, but I can tell you he was murdered at a private club, along with another woman. We are trying to find a link between the two of them."

Sandy Garland smiled. "John, I'm a vegetarian because I can't stand the thought of animals being sacrificed just to feed people, who eat too much anyway. It's getting so that many of them can't fit into one seat on the aircraft and require seat belt extenders to hold them in place." Slobs and perverts, she thought. "I don't believe in killing any living creature, and that includes humans," she added.

"Sandy, I am simply following up on folks who just may have come into contact with the victim and who may recall a detail that can help track the killer. You are not a suspect." I'd like to give you a body search just to be certain. A smile momentarily creased his face.

"A penny for your thoughts?" Sandy asked. Her stare was playful, but Gonzalez sensed something behind her eyes he couldn't put his finger on. He was embarrassed.

"Just trying to follow your comments about people who overeat. I happen to agree with you on that point."

"You look like you keep yourself pretty fit. We share that in common."

"I try. Listen, Sandy, that's about it for now. Here's my card. If you remember something, anything at all, please don't hesitate to call my cell phone at any time. The smallest detail just might help us get the killer."

"The one the news media is calling the 'Swinging Sex Murderer,' or something like that?" she asked.

"Something like that. The local and national media have the scent on this one and are having a field day with so-called expert speculation and general B.S. to keep their circulations and ratings high."

"And here you are having to interview any and all who might have the slightest connection to the case."

"Sandy, sometimes that slight connection can break a case. Remember, the Son of Sam killer in New York during the 70s? A ticket for having his car parked too close to a fire hydrant as he was seeking out his next victim proved to be his undoing. Sometimes, it doesn't take much to stop a killer. Just hard work and a little luck."

"What's your take on this 'swinger' killer?"

"I can't give you much detail, because it's too early in the investigation. We are looking into a couple of other recent homicides and will search the database for older ones that might have matching MOs. Most likely, this guy didn't just begin to kill. I can tell you this. He's strong, smart and seems to be choosing his victims randomly, which is going to make him extremely difficult to catch."

"You're describing a serial killer, aren't you?" she asked, a look of concern clouding her features.

"We're not certain yet, but it's pointing in that direction."

As they reached the lobby, Sandy looked down at his card and said, "Detective, if I remember anything at all I'll be sure and call you immediately."

Gonzalez extended his hand and said, "Thanks. And listen, when you're back in Miami maybe we can get together socially. There's a great restaurant in Little Havana called Versailles, which is a landmark. It serves Ropa Vieja to die for."

Interesting choice of words, Sandy thought. "I might take you up on that. I have your card." With that she turned and headed back to the elevators.

As John watched her walk away, he couldn't help but think that this woman just might be the one he's been waiting for.

Chapter Eleven

Detective Roland Wiggins contacted First Officer Dennis Allison on the cell number that Odyssey provided. "We're checking crew members and passengers who were on specific Odyssey flights that the victims in similar homicides shared," he informed Allison. "At this point, we're following every lead we have, no matter how tenuous."

"I'll cooperate completely with your investigation," Allison said, "but listen detective, I have a date tonight in your fair city, whom I must meet at 7 pm. That doesn't give me a lot of time. Can we hook up at a bar called Crescendos in SoBe around sixish?"

"I know where it is," Wiggins replied. It was a piano bar in South Beach that catered to a mix of upscale gays and straights.

"You'll recognize me," Allison continued. "I'm six foot five, and I'll be wearing a light blue and red flowered shirt. I sort of stand out from the crowd."

"Thanks," Wiggins replied. "I'm five nine, and I'll be totting a .40 caliber SIGARM and a gold shield. I try not to stand out from the crowd."

Allison chuckled. "They say that opposites attract, detective."

Christ, I don't think so, thought Wiggins. "I look forward to meeting you Mr. Allison . . ."

"Please, call me Denny. I'm very informal."

"OK, Denny, see you at 6 pm."

Crescendos Piano Bar was a new, distinctly chic lounge set in the DiLido Building at the Ritz Carlton Hotel in the heart of South Beach. All chrome, marble and leather, the lounge catered to Miami's trendy crowd, who frequented it for strong drinks, top flight piano entertainment and the possibility of a late-night rendezvous. Straights and gays co-mingled peacefully, with the élan of the sophisticated denizens of Miami's nightscape.

Wiggins walked into the lounge a few minutes before six and gave the dense happy hour crowd a quick visual scan. He didn't spot a giant colorfully garbed flamingo but did see a couple of curious looking 'birds' gathered in obvious fellowship around the piano, singing along with the pianist's rendition of Billy Joel's *Uptown Girl*. Whatever floats your canoe, he thought.

He had ordered a vodka and tonic and settled himself at the bar, when Dennis Allison strolled in. Many stopped mid-drink or sentence to take in this extremely tall, good looking man as he made his way to where Wiggins sat at the marble bar.

"You must be Detective Wiggins," Allison said, hand extended.

"Ah, I'm kind of informal myself," Wiggins said. "Just call me 'detective.'" Both men laughed. "What will you have?"

"Hey Johnny," Allison called to the bartender. "How 'bout an MGD64. Got to keep trim and fit for duty at Odyssey," he said to Wiggins, patting his obviously flat stomach. "It becomes difficult to wedge my fat ass into the First Officer's seat if I gain ten pounds."

"When are you due to fly out?" Wiggins asked.

"Not until tomorrow afternoon. All pilots are required to follow the 12-hour 'bottle-to-throttle' rule. That means when I'm done with this beer, no more alcohol until we land the 767 at La Guardia in New York."

"As I told you on the phone, we are interviewing Odyssey flight crew members who were on the same flights with the victims that landed in Miami and Philadelphia on separate days two months ago."

"What happened to these folks?" Allison asked.

"I'm not a liberty to provide too many details. The Miami victims were killed at clubs here in the area. We believe that the assailant was possibly trained in hand-to-hand fighting or the martial arts. The Philadelphia murder had some similarity that was picked up on a national computer database. It may or may not be related at this time."

"Hence, you would be interested in me, because of my combat duty in Vietnam," Allison observed, as he took a sip from his bottle. "I was the commander of an AH-1 Cobra, attached to the 52nd Aviation Battalion in '69. We were based in an oil refining port called Vung Tal, near the Mekong Delta, where the firefights were frequent and fierce. I usually flew close air support for our ground troops and could be called up at a moment's notice. Basically, detective, those years were like living on a razor's edge of insanity, where the line between living and dying was barely perceptible."

"Did any of those 'razor edge' experiences have any effect on your emotional state over the years that might have been a result of combat related stress?" Wiggins asked, watching Allison closely for any facial ticks.

"If you're asking if I have the capability to murder someone, the answer is no. I'm actually a pacifist by nature who happened to be able to pilot gunships through heavy ground fire. After Nam, I flew corporate jets for a time, but ferrying a bunch of business 'fat cats' wasn't my idea of a career. I latched on with Odyssey more than fifteen years ago and have had a great career and a spotless record. You can check it out."

"I already have," Wiggins replied. "As I said, we're following every lead that we have in this case. In fact, flight attendants Sandy Garland, Kirsten Brooks and Elizabeth Charles were also members of the Odyssey crew on both flights. We have completed their interviews."

"Sandy Garland gives me the willies," Allison said.

"The willies," Wiggins repeated, smiling. "What do you mean by that?"

"I don't know really how to explain it. She's never been a problem on any flights I've flown, and she seems quiet and self-absorbed away from work. She just seems cold and uncaring, emotions that are masked by a gorgeous smile and a body even I could go for. I hope that I'm not telling tales out of school. I mean my opinion of her personality has absolutely no bearing on your case, I'm sure."

"I would agree with you, Denny. She just may be what some of us would refer to as a cold, and I won't use the 'B' word here but you get my drift. No, these killings have the earmarks of a man and a very powerful and crafty one at that."

As Wiggins stood up to leave, Dennis Allison's cell rang. "That's too bad," he said to the caller. "We'll catch up with each other the next time I am back in Miami." He looked up at Detective Wiggins. "Well, my companion for this evening tells me that he has come down with a stomach virus and has to cancel. Would you care for another drink?" he said with a wan smile.

"Thanks, Denny, but I am due back at the bureau and one quick drink is my limit. I follow my own two-hour bottle-to-handgun rule," Wiggins said, as he stood.

"That's too bad. I hope that I have been some help. At least you could see for yourself that I don't drag my knuckles when I walk."

"As tall as you are? That would be a feat. I'll stay in touch, Denny."

Odyssey First Officer Dennis Allison left Crescendos after breaking his own rule of 12-hours bottle-to-throttle rule. He had a couple of additional beers and an obviously lonely young man bought him a brandy, but neither seemed interested in any extended conversation. He decided to walk down to Crème Lounge, a jumping place where the lesbians outnumbered the gay men, but that was alright. He'd grab a Diet Coke, check out the scene and see what transpires. He liked a little serendipity in his life.

It was a beautiful Miami night, and Allison took in the invigorating warm, salty air as he ambled along Lincoln Road toward Lincoln Lane, where Crème was located. He was in no hurry, knowing that he didn't have to get up at some ungodly hour for a flight. It was past midnight and unusually quiet, but it was a weeknight. That's when he heard it.

"Denny, hey Denny," the unseen person beckoned in a soft, modulated voice. Allison stopped and looked around but saw no one.

"Who is it?" he called back, sotto voice, as if he and this unseen person shared a secret.

"Over here, toward Bebes," said the voice, which he now identified emanating from a dark alcove besides the closed men's clothing store.

"Who are you?" he asked, as he hesitantly inched toward the alcove's opening. That's when he saw Sandy Garland. "What the hell, Sandy. You scared the shit out of me. What in God's name are you doing lurking about Sobe at this time of the night? You'll end up getting mugged or worse," he warned as he walked toward her. Maybe she's heading to Crème, like I am, he thought. Who knew?

As he approached the tall, statuesque blonde, he instinctively sensed something was wrong. She didn't look right. "What's wrong, Sandy? Have you been hurt?"

It happened so fast that First Officer Dennis Allison, even though possessed of quick reflexes himself, never had a chance to react. Sandy Garland struck him with a precisely aimed knife hand blow to the carotoid artery on the left side of his neck, which shattered the main blood vessel carrying blood and consciousness to his brain. The world went dark immediately for the tall pilot, as he went into a stroke, paralysis and, finally, oblivion.

Sandy Garland strolled unseen out onto Lincoln toward Crème in hopes of meeting some gorgeous young woman who might appreciate her physical perfection. She had a noon flight to New York, and the night still held promise. It's a shame Odyssey would have to recruit a first officer to replace Denny tomorrow, but with his risky lifestyle something untoward was bound to happen sooner or later.

Chapter Twelve

Detective John Gonzalez caught the call at 3:30 am as he was driving to the precinct. He radioed Wiggins. "Didn't you interview Dennis Allison, the first officer with Odyssey Airlines, tonight?" Gonzalez asked.

"Yea, I met him in a bar over in South Beach. He seemed to be clean, why?"

"His body was discovered this morning in an alley near a clothing store called Bebes on Lincoln Road. I'm on my way and will meet you there."

"Ah, shit," said Wiggins as he turned his car around to head for Lincoln Road. Hell, I only left the guy a couple of hours ago. Could the killer be tracking the police and eliminating people we are interviewing? he thought. First Liz Tomkin and now Dennis Allison.

The scene was bustling with police and personnel from the medical examiner's office, as Wiggins pulled up to Bebes. Gonzalez was standing behind the yellow tape in conference with ME Solez. As Wiggins approached, both turned, a look of irritation creasing Gonzalez's face.

"Was Allison with anyone when you saw him this evening?" he asked.

"He was supposed to meet a friend, but the guy wasn't going to show. He called Allison on his cell to say that he had a flu bug or something. That's about when I left him."

"Let's get his cell phone record and find out who made that call when you were with him," Gonzalez ordered.

"Mr. Allison here was killed with what looks like a single blow to his carotid artery," ME Solez said said, looking up at the officers. "The bodies are beginning to pile up."

"Who in the name of God would have known I was meeting this guy, unless it's someone with an inside track at Odyssey," Wiggins mused. "What about that flight attendant you interviewed, Sandy somebody?"

"Sandy Garland," Gonzalez said. "I am going to circle back to her. She may know something about a colleague at Odyssey with martial arts training or who might have a grudge against mankind. In the meantime, I am assigning Cutrazulla and Simmons to dig into her background in Pittsburgh to see if we can shake anything loose. Russo and Keller are doing a little snooping into Brooks and Charles' past, but I highly doubt that either of those two slender, petite women could be involved in these murders."

"I'll let you know what's up, after I perform the autopsy," Solez said. "I don't expect to uncover any revelations. This guy died from a karate-style blow to the neck, precipitating a blunt force vascular trauma to the carotid artery, which ruptured, stopping oxygen to the brain. You can see the unusually large pooling of blood in that area of the neck," she said, pointing to Allison's neck. "You guys have a psycho with a high level of training in karate or some sort of martial art running loose, and he ain't no benevolent 'grasshopper' like that bald guy was in Kung Fu."

*   *   *

Gonzalez's ass was dragging from being up most of the night, as he rifled through notes to find Sandy Garland's cell number. She answered on the third ring. "Hello," the tentative voice said.

"Sandy, this is Detective John Gonzalez. I hate to be contacting you so early, but we found the body of Dennis Allison early this morning in an alley on Lincoln Road, dead from what looks like a blow to the neck."

Silence on the line prompted Gonzalez to determine if the call was interrupted. "Sandy, you still there?"

"Yes," she said weakly. Gonzalez could detect that she was crying. "Oh, God, not Dennis. He was the kindest, gentlest man I worked with at Odyssey. We were like brother and sister," she lied.

"Sandy, I need to sit down with you again. Could you come down to our headquarters this morning? The address is 129 Northwest Avenue; a cabbie will know where we are. I need to ask you a few more questions."

"I have a flight at noon," she said, "so it will have to be in the next hour. John, I thought I gave you everything I remembered."

"We suspect that our murder suspect may work for Odyssey, or in some way be connected to the airline. You may have seen or heard something that could help us. Time is not on our side, especially with a serial killer running loose."

Sandy gasped. "You really think a serial killer may be committing these horrible crimes? It was just a guess on my part. I'll be there at 8:30 am," she promised, breaking the connection. Pretty accurate guess, Gonzalez thought as he snapped his cell shut.

As Sandy Garland entered the South Florida Detectives Bureau, heads swiveled to see the tall, gorgeous blonde as she approached the receptionist. "Detective John Gonzalez, please," she asked the first person she encountered.

"Yes, Miss, let me take you to him," Detective Mickey Russo said brightly, as he nearly leapt up from his desk chair, knocking over his coffee cup in the process. Clearly embarrassed, Russo grabbed some paper towels to soak up the coffee that was permeating his desk and papers.

"That's okay, Mick, I'll take her from here," Gonzalez said, as he beckoned for Sandy to follow him. "Thanks for coming so promptly, Sandy. Let's grab some coffee and sit in the conference room."

After they were settled, Sandy began to tear. "I was devastated by the news of Dennis' death," she said, dabbing at her eyes with a white handkerchief. "I will, of course, help in any way that I can."

"Were you aware that Dennis Allison was gay?" Gonzalez asked.

"Yes, I was, but he was very discrete. He didn't hide the fact that he was gay, but he didn't broadcast it either."

"Did he date someone on a regular basis?" Gonzalez said. "According to Detective Wiggins, he was waiting to meet someone last night, who reportedly cancelled because of illness."

"Dennis was in a long term relationship with a gentleman who owned a chain of flower shops in the Raleigh-Durham area, where he lived," Sandy said. "He wasn't the promiscuous type but probably has . . . had . . . some lovers on the side. I am just speculating. He did mention that he was meeting a person named Richard last night at Crescendos. That's about as much as I know. As a rule, crew members don't mix during a layover. We pretty much go our separate ways."

"I see," Gonzalez said. "Sandy, I have to ask this question. Where were you last night?"

Seemingly unfazed, Sandy said, "I had my usual workout in the hotel, which lasted about two hours and . . ."

"Two hours!" Gonzalez interrupted. "That's a serious workout. Geez, my workouts pale in comparison. What do you do that takes two hours?"

"I do about 45 minutes of cardio, followed by weights and then some specific exercise routines, like Pilates, that I have been doing for years. I find that they keep me sharp."

"They look like they are," said Gonzalez, smiling. "You certainly look sharp."

"Thank you, John. What can I tell you that might help in your investigation? Dennis and I were colleagues and friends, but he never would open up to me. I suppose that his lifestyle was such that he kept everything very close to his vest. He was, you could say, a very private person. I, too, don't socialize with the other members of the crew."

"Could Allison have been mixed up in some sort of group of men who have specific sexual appetites, which might have gotten him killed? He might have been seen meeting with Detective Wiggins."

"I don't know, John. There have been rumors that he had appeared in a number of gay porno films, but I have no way of knowing if that's true. That's just talk, and Dennis seems too grounded to risk his career in commercial aviation to do something like that."

Gonzalez sat quietly for a few minutes, mulling over what she just told him. Ironically, it was beginning to make sense. What began with a killing in a sex club could have been the result of a homosexual involved in the threesome that went very wrong. Roy Stellini, discovering that the other man was more interested in him than Anne Claridge, could have objected strenuously . . . maybe even violently. And the gay man killed them both, in a fit of rage for having been rejected in a club, where indiscriminate sex was the object of the game.

"A penny for your thoughts, John," Sandy said, rousing him from his temporary fugue state.

"Oh, sorry. This case has all of us chasing leads in a hundred different directions, and the pressure being applied by the mayor and city council isn't making it any easier. But you might have helped more than you know, Sandy. I'll let you go, because I know you're on a tight schedule. When will you be back in Miami?"

"Next Sunday, and I'll have a two-day layover. Why?"

"I would like to take you to dinner, if you are interested."

"I would like that, John. I'll call you when I get in Sunday, around 4 pm."

As Gonzalez walked Sandy through the squad room, every detective and staff member stopped what he or she was doing to watch the stunning blond walk by. "Madre di dio," Cutrazulla said, whistling softly.

"I'd let her pee on my face just so that I could see where it was coming from," his partner, Simmons, said aloud, shaking his head.

"You're a pig, Simmons," said Arlene Thatcher, one of the unit's dispatchers, who overheard the comment. "She wouldn't let you within a thousand feet of that part of her body. You'd have to buy a pair of binoculars." Squad members who heard Thatcher's jibe laughed loudly.

When Gonzalez returned, he asked Cutrazulla and Simmons to join him in his office. Thinking they were going to be reprimanded for their sexist comments, they immediately started apologizing as they walked through his door.

"I didn't hear what you said," Gonzalez said, "but coming from you two pervertidos, I can only imagine. That's not what I wanted to talk to you about. I want you two to take a little R&R in Pittsburgh. Dig into Sandy Garland's background, her childhood, what she does in her spare time, lovers she might have had . . . or has. Everything and anything you can learn about her. Do this on the down-low. I still don't think she has any connection to these murders, but I can't afford to risk overlooking anything. I have Russo and Keller canvassing the local gay bars and clubs with Allison's photo to see what they can turn up. They might get lucky and find someone who saw him at Crescendos and who he might have left with."

As the two detectives were leaving Gonzalez's office, he stopped them with a warning. "Don't let Garland get wind you're sniffing around in her hometown. She doesn't seem like the type who suffers fools lightly."

"I'd sure like to fool around with that babe," Simmons gushed, as his partner yanked him out into the squad room.

Chapter Thirteen

Edgewood
1997

Two years had passed since Tom Stanion's accidental death, so ruled by the Allegheny County's uber-coroner Cyril Wecht. Rumors swirled at Edgewood High School that Tom had been murdered. They ranged from a teammate on the football squad, jealous of his notoriety having killed him, to one of the cheerleaders whom he treated like a piece of meat, as was his wont, having him murdered by a jealous boyfriend. The citizens of the small community of Edgewood were seldom without some juicy gossip for entertainment, fueled by a mean-spiritedness and honed by decades of practice.

Sandy Garland was never a suspect in Stanion's death, even though many in the town heard about her molestation in the community club's pool. He was generally disliked by nearly everyone, and no one went out of their way to point a finger at a young lady who was beginning to come into her own academically and socially. Sandy was beginning to develop a charm that would protect her and mask her psychotic behavior for as long as she would live.

Sandy's father, now retired, found that he had more time to drink, which left him in an inebriated state much of the day.

However, he still had enough energy to try to occasionally force himself on Sandy at night. By this time, she was nearly six feet tall and had exercised herself into a level of fitness that made her emaciated, alcoholic father no match for her. After a time, he gave up on his nocturnal activities with Sandy because he was getting the worst of the "dance," from black eyes to puffy lips. Gloria knew what he was trying to do but never interfered for fear of his temper. She knew that Henry still had enough in the tank to beat her soundly.

One night, after a long day of drinking, Henry sat watching Sandy as she said goodnight and headed for her room. She had grown into a beautiful woman and his lust for her trumped any vestiges of good sense that he still might have had left. After a while, he told Gloria that he was beat and headed upstairs. Sandy was waiting for him.

She was laying in her bed on top of the covers, clad in only panties and a small tee shirt, an open school book balanced on her taunt stomach. In a few minutes, the door to her small bedroom began to quietly swing open, as a drunken Henry surreptitiously poked his head into her room.

Sandy looked up from her book. "Hi, Daddy. Have you come to read me a story?" she asked, in reminiscence of Henry's habitual night time sexual exploits. His excuse to Gloria was that he was going up to read Sandy a story. Her cheerfulness caught him off guard.

"C'mon, Daddy," she continued coyly, "don't be shy. I've been waiting for you." With that, she reached down and slid her panties off. Henry, in his drunken state, was mesmerized. He slowly walked toward the bed and reached for her. That's when it happened.

Sandy produced a serrated kitchen knife that she was concealing behind her back and in a motion that Henry's mind couldn't comprehend, she thrust the eight inch blade directly into his chest up to the hilt. With only a quiet gurgle, the already anesthetized Henry fell to the floor, sliding into a permanent slumber. Sandy wiped the blade with her bed clothes, as she rose to go downstairs to her mother, who was watching her favorite TV program, The Tonight Show with Jay Leno.

"Hey, Mom," she said cheerfully to Gloria, who was distracted by a juggling chimpanzee on the show, until she noticed the knife in Sandy's hand and the blood splatter across her neck and face.

"Sandy, what have you done?" she asked her smiling daughter.

"No, Mom, it's what you have done. You've turned a blind eye to me as that drunken bastard raped me night after night. Now, it's your turn to pay the price that was exacted from me."

"Sandy, I love you, but he would beat me, and . . ." Gloria Garland never completed her sentence. Sandy grabbed her by the hair, tilting her head back at an awkward angle, and savagely drew the knife across her throat down to Gloria's larynx, nearly decapitating her. As Sandy walked from the living room she heard her gurgling her last few moments on earth. She turned to see her mother staring imploringly at her, blood spraying from her neck as she took her final breaths. She slumped forward, and then there was silence. The Tonight Show audience suddenly burst into frantic applause for the talented chimp, and with a grin, Sandy curtseyed in appreciation toward the television set.

She then quickly went to work, cleaning up the blood that had splattered on the floors and walls. Sandy was surprised at the small amount there was. She had expected more. After she finished cleaning thoroughly, she wrapped both bodies in plastic that she was saving just for this occasion. Sandy then pulled each body down the stairs into the basement for further processing.

In school Sandy had read with great interest the short story by Edgar Allen Poe called the *Tell-Tale Heart*, a classic horror tale in which the narrator tells of murdering an old man for no other reason than his blue eyes bothered him. He then dismembered the man and hid the pieces of his body beneath the floorboards in the bedroom, only to be given away to the police by the loud beating of the old man's heart. Sandy was inspired by this story but would do a lot better than hiding her parents beneath floorboards. No, she thought, I would certainly do better than that.

Unwrapping the plastic covering each body on the cement floor in the dank basement, Sandy reached into the closet by the utility tubs and extracted her mother's prized Cutco knives, sold to her by a smarmy salesman who, reeking of alcohol, knocked on their door one Saturday, paid mother a single compliment and, voilá, a sale. Mom would appreciate the use of her premium cutlery on this auspicious occasion.

Extracting a nine inch cleaver from the neatly wrapped knives, Sandy began hacking her mother's hands at the wrist, working her way up to her shoulder. This done, she repeated the process on the ankles and legs. After some laborious hacking, Mom was in neatly stacked pieces, like so much cordwood. Dad, to her delight, was next.

After she was finished dismembering Dad, Sandy stuffed her mother and father's body parts into plastic bags and loaded the bags in the trunk of the family car, the Oldsmobile that Henry had loved above all else, particularly his family. She laughed aloud at the thought. Well, enjoy the last ride to your final resting place.

Sandy had planned this night carefully, examining every possible detail and preparing for any possible worst-case scenario. With an I.Q. tested at 140, Sandy Garland was fully capable of developing a foolproof strategy to kill her parents and hide their bodies where they would never be found.

Sandy was familiar with Cook Forest in Northwestern Pennsylvania, more than seven thousand acres of towering white pines and hemlocks so densely huddled together, they reminded German immigrants of their beloved Black Forest. Some of Sandy's older classmates were attending nearby Clarion University and told her of the forest's beauty and desolation. She was reminded of the great line in a book she had read that described the stark desolation of a remote island as "a place where soliloquy went to be alone." This was that kind of place.

Armed with a map, Sandy headed up I-79 North out of Pittsburgh to pick up I-80 East toward Clarion and, eventually, to PA Route 36 which took her into the state forest. It was after dark and Sandy carefully drove through the roads knifing through the dark forest, which, she read, had more than 27 miles of trails. That suited her purposes perfectly, particularly since it was approaching fall and the temperature dipped dramatically at night, keeping hikers and campers to a minimum.

She eased the Oldsmobile into a parking area deep within the forest and turned her lights off and waited an hour to ensure that she couldn't see or hear any movement. She then unlocked the trunk and withdrew the first plastic bag. She looked at her watch. It was a little after midnight, which gave her about four hours to find suitable locations to bury each body. A full moon illuminated her surroundings nicely.

Sandy lifted each bag carefully, while thanking the gods that, although they were in pieces, her parents were small, light people. Grabbing a shovel and pick, she began the long trek on a trail to find their final resting place. The increased level of physical training she had embarked upon during the past year was paying off. She had no problem toting the bags deep into the forest.

Forty minutes later Sandy spotted a dense tree stand about seventy yards off the trail. Mom, you're home, she thought, smiling. She proceeded to walk into the dense underbrush as far as she could, so that she was not seen by a hiker or forest ranger. Sandy began to dig, stabbing her shovel into the forest floor's soft soil. In a little over an hour she had dug a hole deep enough to accommodate the first bag, which she quickly and unceremoniously dumped into the grave and then proceeded to backfill. She toted Dad another half mile up the deserted trail and repeated the process. They would never be found, she thought, and if anyone did find them, it would most likely be one of the forest's scavengers.

As she worked, Sandy hummed the hit song by the Dave Clark Five, called *Bits and Pieces*. Occasionally, she would break out into laughter as the song seemed appropriate background music for her nocturnal endeavor.

It was nearly dawn as Sandy Garland steered her parents' car toward Pittsburgh and her home in the community of Edgewood. A hot shower and a warm bed were going to feel delicious as she guided the car into the garage.

Two days later Sandy reported her parents missing. She told authorities that they had been planning a bus trip for a second honeymoon but hadn't given her any details at all. She was worried when she never heard from them, as they promised to let her know the location her thoughtful father had kept secret as a surprise for his wife. She was frantic at not having heard a word from them.

Without a single lead the investigation eventually fizzled and became part of the cold case files. Her father had no living relatives and her mom's sister, Gwen, had late-stage Alzheimer's and was institutionalized. Gwen was convinced that aliens had assumed control of our government and Jimmy Carter was one of them. She would tell everyone in her facility that President Carter was a Klingon who journeyed to Earth from his planet, Kronos, to rule the United States. Her fellow patients began referring to her as Uhura and would greet her ramblings with the spread finger Vulcan salute.

Chapter Fourteen

Pittsburgh

Detectives Simmons and Cutrazulla walked through the Greater Pittsburgh International Airport to baggage claim and the rental car counters. Hertz gave them a car and directions heading east to the small community of Edgewood, where they planned to quietly make inquiries into Sandy Garland's background. Odyssey had informed the Miami investigative team that Sandy would be on a three-day trip. That gave them enough time to ask some questions to get a sense of her upbringing, education and the years after her graduation.

They knew that she lived alone in a modest house in Edgewood on a street not too far from her old high school, since the disappearance of her parents more than ten years ago, a case that remained unsolved, long relegated to the Pittsburgh Detective Bureau's cold case files. Brief news stories carried in the *Pittsburgh Press* at the time revealed that Sandy was grief stricken by her parent's disappearance and was completely baffled as to where they might have gone for a clandestine second honeymoon. The investigating authorities also were puzzled as to why her father wouldn't have confided in his daughter, giving her some details where he was taking her mother for a getaway. As they delved further into the case, information about Henry's alcoholism and abusive behavior toward his family began to come out. Based on little concrete information and Sandy's willing, yet unhelpful, contributions, the case eventually became unsolved missing persons case No. 4647832. And life went on.

Sandy Garland graduated in the middle of her tiny class of 93 students in 1998 and matriculated at a modeling school in downtown Pittsburgh. It was during this period of her life when Sandy became introduced to the Asian culture and the study of martial arts by a friend who spent only a brief time herself at the Isshin-Ryu school. Sandy took to the never-ending pursuit of perfection as she studied this complicated system of self defense like nothing she had ever been involved in during her life. The pure discipline it required to learn the hundreds of intricate thrusts and blocks in each kata, or forms, appealed to her spirit of determination, which had been hardened and tempered by a life of abuse from her classmates and her parents. With all of that behind her, Sandy could devote her full attention and burgeoning physical power to Isshin-Ryu, translated from Japanese, meaning "one heart-one mind'."

The first stop for Simmons and Cutrazulla was Edgewood High School, located on a tree lined boulevard called Maple Avenue, with spacious old homes, one larger than the next, on each side of the wide street. These stately mansions, many with their own unattached carriage houses, harkened back to a grander time in the small community.

While progress still left the borough pretty much intact, even it had to change with new thinking in society. A for sale sign was never displayed, in fear that a less than desirable family might actually be able to afford one of the homes and invade the sanctity of the community. Now local real estate agents were forbidden to continue the dubious practice of working with lenders to 'redline' minorities from securing mortgages and homes in the 'lily white' town of Edgewood. Now and then an actual for sale sign appeared, and Italians and other ethnic groups moved in, paving the way for others, referred to by the residents as "undesirables." And by this time, an African American could walk through the small town on his or her way to a surrounding community and not be stopped and questioned by the local police. Social progress is a journey, and Edgewood's was taking longer than most.

The high school's administrative office was abuzz with activity as the detectives entered. Cutrazulla discretely showed his badge to the matronly woman manning the front desk and said that they had an appointment with the school's principal, John Major. The stout gatekeeper to the high school's top executive asked them to have a seat while she tracked down Mr. Major, who was most likely in the middle of disciplining some recalcitrant student.

After nearly fifteen minutes had passed, the woman led them to Major's office. If central casting had placed John Major in the role of principal, it couldn't have done a better job. Standing well over six feet three inches tall and rail thin, John Major looked like a modern day Ichabod Crane, dressed nattily in a plain grey suit, white shirt and blood red bow tie. He set this ensemble off with a pair of black sensible shoes that a bus driver might wear and white socks. John Major might not be a fashion plate, but his garb was authoritative and pragmatic. While he may have resembled a middle-aged Pee-wee Herman, each of the school's three hundred students lived in mortal fear of being called to his office.

After initial introductions, Detective Simmons explained why they were visiting the school, which was to obtain some background on a former student, Sandy Garland. This was part of what he described as a routine investigation in Miami, a case in which he was not at liberty to divulge any details. "Suffice it to say, Mr. Major, that while Ms. Garland is not a suspect in the commission of a crime, it's prudent for our department to leave no stone unturned, as they say," explained Cutrazulla.

"But it's important enough for you to travel all the way from Miami to our little town to look into the past of a woman who graduated over a decade ago," Major said, creaking back in his chair with his arms folded over his chest.

A brief silence fell between the men. "Mr. Major, we are investigating a series of murders that have occurred in several locations around the country," Simmons said, with a sigh. "Whatever you can share with us about Sandy just might give us a lead that can point us in the right direction. This has been a tough case because we can't seem to ascertain a motive for the crimes. That's about all I am at liberty to reveal, so please tell us what you can about Sandy Garland. What was her childhood like, how did she do in school, did she have friends, was she a mentally stable child? Give us what you can so that we can form a picture of her early years."

Major reached for a file atop a stack of magazines and papers sitting on the corner of his desk. Scanning the contents for a few moments, he cleared his throat and began to provide an overview of Sandy's childhood and high school years.

"Sandy Garland had an extremely difficult childhood," Major began. "She fought a weight problem as a child, and a group of classmates made her life miserable. She was taunted and bullied mercilessly, which caused her to basically withdraw from her teachers and the other students. This difficult period of her life was exacerbated by suspected verbal and sexual abuse by her alcoholic father. I say 'suspected,' because although there was a suspicion that her father forced himself on her, it was never proven. She made some comments in confidence to a supposed friend and, of course, her friend immediately told another classmate and so on."

"Was there any suspicion that the abuse she received at home was tied into the mysterious disappearance of her parents?" Simmons asked, watching Major's body language carefully.

"There was never any proof, and Sandy denied there were any problems at home, when asked. If there were, one would have assumed that the girl would have reported them to the authorities. No, it seems as if Sandy suffered through the worst of times, and when her parents disappeared she seem to become rejuvenated, beginning a rigorous exercise program at a nearby gym, going on a diet and those types of things. She literally turned her life around. You can probably ascertain that just by looking at her today."

Cutrazulla glanced at Simmons. "Yes, we have ascertained that," he said. And I'd like to entertain that beautiful ass, he thought.

Reading his mind, Major said, "Yes, she is a physical specimen, isn't she detectives? I am sure her immersion in the study of karate at a local school here in Pittsburgh has contributed to her health, well-being and confidence."

Both detectives looked up from their notes. "She studies karate?" Simmons asked, incredulous. "We have no information on that, and she has never mentioned it when interviewed in Miami."

"She doesn't talk much about it," Major responded. "You have to understand that Sandy Garland has always been a very shy, private person. I am sure you can understand how that would occur, given her difficult early years."

"What can you tell us about her karate training?"

"Not much, really. She has been at it for a while, I do know that. Her classes take place at a very large school in the city. I can't tell you the name of it."

Simmons closed his notebook. "Is there anything else you can tell us? Mr. Major. You have been very helpful."

"Not much else. Her grades were adequate, which was puzzling, because her IQ tested at 140, which places her in a select group of very smart people. She should have done better in school."

Major closed the file on his lap. "There is one final thing about Sandy that I hesitate to even broach, primarily due to the fact that privacy laws prevent us from commenting on a health problem. One of her early teachers to her mother, Gloria, that she take Sandy to a psychologist for evaluation."

"What might have prompted the teacher to recommend that?" Cutrazulla asked, his interest heightened.

"I am not sure. Her records here don't provide any details, but I can tell you that the rumor mill in this small community was working overtime during Sandy's grade school days. One particularly vicious one was that she killed her pet dog and hid his body in the basement. Of course, again there was never any solid proof, to the best of my knowledge. I wrote it off to the imaginations of the local gossip mongers."

Simmons noted Major's final comments and stood. "Thanks for your time, Mr. Major, and if anything else occurs to you regarding Sandy Garland, please don't hesitate to call," he said, proffering his card.

As they exited the high school, Cutrazulla said, "Well, that's a revelation. Our girl has been studying karate."

"In my opinion, it's not unusual for a woman to take a self-defense course to protect herself from perverts like us," Simmons said laughing.

"I agree, but just to cover our asses during this investigation let's find out where she studies and interview the head guy or girl," Cutrazulla said.

"Hi-ya," Simmons cried, jumping and chopping with both hands.

"Christ, stop it, Bruce Lee," Cutrazulla said, smiling. "You look like you're having a fucking seizure."

After dividing up the listing of karate schools in the Pittsburgh phone book, Simmons got a hit on his sixth call. After identifying himself as a Miami detective and his shield number, he asked the man who answered if a Sandy Garland was enrolled there. "Yes, she is one of my students," said head instructor Bill Deardon guardedly. "I can tell you that much, but I don't share information beyond that about any of them."

"Mr. Deardon, we are investigating a series of unsolved murders in Miami, most likely committed by someone with knowledge of the martial arts. I'm sure that you can appreciate our need for information on her training. Please understand that Sandy is not a suspect, and the prevailing wisdom is that a man is perpetrating these crimes, but we have to pursue every information trail, regardless of our thoughts on its relevancy. May we come meet with you?"

Later that afternoon, the detectives entered the Academy of Isshin-Ryu Karate in Pittsburgh's downtown. The school, with a nondescript facade, was surrounded by the city's cultural district, including the homes of the Pittsburgh Opera and Pittsburgh Symphony. Students of varying ages, toting gym bags streamed in and out of the school's entrance, above which hung a medallion displaying a half-woman, half-serpent figure with her arms extended, showing an open hand and a closed fist.

Cutrazulla and Simmons peered through the dojo's expansive portal at a class performing rigorous, repetitive punches. In unison they counted in Japanese, "Ichi, ni, san, shi, go . . . ." Fists flew in perfect harmony as the forty or so students punched air.

"This is an exercise that develops focused power or 'chi' to a punch, that in our particular style is called the Ram's Head," Sensei Deardon said, as he approached the detectives from behind. Deardon wore an immaculate white gi, with a black belt tied neatly at his navel. The belt, worn from years of use, had eight red stripes signifying that the head instructor was an eighth degree black belt or Hachi Dan in Japanese. "Good afternoon, I'm Bill Deardon, the owner of the school. You must be the detectives who called me. Please, gentleman, let's go sit down in my office."

After they were seated at a round, Formica topped conference table in Deardon's small office, Simmons got to the point. "Mr. Deardon, we recently were informed that Sandy Garland studies karate at your school. We are investigating a series of homicides that we believe were committed by someone highly trained in the martial arts."

Deardon stared at the detectives thoughtfully. "And you believe that Sandy is a suspect in these murders?"

"We wouldn't describe her as a suspect at this point, but more of a person of interest. She possibly could know someone with the skill level and personality to commit these murders or possibly spoke to someone on one of the flights who fit that profile. I assume students in the martial arts community recognize each other. Any small bit of information she could provide would be helpful."

"Whoever's committing the murders is powerful, smart and very sick. Everything points to a man as our suspect," Cutrazula added.

Deardon smiled and shook his head. "There you are wrong, detective. It's not the gender of this person that matters, it's the skill level. In our world, speed creates force, not muscles. In fact, trying to 'muscle' a technique, like a straight punch, slows it down, reducing its effectiveness. A focused, lightning quick strike does the most damage, much like the end of a whip."

"So what you're telling us is that we could just as easily be looking for a woman as a man?" Simmons asked.

"On the surface, yes, that's what I am telling you. However, all things being equal; that is, a man and a woman equally trained, it then becomes a matter of personality, mental makeup, an inclination toward violence and so forth."

"What can you tell us about Sandy Garland's personality and makeup?" Cutrazulla asked.

"Sandy is the best student, man or woman, that I have ever trained," Deardon said. "She's been with me for nearly eight years, since high school. I have never seen the level of dedication and determination she displays in the pursuit of perfecting the art of the karateka and Isshin-Ryu."

"Would she have the capability of using her skills to hurt or kill someone, in your opinion, Mr. Deardon?" asked Simmons.

"Only in self defense, detective. She has too much respect for both herself and others to ever use what she's learned over the years unlawfully."

Both detectives stood, shaking hands with the sensei. "Thanks for your time, sir. We may be checking back with you. In the meantime, if anything at all should come to mind, please give me a call," Simmons said as he presented his card.

As the detectives left the dojo, Deardon's mind was troubled. He knew Sandy Garland was capable of inflicting great damage to another human if provoked, as he recalled the horrific snapping of Joey Calderon's elbow as she applied a painful arm bar on him during kumite. What concerned Sensei Deardon most about the recent incident was after Calderon screamed in pain, Sandy was smiling beatifically, her countenance resembling the after-glow of sex. If he didn't know better, he'd swear that for a fleeting moment, she almost looked psychotic.

Chapter Fifteen

Chicago

A group of Odyssey's flight attendants, including Sandy Garland, chatted as they walked through Chicago's O'Hare International Airport's Terminal 3 on their way to check in at the Hilton. Sandy, anticipating an extra strenuous workout in the hotel's gym on the sixth floor and then a quiet dinner in the restaurant, quickly broke from the others for the elevators. The team had an early 4 am call for a flight to Newark and then, thank the Lord, she was flying deadhead back to Pittsburgh for a well-earned few days off.

After check in was completed, Sandy headed to her room to change into her exercise sweats. She always liked the Hilton here because its gym was spacious and well equipped, with the additional bonus of floor-to-ceiling mirrors so that she could carefully watch each part of her musculature as she lifted free weights.

Nearly two hours later, Sandy, drenched in perspiration and a towel around her neck, caught the elevator to the eighth floor and her room. After a long shower, she threw on her favorite pair of 7 Jeans and Polo sweater and went down to the hotel restaurant. She was famished, after having burned a thousand calories in the gym and was anticipating a large salad crammed with egg yokes, pecans, almonds and lots of grated cheese and a naked baked potato for the beneficial mixture of protein and complex carbohydrates. The machine that was her body required this level of nutrition for optimum performance.

As she was seated by the hostess at a small table near the window, which afforded an expansive view of the runways busy with arriving and departing flights, Sandy's attention was drawn to a group of men huddled at the bar. Boisterous laughter followed periods of quiet as one after another told the group a joke. Occasionally, one of the men would glance furtively at Sandy, and as she would look his way the voyeur would quickly turn his attention to the jokester. By the looks of the army of glasses and bottles surrounding the raucous group, they had been at the bar for sometime.

Sandy ordered a glass of her favorite wine, Iron Horse Chardonnay, as she perused the menu. Noticing a shadow across her table, she looked up to find a portly man in an ill-fitting blue suit, white shirt and polyester tie hanging loose at the collar looming over her table. She had noticed earlier that he was part of the group at the bar,

"Excuse me, Miss," he said, swaying slightly. It was obvious that he had been imbibing with his friends for a number of hours. "A lovely lady such as yourself should not have to dine alone. Would you consider joining our small band of merry men at the bar? I promise that I won't take 'no' for an answer, as I am one of the top ten Subaru salesmen in the midwest region."

"Thanks anyway, but I am only having a quick dinner and then to bed. I have an early flight in the morning," Sandy said, displaying a forced smile, with about as much patience as she could muster, given the unwarranted intrusion.

Before she could object, the man pulled out a chair and sat down at her table. "Now, Miss, as I said, I am not taking no for an answer. We would all consider it an honor if you would join us," he said, raising his arms to the group, as they, in turn, raised their glasses in salute and invitation.

Sandy was taken aback by the audacity of the rotund little man but realized his brashness was fueled by a friend of his,

Jack Daniels. "Sir, let me make this as clear as I possibly can," she said quietly and evenly. "I am not interested in joining your fucking band of merry men. I'll leave that to Maid Marian. I would like to be left in peace, and if for some reason you see fit to not leave my private table, I will personally lift you and your fat ass up and kick it back to your fellow drunks at the bar. Do you understand me?"

The man, shocked by her threat was speechless. Her cold blue eyes held his, and in his inebriated state, he knew that there was something amiss in her circuitry. This woman was scary, and he sensed that it might be a good idea to get away from her quickly, without losing face with his drunken comrades.

He slowly rose from the table, straightened his rumpled suit coat and in a loud, theatrical voice announced to no one in particular, "Well, I suppose that men don't interest you. If that's the case, then I leave you to wait for your female friend. We all hope that you have a wonderful time tonight," he said, as the others voiced their support.

"Yea, can we watch?" shouted a member of the group, as the others laughed loudly at their fellow drunk's razor wit.

Sandy knew that her privacy was lost in this restaurant and called for the check to pay for the glass of wine. She decided that she would be better off with room service, a little TV and then an early bed. As she left the restaurant, the laughter increased among the men at the bar, all of whom were glancing her way now. She didn't notice the tall, broad shouldered member of the group, who wasn't laughing, break away and head for another exit.

Sandy was angry, but was not a stranger to this kind of treatment from men as she traveled. She took her room key card from her purse and slid it into the lock and opened the door when the light turned green and there was an audible click. As she slid the door open wide, Sandy was pushed violently from behind into her room by the broad-shouldered man from the bar.

"You know," he said, "you were a little hard on our friend downstairs. Who in the hell do you think you are? Do you believe that your ass is made of gold and too good for us hairy apes? I think you need a lesson in manners, and I'm just the one to give it to you." He began to loosen his tie and remove his jacket. Sandy, knocked to the floor by the force of his entry, gathered her wits.

"I think that you had better leave my room now, before you get hurt," Sandy warned, as she stood to face him.

"What are you going to do, call security on me? Everyone heard the threat you made downstairs. Who could possibly doubt that I wasn't forced to defend myself from dangerous person like you?" he said with a smirk.

Sandy abruptly wheeled and walked toward the door, giving the impression that she was preparing to flee. Instead, she closed the door to the room, secured it with the deadbolt and then looked back at the intruder, her eyes locked onto his. During his three-year tour of duty in Vietnam, he had never seen evil and malice reflected in the depths of a person's eyes like hers. With a speed that he was not prepared for, Sandy kicked him painfully inside of his right thigh.

"If I would have wanted to, that could have been directed into your testicles," she said calmly. "But it's just beginning for you. You had your chance and now you must pay the price."

Uncertain what to do next, he began to back up and assume the position for basic hand to hand combat that he been taught in the service. Sweating now, he watched her feet carefully, knowing that she was quick and probably trained, as well.

The element of surprise is the key weapon for a person skilled in the martial arts, who must defend him or herself. That is exactly what Sandy Garland deployed effectively as she feigned an overhead knife hand strike and then, with unanticipated speed, swept both of his legs out from under him. Not expecting that strategy, raising his hands to block the strike, he went down hard, with Sandy on top of him.

His hands covering his face, he pleaded, "Listen, lady, I didn't mean anything by this. I was put up to it by the guys to just scare you, but it looks as though you got the drop on me instead." His chuckle was lame and embarrassing.

"Get up, you dumb fuck," she commanded. "You're lucky I'm in a good mood, because I am going to let you get back to your asshole buddies in one piece. Consider this your lucky day," as she pushed him toward the door to her room.

That's when he made his fatal error. "You bitch," he shouted, "I'm going to tear your head off and shit down your neck." He ran awkwardly toward her, his fists held high. Sandy suddenly produced from her pocket a shuriken or steel fighting star that had four razor-sharp points and with a force honed from years of practice, threw it with deadly accuracy into his forehead. He died instantly, crumpling to the floor of his room with a crash.

"Now look what you made me do, you dick wad," she said to his corpse as he stared at the ceiling. "And we were getting along so well."

She quickly grabbed a towel to soak up the blood pouring from his wound and removed the shuriken, wiping it clean. Opening the door to her room carefully, Sandy checked the hallway and finding it empty, drug his body down the hall and stuffed him into an empty utility closet next to the ice machine.

"There you go, lover, that will keep you on ice for a while until someone discovers your sorry ass." Checking her watch, she saw that she only had a few hours to get ready for her final leg to Newark. Showering and packing quickly, Sandy checked out of the Hilton for her flight hours before the broad-shouldered man was discovered by housekeeping.

In the morning, the Chicago PD and a forensics team ultimately had little to go on. They were particularly perplexed by the wound to his forehead, surmising that he likely was attacked by a local gangbanger wielding a switch blade or dagger. The police were baffled as to how could a man this large and powerful been murdered? they asked themselves. He must have been trying to secure the services of a hooker and the transaction with the pimp went bad. Very bad.

Chapter Sixteen

Miami

Gonzalez was wrapping up a long day following leads on the 'Swinging Sex Murders' case, the most promising of which was the report filed by Cutrazulla and Simmons on what they discovered in Pittsburgh. He was surprised to learn that Sandy Garland was a student at a karate academy there. Somehow, though, his gut told him that a woman like her couldn't possibly have committed these grisly murders. But they agreed that the team might be able to take advantage of her expertise to help catch the killer. His cell phone rang.

"Hi, John, it's Sandy Garland," the voice said. I am flying into Miami tomorrow, and you told me to let you know the next time I'm in town. If you still want to get together for dinner, I'll be getting to the Embassy Suites at the airport around 7 pm."

Pleasantly surprised to hear from her, he said, "I was just thinking about you."

"I hope they were good thoughts," Sandy replied teasingly.

"Of course, how can anybody have anything but good thoughts about you?" he responded. "How about I pick you up in the lobby at 8 pm, and we'll go to that restaurant I told you about in Little Havana, Versailles. I remember that you told me that you were a vegetarian. You're going to love their Moros, Platanos Fritos

Y Ensalada Verde. It's a combination of beans and rice cooked together in a salad."

"Sounds good, John. I'll see you in the lobby tomorrow at 8 pm."

As he pocketed his cell, he noticed Simmons still at his desk. "What's your take on what you found out about Sandy Garland?" he asked, sitting down in a chair next to his desk.

"According to her instructor, she is a very responsible student who, in his opinion, wouldn't use what she's learned over the years unless it was in self defense. He told us that she is extremely dedicated and somehow through her studies, she has learned to respect herself and, likewise, shows people the respect they deserve."

What if they don't deserve her respect? Gonzalez wondered. "Your report indicated that she had a tough childhood and suffered the brunt of bullying from her classmates."

"That seemed not untypical for an overweight kid growing up and taking his or her daily ration of shit from other kids. The most troubling to us was the suspected abuse by her father, who was an alcoholic. Supposedly it consisted of both verbal and sexual abuse. But they were only rumors, nothing substantiated. Tell you the truth, Sarge, I think it's a coincidence that she studies karate. Hell, millions of people around the country study some sort of martial art, from children to senior citizens."

"I don't disagree with you on that point. She strikes me as a woman who knows what she wants and is comfortable in her own skin. I still think a man is our killer. I just can't wrap my head around a woman having the strength or skill to commit these murders. Not the way the bodies were twisted and broken. No way, not a woman."

*　　*　　*

Gonzalez pulled up to the ornate portico of the Embassy Suites on South River Drive. The main entrance to the hotel, which was designed in typical Mediterranean architecture painted in bright art deco pastels common in Florida, displayed three flags, giving it the air of an official embassy of a foreign country. Parking his unmarked in a guest check-in slot, he entered the revolving glass doors leading to a spacious lobby. Glancing at his watch, he noticed that it was only 7:45 pm, so he headed into the lounge and took a seat at the bar, affording him a clear view of the lobby to watch for Sandy.

At precisely 8 pm, Sandy Garland emerged from a bank of elevators near the reception desk. Gonzalez was stunned by her beauty. She wore a form fitting little black dress, which accented the curves of her toned, muscled body. Her thick blonde hair draped over her shoulders, ending in a mass of curls at her shoulder blades. As she walked toward him, she was strikingly conspicuous among the short, squat, thin, homely, plain and downright ugly guests scurrying back and forth in the lobby. Gonzalez was smitten.

"Hey, Sandy," Gonzalez said, waving in greeting. She saw him and joined him at the bar. "You look lovely, and as we say in Spanish, 'belleza que trasciende la vida, Misma,'" he said, touching her arm lightly.

"Gracias, amable señor, usted es un caballero y un romántico," she responded with a smile.

"Como tú, tu español es impecable. Estoy impresionado," Gonzalez said, a look of amazement on his face.

"Don't be," she countered, laughing. "That's about the extent of my high school Spanish."

Gonzalez paid the bar tab and suggested they head to Little Havana and the Versailles Restaurant for dinner. As he drove to west Miami, he carefully broached the subject of her involvement in the martial arts.

"Sandy, you never told me you studied karate," he said, watching her body language and eyes for any non-verbal reaction to his statement. There wasn't one. Sandy remained relaxed, an air of serenity surrounding her.

"Actually, I was never asked about it," she replied, "and the word 'study' doesn't apply in this instance. It's a hobby that keeps me in shape. I only occasionally get to the dojo, given my travel schedule. Some of the kids at the school take the whole karate thing very seriously. I'm not one of them. Why is my silly little leisure time activity of interest to you?"

"The murders that my squad is working on were committed, we believe, by a person who has been trained and is highly skilled at karate or some form of martial arts," Gonzalez said.

"And you think I may be this person?" Sandy continued to smile as she posed the question. "I'd like to think that I'm a student of the art of love not violence."

I sure hope you are, he thought. "I know that you've heard this before, but it's simply routine. You can understand that if our killer is someone who is trained in some sort of martial arts, then we must look closely at anyone involved who studies karate or jiu jitsu. Also, we may call upon you as a sort of technical consultant to help us nail this guy."

"I'll certainly help you in any way that I can," Sandy said. "From what I have read, the person who perpetrated these crimes is probably suffering from some sort of mental illness that would compel him to so violently mutilate the bodies of the victims."

Gonzalez glanced over at her. "I notice that you use the pronoun 'he.' What makes you think it's a man?"

"John, we have at least two hundred students at my school in Pittsburgh. The majority of them are men, and I am pretty sure that demographic applies to other styles and schools across the country. Besides, men are inherently more violent than women."

"That I can attest to," Gonzalez replied. "Nearly ninety percent of violent crimes are committed by men."

"My point exactly, John. You're looking for a man trained in some sort of martial art, who also may be a sociopath. That could be a bad combination. His lack of feelings and remorse, and a virtual disregard for society's standards' are going to make him difficult to catch. Any person who is dedicated to the art of karate respects not only the particular style he or she studies, but also learns to respect other people, both fellow students and those outside of the dojo. The man you are seeking is someone highly trained and proficient in inflicting pain and injury to people and has grown to enjoy it. In fact, it may have become a sexual thrill for him."

"You mean we may possibly have a nut case who gets his rocks off by killing strangers?" Gonzalez asked, glancing briefly over at the woman seated next to him.

"That's one way of putting it, John. "Crude, but descriptive. Yes, this individual may be killing for sexual release or to satisfy some compulsion, such as sadism, latent homosexuality or a death fetish, in which he displays a morbid fascination with ending another person's life with the skill he has honed from years in combat or some sort of training."

"You seem to have some knowledge of what may make our suspect 'tick,'" Gonzalez responded.

"I've always had an interest in psychology and understanding why people are the way they are. It has helped me immensely as I try to ensure the safety of my passengers on Odyssey flights. Their psychological makeup at any given moment can range from frightened to angry to drunk and surly, and I have to be able to deal with all of them effectively for the safety of the collective."

As Gonzalez pulled his car up to the Versailles' valet, he said, "We'll get him, Sandy. These guys eventually make a mistake, and it's usually something small that gets them caught."

They entered the restaurant, which was nothing more than a glammed up diner, with mirrors and chandeliers meant to invoke thoughts of a French bistro. But the pungent aromas of true Havana cooking caressed the senses like an expensive Cuban cigar, telling those who entered, "This is where real Cubans come to eat."

"Detective Gonzalez, es muy agradable ver nuevamente. ¿quién es su hermosa compañera esta noche?" asked the flamboyant owner, Felipe Valls, Jr., the son of the founder, who claimed it was the most popular Cuban restaurant since he established it in 1971.

With a brilliant smile and nod of her head, Sandy replied, "Usted es demasiado bueno, sir. Soy apenas uno de John' s muchos amigas."

Valls, surprised, became animated. "Hermoso y también domina el español. Usted es un hombre afortunado, Senor González."

After they were seated at a table and had ordered cocktails, Gonzalez announced that he was going to order for them, knowing that Sandy was a vegetarian. "Versailles has a great selection of great vegetarian dishes using black beans, rice and imaginative uses of fruits and vegetables," he said, as he perused the menu.

Sandy noticed that two young black males entered the restaurant, both nervous and wearing windbreakers, although it was humid and in the low seventies this evening. Her antenna went up, and she placed her hand lightly on Gonzalez's arm. He looked up and caught the same vibe she was feeling. These two weren't here for the Empanadas and Croquetas.

One of the men looked over at the table where Sandy and Gonzalez were seated and recognized the detective. In an instant he produced a 357 magnum from beneath his windbreaker and pointed it at them. "OK, motherfucker, let's see bof yo' hands on da table!"

Gonzalez hesitated. "I ain't gonna axe you again," the young man warned. His partner produced a Sig Sauer P250 and also pointed it at the couple. "This motherfucker is heat," he said to his partner.

"Well, den mistuah Heat, les sees dat piece you pack up on da table. Now, muthafucker!" he screamed. The other restaurant patrons were frozen. Gonzalez complied, producing his 45 caliber Glock and carefully, slowly laying it on the table.

One of the men snatched his gun, while his partner jumped over the counter and struck the woman tending the register in the temple with his handgun, knocking her to the floor. He opened the register and began scooping up the money. It was at that time the man pointing his weapon at Gonzalez noticed Sandy.

"Hey, mama, ain't you one mad looker," he said, licking his lips lasciviously. Gonzalez began to rise from his chair, and as quickly as a coiled snake, the young black male struck him on the head with his handgun, rendering him unconscious. "Dat cool yo' ass, mistah Heat," he said chortling.

The men ordered everyone in the restaurant into a storage area in the back. They dragged Gonzalez's inert body into the small room and instructed the group to cluster together so they could lock the door, or they would be shot. Everyone, except Sandy Garland, that is.

"Hey sweet thang," one of the males said. "Yo' come on out heh with us dogs so's we can part-tay," he said in a lilting voice. "Or we gotsta put a cap in mistah Heat's ass. Ain't dat right, bro?"

"Word on, dog," his partner responded. "This foxy thang's gonna' love the pipe we gonna be laying on her."

Sandy slowly walked out of the storage closet, as the men bolted the door, locking the twenty five customers, staff and the unconscious Gonzalez in the confined space.

"OK, straight up, bitch, we gonna' get dis candle lighted," said one of the males, as he reached to yank the front of her dress down.

With speed and a fury that her assailant didn't expect, Sandy grabbed his wrist and jerked him toward her, as she drove an open hand directly into his throat. His forward momentum coupled with her throat strike immediately crushed his larynx. Dropping his handgun, he fell to the floor as his dwindling oxygen supply began to rob him of air to his brain.

His partner didn't react quickly enough, and as he tried to wheel his Sig around to shoot Sandy, without a second's hesitation, she stepped toward him, positioning herself inside of the hand wielding the pistol. She grabbed the thumb of his gun hand, jerking it up and away from her. She pointed his gun at him and helped him pulled the trigger. A deafening blast erupted, as the top of his head exploded, blood, brain matter and skull fragments sprayed the ceiling and wall of the restaurant. He collapsed next to his partner, and all was quiet.

*   *   *

Gonzalez sat with a bag of ice on the back of his head, as an investigator from the coroner's office zipped the body bags and prepared to remove them from the scene. Miami PD was interviewing the Versailles patrons who were seated at tables, some with stiff drinks gladly supplied by the still shaken Mr. Valls. Sandy, looking as radiant as the moment she entered the establishment two hours earlier, was talking to Detective Wiggins.

"Sandy, you are either a very brave lady or a very foolish one," he said, gazing at her with admiration.

"Detective, as I have said, I really didn't have many options," she replied. "It was painfully obvious to me that I was about to be raped by those two thugs, and I wasn't going to let it happen."

"And you used your skills in self defense to not only subdue the perps, but you managed to kill them both."

"That's not accurate," she said quickly. "As I stated, when the one male tried to tear at my dress, I struck out at him and managed to hit him in the throat. It was a lucky blow. His partner then swung his gun around to shoot me, but I grappled with him and his own gun discharged in his face. I have no idea how that happened, but I can tell you that I am very lucky to be standing here talking to you."

Wiggins shook his head in amazement and looked over at his partner. "You okay, Sarge?" he asked.

"When this mother of all headaches lets up, I'll feel a lot better," Gonzalez said. Looking at Sandy, he said with a smile, "Tonight was certainly an auspicious first date."

"John, it certainly didn't lack for excitement." She then whispered quietly in his ear, "I layover for another night here in Miami. How about tomorrow evening, we order room service at my hotel and put on reruns of *Cops*. At least we can have some fun watching other people get in trouble."

Gonzalez began to feel better already.

*   *   *

John Gonzalez and Sandy Garland didn't watch reruns of Cops in her hotel room at the Embassy Suites. For two days they made love, exploring each other's bodies voraciously, licking and tasting each other. They only took brief intermissions to order room service, to refuel. Then they fell back into bed, into each other's arms. Gonzalez had never met anyone like her. And she finally met the man who would transport her to where she longed to be. They were falling in love.

Chapter Seventeen

As his men assembled for their Monday morning briefing, Gonzalez sat on the edge of his desk idly bending a paper clip into various contortions. With everyone seated and waiting for his status report, the chief of detectives didn't seem to notice them.

"Sarge," Wiggins called softly. "You okay?"

Pulled from his reverie, Gonzalez grabbed a sheath of papers and attempted to clear his head. "I would assume you've all heard what happened Friday night?"

Murmuring among the men was accompanied by head nods.

"It seems as though we were in the wrong place at the wrong time and both Ms. Garland and I dodged a bullet, pun intended," Gonzalez said. "The gunmen were two career criminals we all know very well," he continued, referring to his notes. "Lamont Johnson and Daray Watkins were middle level dope dealers with a specialty in crystal meth. Both now deceased . . ."

Ripples of laughter interrupted his report. He looked up, clearly irritated.

"Both now deceased," he continued, "the city can close the chapter on these two violent men."

"Sarge," said Simmons, "how in the hell did Sandy Garland manage to subdue those two and escape with hardly a blonde hair out of place? I mean they were packing heavy artillery and were higher than kites. Is she that good or just plain lucky?"

"Actually, no one really saw what happened. Except for Sandy, we were all locked in a storage closet. She explained that when they attempted to rape her she just struck out and luckily hit one of the men in the throat who was obviously caught by surprise. As he fell backwards, he stumbled into his partner, knocking his gun to the floor. It discharged, blowing the top of his skull off. According to Ms. Garland, it all happened so quickly it was difficult for her to recall the exact sequence of events."

"The ME's report," Cutrazulla said, "indicated that Watkins, the guy who lost his head over the encounter with Sandy Garland," . . . more laughter, "and who somehow shot himself with his own gun, had a fractured wrist and thumb."

"Where you going with this?" Gonzalez asked, looking impatiently at Cutrazulla.

"Well, Sarge, if it was a stroke of fate and the lucky blow that Sandy Garland described, how in the hell did Watkins break his own wrist and thumb?"

"Any number of ways," replied Gonzalez, patiently. "The recoil of his 357 could have snapped them, it could have happened when he fell . . . . who the hell knows or cares. Ms. Garland, by the fate of the gods, was unharmed."

"We get that, Sarge," Simmons spoke up. "But we're chasing a serial murderer here in Miami, who happens to be highly trained in the martial arts, judo or some other form of hand-to-hand fighting. Sandy Garland, at least at this point in time, seems to be an extremely viable suspect."

"Everyone's a suspect, Simmons," Gonzalez said. "And we've all agreed that it's a powerful man who is trained in karate or whatever, who's committing these violent crimes." I hope it's a man, he thought.

Simmons began to object, when Gonzalez cut him off. "Look, let's not spin our wheels on this point. I have some news that may help clear this case sooner rather than later. Chief Martinez informed me early this morning that the mayor and commissioners have agreed to ask the FBI to join our task force . . ."

Groans erupted among the detectives. "Now hold on," Gonzalez directed, raising a hand as if quieting a high school classroom, "I agree with the chief that the FBI's experience in tracking and apprehending serial killers will be of immense value. For now, the bureau will be functioning in a consulting role."

As if on cue, the door to the squad room opened and a man entered, carrying a thick manila file folder under one arm and a laptop computer in his right hand. Dressed in a tailored grey suit, which was fastened precisely with the second button, shoulders squared, he strode purposefully to Gonzalez. He wore a bright white shirt, adorned with a simple, yet elegant grey and blue rep tie. He would have been at home in the board room of IBM.

"Gentleman, timing's everything in life," Gonzalez announced. "Let me introduce Special Agent Randall Miles, who heads up the FBI's Violent Criminal Apprehension Program, known as ViCAP."

"Good morning, Randy," said Gonzalez, extending his hand.

"Agent Miles and ViCAP are part of the bureau's Critical Incident Response Group, or CIRG and have more than 20 years experience tracking serial killers. We are pleased to have him lend his analytical skills and expertise to this case. I have asked him this morning to brief us on the likely profile of the unsub we're looking for and how we will work together going forward. Agent Miles."

"Thanks, John," Miles said, as he connected his laptop to the digital projector that had been sitting on the conference table. "First, let me begin by saying that it's an honor to be asked by our city officials to join your team. I am here to lend my expertise in what is referred to as 'profiling' serial killers. By working together, sharing all levels of information and using the bureau's massive database of violent crimes and behavioral analyses, we can apprehend this individual quickly, before anyone else is murdered here in Miami or in another city."

Cutrazulla raised his hand, and Miles nodded slightly toward him. "Agent Miles, one of the critical points in this case seems to be whether these homicides are being committed by a man or a woman. What are your thoughts?"

"Before we begin profiling our unsub, let me provide a little background on serial killers and ViCAP's role in their apprehension," Miles said evenly. Turning on the projector, which displayed the recognizable FBI logo with ViCAP spelled out beneath it, Miles clicked to the next screen, which said, 'Serial Killers—A Definition.'

Glancing at the screen, Miles began his briefing. "Let's toss out what we've seen in the movies or on TV about serial killers. For one thing, they aren't as flamboyant and menacing as our friend, Hannibal Lecter, in the *Silence of the Lambs*. You could be standing next to one in a crowded elevator and he would look like you or me. Our database has collected thousands, if not millions of pieces of information gathered during the interviews of apprehended serial killers and other types of murderers and violent offenders."

"You just said 'he' Agent," said Russo. "Are we to assume that you consider this person to be a man?"

"Let me answer that question this way. The vast majority of serial killers are men, who are intelligent, with IQs in the normal to bright range. Most of these are Caucasian, but a growing number are of other races and ethnic groups. Consider the recent case of serial snipers John Muhammad and Lee Malvo. Muhammad was an African-Amercan who later joined the Nation of Islam. Malvo was born in Jamaica."

Miles turned back to the screen. "Serial killers are most often products of unstable families, in which an alcoholic or mentally unstable parent abuses them sexually, emotionally or physically . . . or all of the above. They exhibit narcissistic tendencies and most often have a delusional feeling of self-importance. They have no compunction about lying, cheating, stealing or killing to further their own means. In short, they are sociopaths who murder, nearly all of them beginning with the torture and killing of animals, eventually graduating to humans.

"To answer your question, detective, female serial killers are, indeed, rare. They tend to murder those close to them, primarily for material gain, and most often use more subtle methods to kill their victims, such as poison or suffocation. The most notable exception to this profile is the case of Aileen Wuornos right here in Florida, who killed her victims outdoors with a handgun. She posed as a prostitute to lure seven men—who were strangers—to their deaths, killing them for her own gratification and personal reasons known only to her. Her profile fit that of a male, rather than a female. But serial killers do share commonalities, whether they are male or female. They are psychopaths but technically as sane as you and me; they look as normal as you and me, and they were born without a conscience."

"So you are saying that the unsub we are looking for is a man, while highly skilled in the art of hand-to-hand combat, may be of higher intelligence, acts as normal as anyone else and is probably a product of an abusive family?" asked Detective Keller. "And with delusions of grandeur, so to speak, he kills for the thrill of killing. Hell, that narrows the field down to a couple thousand or so guys running around Miami."

Quieting the laughter, Miles replied, "Not really, detective. I would profile your killer of very high intelligence, who is quite organized in his behavior. In other words, he plans his killings very carefully, is knowledgeable in ways to not only kill quickly and effectively, but also to avoid detection. This is a game to him, a way to satisfy his sexual compulsions while turning the Miami detectives' bureau into the Keystone Cops. Much like Jack the Ripper and more recently, Ted Bundy and John Wayne Gacy, our unsub is smart, under control, powerful and likes to kill with his bare hands. He is exhibiting his total control over his victims with an unbridled blood lust. However, often times there comes a point when his thinking becomes what we call 'disorganized,' during which he begins to become delusional and has feelings of invulnerability. At this point, he begins taking chances and making mistakes. That's when he actually may become most vulnerable."

"I agree with you on many of your points," Gonzalez added. "This guy has been like a ghost, coming and going without detection. Also, the violence and strength it takes to literally twist a person's head around like a rag doll can only be the work of a man who has seen military action, a combat veteran who is used to killing up close and personal. My question to you, Randy, is that the victims are both men and women, all of whom are connected in some way to a case which started at a sex club here in Miami. It seems as though the killer is following what we do and murdering links to the crime we are establishing. Is this possible?"

"Not only possible, but highly probable. Like The Ripper, David Berkowtiz or 'Son of Sam' and The Zodiac killer in San Francisco, he is taunting you by killing right under your noses. He's literally telling you that he is superior to you in intellect, strength and stealth. The only thing he hasn't done yet is contact the news media. That may be next."

"How do we catch this guy?" asked Wiggins. Other detectives nodded in agreement with the question.

"Ah, here's where the rubber meets the road. We're not dealing with some killer on a spree. There's, in his mind anyway, a rationale of why he is committing these murders. They're not random, which makes him more vulnerable. Therefore, I suggest that we draw him out by creating a sting operation. Let's consider establishing that next link in our investigative chain, and use him or her as bait to see if the killer strikes. Rather than allow him to set the schedule, we'll set it and be ready for him."

"Agent Miles and I will be discussing this operation, which will involve all of you. A word of caution, no one can mention any part of this plan to anyone. I mean anyone, including your spouse, significant other, buddy or priest. This has to stay inside this room until the killer is caught. Is that clear to everyone here? He's getting his information from some source close to us and the investigation. Let's not help him."

Nods of agreement among the detectives. "You got it, Sarge. Okay."

"Dismissed. Let's plan on meeting here at 8 am tomorrow to strategize our approach."

Chapter Eighteen

1999

After she graduated from Edgewood High School in 1998, Sandy Garland wasn't interested in applying to one of Pittsburgh's many colleges. She was, instead, intent on pursuing a career in modeling and filled out an application to the Duff School of Modeling. In her mind, her beauty and height were part of what she considered the perfect package for modeling.

Three weeks after sending in her application and photos, Sandy received her acceptance in the mail. She was pleased and knew that her good looks and perfect body would make it difficult for her to be rejected. Since she became a senior in high school, Sandy used her beauty as a weapon to lure and, ultimately, humiliate, salivating young men who would have gladly donated a testicle to cup their sweaty palms around her round, juicy buttocks. She was every boy's dream and every boy's nightmare. Sandy Garland was getting even.

Classes began in September and Sandy was more than ready for the next phase of her life. With the money left to her by her deceased parents, may their souls burn in hell for eternity, she had more than enough to pay her tuition, while living comfortably in the small frame house in Edgewood. She sometimes wondered whatever became of her mother and father. It was just like them to abandon her in her final year of high school. Some people just couldn't handle responsibility.

Sandy had adopted a small terrier mix from a local humane shelter, thinking that having a companion around the house would bring some measure of comfort after her parents disappeared. But the tiny dog barked incessantly, driving Sandy to distraction. She eventually had to dispose of the little beast but decided to do it with some flair. One dark evening she walked the dog she had named 'Henry,' in honor of her loving father, into the back yard, poured kerosene on it and lit it with a single match. Its screams of anguish actually didn't last long, and after it was incinerated, she scooped up its ashes and bones into a plastic bag and sat it by the curb on Thursday morning for trash pick up. Barking dog problem solved. Sandy decided at that point to keep her own counsel and not complicate matters with pets, canine or otherwise.

Duff's urban campus, a single red brick building with classrooms on the first three floors and administrative offices on the top floor, was located in the city's center, near the Civic Arena, referred to locally as the Igloo, the domed edifice with the retractable roof, that was home to the Pittsburgh Penguins. The Pens were the city's beloved hockey club that was in danger of folding until a bankruptcy court granted former player and hockey icon, Mario Lemieux ownership. The team still attracted standing room only crowds of dedicated hockey fans. Pittsburgh hockey fans couldn't care less about the team's financial situation. They came for the fights, and the team's goons didn't disappoint.

Sandy arrived at the Duff School early for her first class called "An Introduction to Modeling," taught by former professional model, Samantha Anderson. Sam, as she was called by her friends, was in her forties, yet still a beauty. Like many models, she was over six feet tall and rail thin. The only apparent flaw seemed to be her habit of chain smoking, which probably contributed to the series of burgeoning wrinkles around her mouth and eyes.

Sandy was the first student to arrive in the cramped classroom on the second floor of the Duff building. Sam looked up, smiling, as she entered the room.

"Good morning," Sandy said brightly, "looks like I'm early. My name is Sandy Garland, and this is my first year."

"Hi Sandy, welcome to Duff. I am Samantha Anderson, the instructor for this class."

"Yes, 'mam," Sandy responded. "You worked for Ford for nearly ten years and appeared on more than twenty major magazine covers, from *Elle* to *Cosmo*. You were on the runway for just about every major showing, from New York to Rome, modeling couture designed by the world's leading designers from St. Laurent to Chanel. You retired in 1975, after having achieved every honor a super model could possibly earn."

Sam stared at Sandy, a smile frozen on her face. "Wow, you've done your homework. I'm impressed. Most students are too lazy to dig out that information at the library."

"It's a real thrill for me, Ms. Anderson, to be part of your class. I am truly looking forward to learning from the best of the best."

"Flattery will get you everywhere, Sandy," she said with a laugh. "Grab a seat and we'll get this party started when the others arrive."

Her first class with Sam Anderson was fascinating, as she summarized what they would be learning during the semester. She would cover subjects from the runway to makeup and everything in between. Sandy was ecstatic and enthusiastically hung on the former model's every word, taking copious notes. If only the subsequent class was nearly as interesting and taught by a former star. It wasn't.

Portfolio 101 was led by a disheveled man in his twenties, who wore his hair long in the back and short on the top and sides. It looked unkempt and greasy and as if it hadn't been washed in months. His hair matched his wardrobe. His tight jeans looked grimy and sported so many rips and holes Sandy was amazed that the pants didn't disintegrate at any moment. This sartorial splendor was topped with a black T-shirt, also tight, with rips and tears. This kid looked like a vagrant. Sandy was repulsed.

"My name is Dirk Allen," the photo instructor announced to the class of fifteen smiling girls, in a bored monotone. "I am a professional photographer, actively working here in Pittsburgh, with a specialty in creating portfolios for aspiring models not unlike yourselves. I will be working with you to get you comfortable in front of the camera, so that it captures the very essence of your individual beauty, be that as it may." Laughter from the class elicited a smile from Allen.

"This class is not going to be easy. Posing so that the clothes you are wearing look their best is tedious and sometimes frustrating. You are not all going to become super models. Most of you will go onto pursue careers as secretaries or waitresses. A few of you will model clothes for a JC Penney's catalogue or sexy underwear for Freddie's of Hollywood. One of you, possibly, will latch onto an agency and hit the runway in a major showing. Let me emphasize the word 'possibly'."

Sandy looked around at her fellow classmates. No one was smiling. This kid was a pompous jackass, and she wondered if she could transfer if she did it quickly. But she decided to hang in for a while to get an idea of where he would take the class. Besides, she wasn't going to let some jerk who looked as though his clothes were a series of body stains chase her so soon.

As her first semester progressed, Sandy was not impressed with the quality of instruction at Duff. Except for Sam's class, the level of expertise was low and arrogance was high, particularly Dirk Allen's portfolio class. He was condescending, self-centered and he smelled bad. Sandy hated his guts.

One late fall afternoon, Allen asked Sandy to stay after class, so that he could have a word with her. Reluctantly she complied. After all the other students left the room, Allen motioned her to join him at the front desk.

"Sandy, I've been monitoring your progress in this class, and I've got to confess, I think you have what it takes to make it in the modeling business."

"Thank you, Mr. Allen," Sandy said unenthusiastically.

"Hey, don't thank me just yet. You've got a lot of work to do and a lot to learn, but I'm willing to go the extra mile with you if you're up for it."

Sandy brightened. "What do you have in mind, Mr. Allen?"

"Please, call me Dirk. What I suggest is some extra work at my studio. I have a client who has retained me for a series of photo shoots to create erotic photos that appeal to a special group of his customers. It will be good experience for you to model sexy lingerie and other costumes in a professional environment. And the even better news is that this gig pays $700 for the day. You can get on-the-job experience and get paid doing it."

"You mentioned lingerie and other 'costumes.' There is no nudity involved is there?"

"There may be some," Allen replied irritably, "but Sandy, you had better get used to it straight away. If you're going to make it in the business you better be flexible and able to flaunt your sexuality, whether it's in the studio or on the runway. Keep in mind, the shy, reluctant types inevitably get left behind."

"If you think so, Dirk. I surely don't want to be left behind."

"That's the spirit." And what a gorgeous behind it is, he thought lasciviously. "Here's my card. Be at my studio at 10 am this coming Saturday. I'll have a makeup girl there, so don't worry about bringing anything of your own. She'll have you looking tremendous."

When Saturday arrived, Sandy called one of the few Yellow Cabs that still plied the streets of Pittsburgh and directed the driver to take her to First Avenue. Allen's studio was nestled among a series of office buildings. Formerly a grain warehouse that supplied the cargo ships that docked along the sloped banks of the Monongahela River in the 1800s, the building was renovated, retaining the original bare brick walls and stout wooden support beams. In the building's foyer, a single black buzzer protruded below a small card that simply read in black script, "Allen Photography 301," next to a cheesy clip art design of a camera.

Sandy pushed the buzzer and waited until Allen's tinny voice scratched through the intercom. "Who is it?"

"Sandy Garland." Who were you expecting, Judy Garland? she thought.

"C'mon up. Elevator's busted. You'll have to take the stairs."

Sandy jogged up the three flights, as if she was taking a leisurely stroll. Her strenuous daily exercise routine of running and free weight training had her in top condition. She was considering enrolling in a local karate school that a classmate had recommended. She told Sandy that the Academy of Isshin-Ryu Karate on Penn Avenue had one of the top instructors in the country, and it was a style of empty-hand self defense similar to kick boxing that was tailor made for a woman who needed to defend herself in a tight situation. Her classmate told her that karate was nothing like the crap portrayed on television, where combatants flew around like birds, acrobatically kicking each other and yelling like banshees. Most often, your attacker tried to grapple, grabbing your arms or choking you, while attempting to throw you to the ground. People trained in karate, she said, wouldn't let that happen and used precise strikes and kicks to keep distance between them. Sandy couldn't help but think that she knew a few guys that she'd like to precisely kick . . . right in the nuts.

The door to Allen's swung open and Dirk the Dirt Bag, as some Duff students referred to him, emerged like some grimy Neanderthal from his cave. "Hey, Sandy, right on time. Let's get rolling."

He led her into an expansive studio that was littered with lights, coiled power cords, brightly colored backdrops, power packs and hundreds of other pieces of photographic paraphernalia. This guy may be a cocky little grease ball, but it looked as though he knew what he was doing, she thought.

"Okay, let me explain the first shot sequence," Allen began as he offered her a seat by his desk. Like the studio, his desk was a disaster zone, piled with photos, a light board, magnifying loops, envelopes of all types and opened bags of potato chips and pretzels. Crumbs covered everything, like SO2 emissions that used to spew daily from the stacks of Pittsburgh's ubiquitous steel mills. Sandy thought this guy was a slob, but she had no idea.

"You will be wearing only a bra, panties, garter belt and nylons and patent high heels, all black," he explained. You'll be cracking a black whip and wearing black leather gloves. This black diamond-studded collar will be around your neck," he said, holding up what looked to Sandy like a fancy dog collar. Juxtaposed against your white skin and blonde hair, your S&M attire will literally jump out of the photo."

"S&M?" Sandy said, with a puzzled look.

"Stands for Sadism and Masochism, which is a sexual practice that some people enjoy participating in. They derive pleasure from inflicting or receiving pain, such as spankings, whippings, nipple clamping, bondage and other cruelties too numerous to mention," he said with a snicker. "Getting beat on, pinched or slapped turns them on. I personally don't get it, but that's just me. I photograph what the client asks for."

As he ushered Sandy back to the dressing room, she noticed that they were the only people in the studio. "Where's the makeup girl?" she asked.

"Had to cancel at the last minute, the bitch. But we'll be okay, there's plenty of makeup and a lighted mirror. This will have to be a do-it-yourself shoot." He handed her a leather bag. "You'll find the outfit and props for this sequence in this bag. There's a white robe hanging in the dressing room, which you can put on after you've changed. I'll be setting up lights and a backdrop. Just come on out when you're ready."

Alone in the dressing room, Sandy had an uneasy feeling about this whole setup, especially being completely alone with the little worm. She then recalled Dirt Bag Dirk's warning of how the "shy and reluctant invariably get left behind," and she strengthened her resolve, opened the bag and began to change.

A half an hour later, Sandy walked into the studio, balanced carefully on ultra-high stiletto black patent heels and wearing the white robe. Allen appraised her intently, assuming a professional attitude. "Take off the robe and let me see what I'm working with," he ordered.

Sandy was self-conscious as she slowly took off her robe. For one of the few times in his life, Allen was speechless. Her body was as near perfection as any he had ever seen or photographed. Her legs were well muscled, but in a feminine way with alluring curves in her calves and thighs. Sandy's small taunt stomach displayed a six-pack the likes of which he had never seen. As if these qualities weren't enough to be bestowed upon one lucky woman, she was well endowed with perfectly round breasts that threatened to burst out of the flimsy black décolleté bra he had given her. He could barely pry his gaze away from her.

"Okay . . . good. Looks like the outfit will work," he said nervously as he fiddled with his camera which was tethered to a series of slave lights. "Go ahead and stand right on the black tape on the backdrop there. I need to take a light reading."

As instructed, Sandy grabbed the whip and walked onto the paper backdrop and turned toward Allen. He walked slowly up to her, holding a light meter up to her face. He was perspiring and his body odor wafted under her nose, and she nearly gagged. Jesus, she thought, take a fucking bath once in a while.

Getting closer than she would have wanted, he finally got his reading and walked over and grabbed a Nikon that was linked to nearby lights that were momentarily off.

"Okay, Sandy, now I don't want you to look at the camera. Imagine that you are a dominatrix . . ."

"A what?" Sandy interrupted.

"A dominant woman in an S&M relationship who doles out the punishment to her naughty partner," he explained, with a hint of impatience in his voice.

"Just wanted to know who the hell I'm supposed to be, that's all."

"Okay, no problem, Sandy. Imagine that you are punishing some guy who's hurt you in a relationship."

"Oh, I can do that," Sandy assured him.

Allen lifted the Nikon and said, "Go, Sandy. Start cracking that whip." His two lights exploded as he began pressing the Nikon's rapid-fire shutter. Whack, whack, whack. Sandy tried to get into character and actually thought she was looking like Ms. Domin-whatever, as she continued to fling the whip forward so that it was making a loud snapping sound.

Allen abruptly stopped, sat the camera on the floor and "Sandy, you look like you're casting for bass, with about as much emotion in your face. You are in a sexual frenzy, wanting to inflict pain on this guy, before you have crazy sex. You are pissed and really want to make him hurt. Let's try it again."

This time, Sandy thought about the miserable bastards who mistreated her in school, as she cracked her whip in perfect rhythm. The cracking sounded like the shooting gallery at Coney Island.

"Yes, that's it, Sandy. Now you're into it." Whack, whack, whack, went the whip in cadence with the lights, firing in rapid succession. "Beautiful, sexy. Keep going."

After 15 minutes, Allen stopped. "Let's break and talk about the next shots. These are going to be a little trickier. It will require some nudity on your part, but since you handled the lingerie sequence so well, this shouldn't present a problem for you."

"What kind of nudity?" she asked, suspiciously.

"You have on the same garter belt and hose, except you won't have on any bra or panties. This represents the natural progression a dominatrix makes as she works herself into a frenzy."

I hope this guy is legitimate, Sandy thought. For all I know he's nothing but a little pervert who runs this scam on aspiring, unsuspecting models. "Okay, Dirk, I'll cooperate but let's get these shots over with." Without warning, she quickly removed her bra and then slipped out of her panties.

Allen was once again mesmerized, as she stood towering over him. Her large breasts swayed as she began to move back onto the backdrop. Her buttocks were perfectly round and shapely, like two ripe peaches sitting side by side. "Now what?" she demanded, yanking him from his reverie.

"Ah . . . I need another light reading." He approached her with the light meter, but this time he couldn't control himself. As he held it over her chest, his hand came down on top of one of her ample breasts. Sandy immediately slapped him across the face, nearly knocking the diminutive photographer off his feet. He retaliated by slapping her back. This time Sandy didn't slap him. With an overhand right reminiscence of Muhammad Ali, she knocked Allen on his back, his light meter flying from his hand, breaking on the studio's hardwood floor.

"You bitch," Allen cried, as he got back to his feet. Sandy attempted to head back to the dressing room, when the Dirt Bag tried to tackle her from behind. It did little more than knock her off stride. She again slugged him, this time catching him directly on the bridge of the nose, with a sickening crack. A geyser of red began spurting from his nose, as he sunk to one knee, clutching a light stand. He went down, along with the stand and light.

"You, uh, fail my course, you whore," he gasped, trying to stem the flow of blood by holding his nose toward the ceiling. "You have no fucking talent and . . ."

His words were abruptly choked off as Sandy wrapped the whip quickly around his scrawny neck, and with all the strength she could muster, pulled it tight. Allen tried to break free as she twisted the whip tighter and tighter. She was thinking of her bullying classmates, as they made her life at school a living hell, and her father, who had sex with her whenever he could get it up, the drunken bastard. The whip tightened like the tempered wire whirring around a massive reel as Allen fought for his life. He lost. Sandy let him slump to the floor as she hurried into the dressing room to change.

Son of a bitch, she thought, as she changed into her clothes. Now what the hell do I do? This isn't going to look good on my transcript at Duff. Then she thought of her little toasted puppy,

Henry, and the solution came to her. Well, then, he fired himself up by groping me. I'll just help the process along.

Sandy located his darkroom stocked with developing chemicals marked "Danger Flammable." Perfect, she thought. This will heat up the little bastard. Sandy began pouring the chemicals over everything, soaking Allen, his papers, film, everything that would burn, until she exhausted her supply. Grabbing a pack of matches lying on his desk she walked slowly over to Allen's body.

"Well, Dirt Bag, I can't say it's been fun, but it hasn't been boring." She struck a match and dropped it on Allen, igniting the chemical with a loud swoosh. It was only a matter of seconds until the whole studio began to be engulfed in flames. Sandy grabbed her bag and quietly let herself out. Once on the street, unnoticed, she was now just one of a group of pedestrians who happened to spot the flames shooting from the windows on the building's third floor.

"Quick, call the fire department," one passerby shouted to a man entering the building next door. Sandy was smiling as she strolled down First Avenue to hail a cab.

The following Monday, the fire and discovery of a charred, unrecognizable body, later identified as Dirk Allen, was all anyone talked about. Sandy and her classmates in Portfolio 101, while outwardly saddened, were personally pleased at the prospect of a new photographer taking over the class. Sandy couldn't stop herself from giggling. Dirt Bag certainly went out in a blaze of glory. The next time, the little shit wouldn't get so fired up over an innocent young student.

Chapter Nineteen

Gonzalez forced a heavy swoosh of air between his teeth as he forced the barbell up off his chest. Trying to complete ten repetitions bench pressing the more than 300 pounds of weight was about his maximum.

"C'mon, John," urged his spotter Wiggins. "You have this last one. Push!" Gonzalez and Wiggins were exercising in the spacious new athletic center on the sixth floor of Miami PD headquarters. The gym was stacked with top line machines and enough iron to please the most fervent gym rat. Gonzalez's team of detectives each exercised three or four times a week there.

Gonzalez managed to squeeze out number ten and let the bar clang onto the heavy duty bar catcher. "Geez, I must be getting old," he gasped, perspiration soaking his tee shirt.

"Either that or la vida loca you live is catching up with you at age 35," Wiggins chided.

"Probably all of the above. I have to shower. Sandy's in this weekend, and I'm taking her to Mango's over on Ocean Drive. The club has a great salsa band I want her to hear."

"Listen, Sarge, do you think it's a good idea to get involved with a woman who's still a suspect in these murders? You two are spending a lot of time together. There's something about her that doesn't quite ring true with me, no disrespect intended."

"None taken. Listen, we're just getting to know each other. No strings, no commitment. But ya gotta admit that she's awfully easy on the eyes."

"That I don't disagree with. I just don't want to see you tangled up with her personally during our investigation, which may lead us who knows where."

Gonzalez smiled. "Look, Wigs, I'm a big boy and know what I am letting myself in for. Besides, I personally haven't ruled her out as a suspect. These murders may look like the work of a man and a powerful, highly trained one at that. But women today are bigger and stronger, and can outperform men in some sports and physical activities. The problem is we can't identify a motive yet. That makes catching this guy . . . or woman . . . problematic."

"I ordinarily would agree that the murders look as though they have been committed by a man, but being around Sandy Garland has dispelled that notion," Wiggins responded. "She looks strong enough to crush concrete blocks, let alone a person's neck."

"Maybe she looks fit and strong," Gonzalez said, "but what bothers me is that she seems calm, level headed and intelligent. And regarding motive, she doesn't have one. In fact, she doesn't have the temperament either. It just doesn't add up. I'd stake my reputation that the killer we're looking for is an ex-Navy Seal or Green Beret, with a burning hatred for women and gays. Probably some religious fanatic who's cleansing the streets of those who don't fit his concept of a righteous lifestyle."

"You've been meeting with Randy Miles. What's the FBI have in mind to help us trap this nutcase?"

"At this point I can't reveal any details because I was told to wait until the team was briefed to avoid any possible leaks. I'm just following directions given to me by the Chief, that's all. Come Monday morning, and we'll all learn together how we're going to lay a trap for the so-called 'Swinging Sex' murderer."

*   *   *

Randy Miles and Gonzalez were waiting for the task force team, as they filed into the conference room. Most of them were holding coffee cups from the Starbucks located on the first floor, as well as notepads and pens.

"Good morning, men," Gonzalez said. "First, let me welcome you to our briefing, and secondly, put away your notepads and pens. We want nothing in writing, so we're all just going to have to commit details to memory."

"Sarge, I can't remember anything anymore," Cutrazulla said. "My doctor told me I had Alzheimer's. He said the good news is that I'd meet new people every day."

Laughter. "Okay Cut, Bada Boom. Old joke. Those of us with damaged memory circuits will just have to rely on his partner for information. If you both can't remember the plan, then you're screwed." More laughter.

Randy Miles spoke up. "As I said last week, we believe there is some way the killer is getting information from our investigation, either from an informant here in the agency, such as someone he knows or a girlfriend, or from another source. Possibly someone at Odyssey Airlines is leaking information, such as the flight attendants who I'm sure spend a lot of time chatting among themselves. One of them could be connected to the killer, either directly or tangentially."

"The only thing in this case that doesn't square is the murders in Philadelphia and Chicago, that resemble our boy's MO," Simmons offered. "Why would the unsub fly there to kill a person at random?"

Miles hesitated a moment before he replied. Choosing his words carefully, he said, "While the majority of victims know their attackers, there are murders committed that are totally random or that may resemble others but, in fact, have no relationship to each other. These are the ones that I am afraid to say may never be solved. I believe that's what we are looking at in those other cities."

"Are you suggesting that the murders we thought were connected were actually coincidental?" Russo asked, eliciting murmurs of discussion among the assembled detectives.

"Yes," Miles responded emphatically. "One of the early pioneers of psychological profiling David Canter, in his book *Mapping Murder*, wrote that crime is most always a coincidence.

People and places come together in a dangerous juxtaposition to create the circumstances for the crime. He theorized that 'chance' plays an important role in these scenarios. In other words, the victim is at the wrong place at the wrong time."

"That leaves us with a serial killer here in Miami who seems to be attacking at random but may or may not be. Do I have that right, Agent Miles?" Simmons asked, seemingly perplexed.

"I don't think this unsub is killing at random," Miles said. "He has a purpose, which I believe will be revealed very soon. We need to make a preemptive strike to stop him before he shows his hand. I am going to let John explain what we have in mind."

Gonzalez stood up and positioned himself before the detectives. "We believe that the trail to our killer runs through Odyssey Airlines. We do know this much. The unsub murdered Roy Stellini, who flew into Miami on one of its flights and Anne Claridge, a woman he met at a sex club. Once we initiated our investigation, Claridge's roommate and lover, Liz Tomkin, was murdered, soon after we interviewed her. Then Odyssey Airlines First Officer Dennis Allison was murdered following his interview with Detective Wiggins. He seems to be acting on information gathered by this task force or within the airline company itself. To that end, we have been working very quietly with Odyssey Airlines to imbed one of our own detectives in a flight crew that routinely flies into Miami. No one at the airlines will know her real identity, except its chief of operations Fred Gladstone, who sanctioned the operation. First let me introduce Detective Molly Vincendo, who is on loan to our division, courtesy of Northwest Homicide Unit."

Gonzalez opened the door to the conference and gestured to someone in the waiting area. Molly Vincendo walked through the door, amid admiring stares from the assembled detectives. A former college water polo athlete, Detective Vincendo was a 5 foot 10 inch attractive woman, who had thick auburn hair and striking amber colored eyes. She was muscular, with the broad shoulders of a swimmer. With a gaze that was nearly wolf-like in intensity, Vincendo looked like she could handle herself.

"Detective Vincendo is a ten-year veteran of homicide and has earned numerous commendations for bravery and is credited with having infiltrated one of the most dangerous drug operations in Florida," Gonzalez said. "She gained the gang's trust acting under cover as a so-called reliable connection to a cartel operating out of Mexico. After gaining their trust, she was responsible for providing critical information that led to the arrest of not only the dealers here in Miami, but also their suppliers up the chain. Some $4 million dollars of heroin and crack a day were taken off the streets and a whole bunch of bad guys are behind bars, due primarily to her great work."

Agent Miles picked up the introduction. "Detective Vincendo has agreed to go under cover at Odyssey Airlines and will assume the role of a flight attendant. She will subsequently be identified as a 'person of interest' in our investigation. In effect, we will be using her as bait to see if we can get the killer to show his hand. She will have knowledge of the murders and will discuss them openly with other members of the crew, in hopes of drawing interest from one of them who may be our murderer or who has some connection to him."

"Detective Vincendo will, of course, be wired and tracked 24/7 with a global positioning device," added Gonzalez, "and will be monitored by local police no matter where she is at any given time. And if you think Ms. Vincendo will be at risk during her undercover role, let me add that she is a fourth degree black belt in Jeet Kune Do, considered to be the most deadly form of martial arts. Please introduce yourselves and get to know Detective Vincendo before she joins the other team at Odyssey, and I must warn you again to say nothing of her role in this operation to anyone, and that includes your spouse, significant other, friend or even your dog. To expose her could comprise the entire effort and put her in harm's way. Now let's introduce ourselves to her."

Chapter Twenty

Pittsburgh
2000

Sandy Garland grew disenchanted with the quality of her education at Duff, as well as the entire notion of modeling. There was something demeaning, she believed, in using her perfect body to show off the bizarre creations of some effete, emaciated designer with spiked hair, a nose ring and probably wearing women's panties.

Just before the start of her sophomore year, she withdrew, much to the chagrin of Sam Anderson, who was, in Sandy's estimation, the only competent instructor in the entire school. That slime ball Dirk Allen was the absolute worst, and he ultimately couldn't keep himself from getting "hot and bothered" by Sandy. The very thought of his 'flashy' exit from this world brought a smile to her beautiful face.

"Sandy, you must be kidding," Sam said angrily. "You can't just up and quit. You have too much potential. What about us?"

They were sitting in Sam's penthouse in the new Trimont Tower perched atop Pittsburgh's scenic Mt. Washington, a veritable cliff overlooking the city. The view from her two thousand square foot apartment was magnificent, looking down on the steel and concrete of the city, with its scores of bridges traversing the

Monongahela River. The tributary sliced through Pittsburgh to join up with the Allegheny River to form the Ohio River at what was called the Golden Triangle. During the summer, the city's Three Rivers were dotted with pleasure boats and barges laden with coal making their way to the few steel mills still in operation.

Pittsburgh had come a long way from it smoky, ash-laden days of Bessemers, open hearth furnaces and ladles bubbling over with molten steel, when at 10 am the skies were black with fly ash and SO2 emissions. The city was now a center for medical research, education and small, hopeful technology firms. Miraculously the air was clear and blue skies were evident when clouds and rain from the Great Lakes didn't loom over the city.

Sandy and Sam sat side by side on a massive white leather u-shaped couch, their bare feet entwined. Sandy leaned over and gently kissed Sam on the neck. Sam turned her head and accepted a deep kiss. Sandy pulled back and looked into her eyes.

"Sam, I can't do it anymore. The whole idea to me is so much bullshit, and you are the only instructor in the whole program who knows what she's doing. I'm thinking of applying to the airlines."

Sam jerked her head in Sandy's direction. "You have aspirations of being a waitress with wings? You're better than that."

"Do you have any contacts at Odyssey here in Pittsburgh?" Sandy persisted.

Sam sighed. "I do, but I really think you're making a mistake."

Sandy pulled Sam closer to her and began to unbutton her blouse. "I'll make it worth your while," she whispered huskily.

*   *   *

Sandy's interview was scheduled for the following Friday with Bert Avanides, director of Odyssey Airline's human resources division, and former lover of Samantha Anderson. Avanides' office was on the sixth floor of the company's modern, black glass building three miles from the Greater Pittsburgh International Airport. The spacious, bright lobby had a full-sized, vintage Odyssey DC3 passenger airplane suspended from its massive ceiling. The aircraft, built in 1936, had the airline's recognizable stylish red "OA" logo painted on the sides of its Pratt & Whitney Wasp engines. Considered a giant step forward in commercial aviation at the time, the DC3 had a cruising speed of 150 mph, a virtual "slug" by the standards of today's passenger jets.

"May I help you?" the obese woman seated at a massive reception desk asked pleasantly, as she looked up from her keyboard. She was wearing a set of headphones that looked miniscule against the backdrop of her "big hair."

This cow looks like a sumo wrestler in drag, Sandy thought as she replied cheerfully, "I have a 2 pm appointment with Mr. Avanides in human resources."

"Name?" she asked.

"Sandy Garland."

After signing Sandy in, she nodded to a couch. "Please take a seat over there. Someone will be with you shortly."

Bert Avanides' secretary soon appeared and escorted her to his office. He stood as they entered and extended his hand. "Hello Ms. Garland. Please, have a seat." He beckoned to a couch flanked by two chairs.

Avanides was slender and well-dressed, in a form fitting grey suit, blue and white rep tie and a tasteful silk pocket handkerchief in complementary shades of grey and blue. Sandy could smell his cologne, which was a mild, pleasant wood scent. His office occupied a corner of the building and was filled with photos of him with his family, golfing buddies leaning on their golf clubs and the Mooney aircraft he owned with two other business associates. Four large windows afforded a view of the main highway leading from Pittsburgh to the airport. Aircraft could be seen in the distance circling and making their slow descent into the airport.

"I received a call from my good friend, Samantha Anderson, that you were interested in joining Odyssey Airline's team of flight attendants."

"Yes, that's correct. I believe that my personality and attitude gives me the foundation to be a good flight attendant. I can relate to people well and can adapt to any situation."

Avanides jotted notes as they spoke. After an hour, Avanides said, "I can see that you are confident and certainly have the requisite physical requirements." I'd like to personally inspect your physical attributes, he thought. Clearing his throat, he added, "I refer to proportionate height and weight, good grooming, no visible tattoos and so forth."

Sandy smiled. "I'd never have a tattoo anywhere on my body." It would ruin perfection, she thought.

During the interview the subject of pay, benefits and work requirements were discussed. "Here are some forms to complete," Avanides said, producing a file folder. "Mail these back to us and we'll schedule you for six weeks of training here at headquarters for certification by the FAA. The timing is good, because our next class is scheduled to begin two weeks from today. That is, provided you clear a background check. Once that's done, you'll be enrolled and on your way. Any other questions?" he asked.

"I was thinking of enrolling in a self-defense course," Sandy said, "strictly for conditioning and self-awareness. Can you recommend one in the city that I can contact?"

Avanides smiled and said, "Many of our employees take part in various types of martial arts or self-defense training. It prepares you mentally and physically for many situations, particularly in today's society. I hear good things about the Academy of Isshin-Ryu Karate downtown. The head instructor is a gentleman by the name of Bill Deardon." He jotted contact information for the school on a sheet of note paper and handed it to Sandy.

They both rose as Avanides said, "It's been a pleasure speaking with you, and allow me to welcome you in advance to the Odyssey family. I'm sure you'll pass with flying colors, so to speak."

*   *   *

Sandy stood in front of the Academy of Isshin-Ryu Karate and looked up at the medallion that hung over the dojo's entrance. On it in colorful relief was an Asian woman who was half serpent, with her arms spread, one displaying a closed fist and the other, an open hand. She was submerged in an ocean to her waist, with a fierce dragon floating above her head.

"That's the Goddess of Isshin-Ryu," said the silver haired man with the countenance of a boxer, who suddenly appeared behind her. Sandy looked around at him and was taken with his blue eyes, which held her own gaze. She was four or five inches taller than him, but he had a physical presence that bespoke coiled violence.

"The Goddess was designed by our master, Tatsuo Shimabuku, who had a vision for the style of karate he was creating. He believed that this woman embodied the philosophy of the self defense system he called Isshin-Ryu. Notice her open hand, which indicates that she comes in peace. However, the the other hand is a closed fist, meaning that she has the strength to defend herself in the face of any intended aggression."

"What do those three gold stars floating above her head mean?" Sandy asked, pointing to the medallion.

"They symbolize the three forces inherent in our style . . . the spiritual, mental and physical aspects of Isshin-Ryu Karate."

"That's fascinating," Sandy said. "I've heard about the mysteries of the Asian martial arts. I am eager to learn more."

"Hi, I'm Bill Deardon, the head instructor at this school, or 'sensei' in Japanese." He extended his hand, and Sandy couldn't help but notice his bulging knuckles. She grasped it firmly.

"I'm Sandy Garland and was just about to enter the school to learn more about enrollment."

"We are about to begin our 5 pm class," Deardon said. "Why don't you come in and watch and then we can talk." He led her into a spacious room, with a beautiful natural wood floor. Various weapons hung on the walls above mirrors which surrounded the entire room.

"This is called a dojo, a Japanese term for what is our training room," he explained as he led her to a bench outside of the white striped area that delineated student-only area. "The students, around thirty to forty in number, usually participate in each class we hold at various times during the day. The dojo's open from 7 am until 9 pm to accommodate our students' personal schedules, and black belt instructors are always available to answer questions, help with training or referee kumite or sparring matches."

Sandy hung on his every word. This was a completely unknown world to her and she was enthralled by it. Students were already on the floor and stretching or practicing what looked like a dance routine to her. "What are they doing?" she asked, pointing to the group of dancers.

"They are practicing kata or forms," Deardon explained. "This is an important part of karate in which you are defending yourself against an imaginary opponent or group of opponents. It also encourages excellent conditioning as well as speed and accuracy of techniques. To earn a black belt, our students have to be able to learn sixteen kata, eight of which are empty handed and eight require the use a weapon, like the ones hanging on the wall. Some katas have hundreds of movements and a student will spend a lifetime pursing perfection in their execution but will never really achieve it. It's a lifelong journey."

More students were now assembling for the class, and Deardon excused himself to change. He was leading the class himself tonight and a larger turnout was expected.

One of the black belts, Jean Bucklin, was watching Sensei Deardon intently as he spoke with Sandy Garland. She was having an intense sexual affair with him, and her mood darkened as she assumed he, a notorious womanizer, was on the prowl for another bimbo to bed. Women were attracted to him, his rugged looks and the power he exuded. Jean was pissed, and couldn't wait until this blonde bitch put on a gi.

The class began with Deardon's bow of humility to his class, and thirty students bowed in unison in return. Then the exercises commenced; a grueling series of kicks, punches and thrusts, everyone counting loudly in Japanese, "ICHI, NI, SAN, SHI, GO, ROKU, SHICHI, HACHI, KYU . . . ," they grunted gutturally in unison. Sandy was mesmerized by the scene before her. She decided that she wanted to be part of this as soon as possible.

When the class concluded nearly two hours later, the students were drenched in sweat and made their way slowly to the locker rooms for a shower. Jean Bucklin hung back as she feigned interest in some heavy bag work, while Deardon took Sandy into his office. She watched them through the glass as they smiled and chatted, which infuriated her further. She learned later that Sandy Garland signed up for the black belt course, a minimum two years of grueling training. Bucklin vowed that she would see to it that this whore never made it past green belt.

*　　*　　*

Sandy, wearing a white gi tied with a white belt, walked onto the dojo floor in her bare feet twenty minutes before her first class was to begin, looking like a super model who was preparing for a photo shoot. Students, particularly the men, walked up to her and introduced themselves.

"The lead black belt today is Jean Bucklin," one of her fellow students whispered to her. "She's a fucking bitch, and the rumor is she's Sensei Deardon's squeeze. Be careful of her. She likes to hurt people."

Jean Bucklin assumed her place in front of the forty students who were lined up according to rank; black belts in the front rows, brown belts, green belts and then came the white belts, considered beginners. Bucklin spotted Sandy Garland in the far back row and smiled. She bowed and all others returned her bow. Then it began.

Bucklin led a frenetic pace of kicks from the front, the side and the back. Then it was onto punches, from every angle, the speed intensifying. Some students began gasping, never having been part of a grueling workout like this. Even the other black belts were feeling the exhaustion and pain burning in their thighs and shoulders. They began to glance at one another, signaling that possibly Bucklin was out of control. Suddenly Bucklin halted the calisthenics and so-called warm-up beginning of the class. She broke the colored belts into separate rooms, announcing that she would work with the white belts today, and that they were to assemble in dojo B for some work on kumite or sparring.

Bucklin paired the students to begin training them in hand-to-hand fighting, blocking punches, using a kick to set up a straight punch, how to leg sweep an aggressive opponent and other techniques requisite to defend oneself. Bucklin's catch phrase was "a good offense is a good defense. Don't back up and create space between you and your attacker. That only gives him room to kick your ass. Remember, a 255-pound drunken street fighter's objective is to get you onto the ground and snap your neck. We will never, with the emphasis on 'never,' allow that to happen. Right class?"

"Hai, sensei," they responded with enthusiasm. She walked over to Sandy who was not paired with anyone and said, "I'll work with you, uh, your name?"

"Sandy Garland. This is my first class at the academy."

"Well, Sandy Garland, let's begin with kumite, which is a way to use what you will learn on the dojo floor and the katas you will study. Front and center," she said, pointing to a spot on the floor.

Sandy walked toward Bucklin, and bowed, assuming that the black belt would continue her tutorial on fighting. She didn't. Just a nanosecond after Sandy bowed and assumed the fighting stance, feet spread shoulder width, fists up and protecting the face and side, Jean Bucklin unleashed an overhand right into Sandy's jaw. Sandy dropped like the Times Square Ball at midnight on New Year's Eve.

Sandy lay on the floor dazed, staring up at the colorful ceiling, painted in shades of blue and green, the color palette established to serve as background for the Goddess of Isshin-Ryu Karate above the dojo's front entrance. She was having difficulty orienting herself. When the clouds lifted, and she saw Bill Deardon looking down at her.

"What happened?" he asked Jean Bucklin, continuing to stare down at Sandy, concern furrowing his brow. He looked up at Bucklin, expecting a quick answer from one of his instructors and his lover.

"I was just beginning to show her how to use a straight punch to set up a front kick during kumite, when she moved directly into the punch," she said, feigning anxiety. "I didn't expect her to walk toward me as I was demonstrating a technique. Maybe I expected too much of her."

"Expected too much of her?" Deardon asked irritated, glancing over at Bucklin. "This was her first day in the dojo. What were you thinking?"

"Sensei, I had no idea that she was new," Bucklin said. "I humbly apologize. If I had known, I would have paired her up with another beginner."

"Let's get her onto the couch in my office," he ordered, as they all lifted Sandy gently to her feet. She was barely able to walk as they guided her into Deardon's office, her bare feet barely touching the floor. After she was laid gently on the couch and an ice bag applied to the back of her neck, Deardon asked everyone to leave them alone, including Bucklin. She received this command poorly, her face contorted with anger. She reluctantly joined the others as they filed out.

Deardon sat watching Sandy intently as she began to regain her faculties. He marveled at how gorgeous she was, even as she lay with her senses momentarily gone. She could have been posing for a magazine, he thought.

Sandy finally focused on Deardon and groggily said, "What happened?"

"You were accidentally struck by one of my instructors during a lesson in kumite. She claims that she didn't know this was your first day in one of our classes. Is that true, Sandy?"

Sandy hesitated a moment. "Yes, that's true, sensei," she replied with a smile. "I suppose I should have said something. It just didn't occur to me."

"That's a good way to get hurt, because my class leaders don't know who has what experience and, therefore, what level of instruction to provide. I am very upset with Ms. Bucklin for not determining that you were a beginning student before she initiated kumite instruction. She claimed you walked into her front strike."

Hesitating again, she replied, "That's true. I have no idea what I'm doing. The fault lies with me." I'm going to fuck that bitch up good, Sandy thought.

*　　*　　*

It was past 9 pm as Jean Bucklin walked toward the parking garage near the dojo. She always parked there for the evening classes but resented having to pay the exorbitant rates that the municipal facility charged, which was tantamount to rape in her eyes. She used the pay station on the ground floor to get her ticket and pushed the up button to retrieve her car on the fifth floor. Although it was relatively early by big city standards, the lobby was deserted. That's what Bucklin liked about Pittsburgh. It had big city chutzpah with a small-town attitude. Most of the downtown work force escaped the city at 5 pm and fought their way through traffic to their own neighborhoods where they stayed put until the following day.

The elevator door opened on five and Bucklin saw the familiar ass end of her silver Toyota sticking out of the row near the bank of elevators. As she approached the automobile, Bucklin couldn't help but notice the eerie silence that enveloped the garage like it was baffled for soundproofing. She could hear nothing except for an occasional car horn in the distance. This is freakin' weird, she thought.

Then she heard the voice. "Bucklin, I've come for you." It was a woman's voice, and she was struck by how calm and articulate it was.

"Who's there?" she demanded. "I'm bound by law to tell you that I'm a black belt in karate. So, you've been warned." Her words sounded hollow and silly. She heard a scraping sound behind her, and she whirled quickly, dropping her purse and gym bag, crouching into a seisan stance, feet spread shoulder width apart, arms stretched in an offensive posture, one palm open facing the voice. The other clenched into a fist, top two knuckles pointing downward; the classic Ram's Head.

"C'mon, bitch. Show yourself, or are you afraid I'll kick your fucking ass?"

Sandy Garland appeared behind Bucklin and said, "Your ass-kicking days are at end, I am afraid to tell you," she said, producing a lead pipe from behind her back. Bucklin, a trained martial artist and self-proclaimed bad ass, never saw it coming as the heavy pipe slammed down upon her skull like someone trying to win a stuffed animal at Kennywood Park by ringing the bell with an over-sized hammer. Bucklin, her skull split like a watermelon, dropped onto the pavement of the garage floor. Blood, tissue and grey matter had sprayed across the trunk of her Toyota, as Bucklin crumpled in a heap, a gurgling sound bubbling up from her chest.

Sandy wasn't finished quite yet. She produced a 12-inch serrated knife and with great care, expertly slit Bucklin's throat so deep that her spine was visible. She took the pipe and knife, wrapped them in a towel and dropped them into her gym bag. Picking up Bucklin's purse, Sandy calmly jogged down the five flights to ground level and disappeared into a group of people planning to catch some live music by the well known trio, the Jazz Express, which was appearing at the Red Door near Liberty Avenue.

Sandy was a welcome addition to the regular Red Door crowd, all of whom, in their inebriated states, would swear that she had been with them since happy hour. Hell, they didn't know where they were at that time. They were so shit faced that they would have claimed that President Obama was making martinis at one point.

As the male patrons were treating Sandy to drinks, one of them asked her what was she doing in town this fine evening.

"Oh, nothing special, just 'cutting up' a little," and everyone laughed. Sandy joined the laughter but wasn't smiling.

Chapter Twenty One

Pittsburgh

Detective Molly Vincendo was dressed in the blue and white Odyssey flight attendant's uniform, a form-fitting blazer and skirt designed especially for the company by Richard Tyler. Pulling her rolling bag behind her, she strode purposefully through the Greater Pittsburgh International Airport. As a senior flight attendant, she qualified as a 'line holder' and could choose her flights. She chose to work a 9 am flight to Raleigh aboard an Airbus 321-200 leaving from Gate B29. One of the older aircraft in Odyssey's fleet, the medium range jet could accommodate 146 passengers in its stretched fuselage with a single aisle configuration. Six crew members were required: two pilots on the flight deck and four cabin attendants. This was Detective Vincendo's first day on the job, and she'd be reporting to lead flight attendant Sandy Garland.

Vincendo was told to make her way to the Odyssey crew room located under the main concourse of the Pittsburgh airport. It was there that the crews were checked in, received safety and operational briefings and then was dispatched to their respective gates thirty minutes prior to passenger boarding.

She swiped her ID card through the magnetic security system and entered the room. Odyssey personnel in the lounge were listening to an in-flight supervisor conduct a briefing on updated security measures the major airlines were adopting to protect passengers from terroristic acts. As he was pointing to bullet points on the screen with a light pen, Vincendo saw her. Sandy Garland was seated at a table, staring into a laptop. The photos Vincendo had seen of her didn't do her justice. This woman was breathtakingly beautiful. She approached her.

"Are you Sandy Garland? I'm Gloria Hernades, and I believe I'm assigned to your crew for the flight to Raleigh." Vincendo extended her hand, which Sandy accepted with a bright smile.

"I was expecting you. It's a pleasure to meet you. Your personnel profile says that you are new with Odyssey but have had other flight experience."

"Yes, that's true, Sandy. I was with Continental for four years, but they had some personnel cutbacks a few months back, and I got caught in the backwash. So, I applied to Odyssey and luckily the company was hiring."

Sandy's smile displayed perfect white teeth. "Well, we're certainly lucky to have you. You're going to service the forward galley with me on 7365 to Raleigh. The team will be ready to leave in a few minutes for the pre-boarding check. I'd like you to make sure the emergency equipment is stowed and has current certification. About forty five minutes prior to passenger boarding, Captain Jurgensen will give us a briefing report on weather conditions, safety procedures and any other related issues."

Vincendo thanked her and walked over to an unoccupied couch and pulled out her BlackBerry. "Have made contact with lead attendant, Garland, and have assignment. Going to introduce myself and take some soft soundings," she typed and then emailed to the Miami task force mailbox set up for this specific effort. Every member of the force had access to it.

Rising from the soft leather couch, Vincendo began introducing herself to Odyssey staff and crew members. One strikingly handsome man approached her. He was tall, with a head of thick, silver hair combed neatly back from his face, setting off a pair of clear blue eyes and square jaw that morphed into a deep cleft at his chin. He wore an Odyssey uniform with four white stripes on his sleeve. "I am Bob Jurgensen, a senior pilot. I drive one of Odyssey's big blue and white birds," he said smiling, as he extended his hand. Molly took it firmly, surprising the captain by the strength of her grip.

"I'm Gloria Hernades, a new flight attendant. Actually, today is numero uno."

"Well, welcome aboard," Jurgensen said. "I saw your name on my crew manifest, and I look forward to working with you. I was told that you used to fly for Continental. Good company, that one."

"It is but is experiencing some rough times financially."

"What company isn't these days? The rising cost of fuel, empty seats, personnel required on flights and other factors make it extremely difficult. Southwest seems to be the only one able to make a profit."

Gloria listened and replied, "Yes, that's true, but they have been able to do it by cost reductions in personnel through attrition, reducing the number of employees per flight and through write-downs of fuel hedging contracts."

"Well, Gloria, you seem to know the airline industry very well. Let's continue this conversation when we get to Raleigh. It's time for the crew to go over a few details before heading to the gate. We are meeting in five minutes in the smaller conference room B over there," he said, pointing over Gloria's head. "See you in there shortly."

As the crew was gathering in B, Sandy Garland intercepted Vincendo. "Gloria, be wary of that one," she said conspiratorially. "Captain Jurgensen has a lot of notches on his belt, and they're not there because of his ability to land an aircraft in multiple instrument approaches in a storm, if you catch my meaning."

Gloria smiled. "You refer to his expertise in using another instrument, I gather."

"You gather correctly," Sandy said, smiling grimly and walked ahead of her into the room.

*　　*　　*

Odyssey flight 7365 landed without incident at the Raleigh-Durham International Airport at 10:23 am. The flight crew, happy to be free of over a hundred passengers, some of them continually complaining and abrasive, a few inebriated and a couple of them just assholes, gathered at the departure area to catch the shuttle to the Embassy Suites. Vincendo spotted Sandy sitting on a bench adjacent to the exit.

"Sandy, does the hotel have a decent gym? I would kill for a hard workout."

Interesting choice of words, Sandy thought. "It does, on the second floor. I am an exercise freak myself. Maybe I'll see you there."

At noon, Vincendo was on her sixth set of crunches when Sandy entered the gym. Molly was impressed at her muscular development and low body fat ratio. This was a woman who took her workouts seriously. Dressed in a solid blue track suit with wide white stripes down the legs, Sandy was clearly intense during her routines. She didn't hang out at gyms to impress the guys. She was there to work.

"Hey, Gloria," Sandy said, as she began to stretch.

"Sandy," Molly acknowledged cordially. She was just beginning a series of Jeet Kune Do parries and thrusts, watching her form carefully in the mirror. Like water flowing around rocks in a stream . . . . flexible, taking different shapes, she thought as she moved quickly and easily. Strike, move toward your opponent and parry. Redirect his attack, use his own force against him, intercept his fist, breathe and be calm, as the water's surface, she recited to herself, a mantra she knew well.

Sandy, who was stretching the muscles in her thighs and lower back, watched with fascination as Hernades trained. When she was finished, Molly grabbed her towel and began to wipe the perspiration streaming down her face. She noticed Sandy watching her.

"That's just a training regime I follow," Molly said, embarrassed that she attracted Garland's attention.

"Is that Jeet Kune Do, the style of martial art developed by Bruce Lee?" Sandy asked.

"Actually, Master Lee created Jeet Kune Do so that it had no label, no style and was free of rules. It is free flowing, like water, able to surround, intercept and overcome."

"Interesting," Sandy replied. "I don't know much about that stuff, but I've always been impressed by the body control and discipline it requires. Have you been studying long?"

"I've been a disciple of Lee's philosophy for a time. I understand that you are a student of the martial arts."

How would she know that? Garland asked herself. "Oh, I've been an occasional student at a small school in Pittsburgh. I'm a little too skittish for fighting."

"I see," Molly replied. "I enjoy it but don't allow it to become my life, which some let happen. I guess it's easy to get so immersed, a person ends up living and breathing martial arts."

"Where is your hometown, Gloria?" Sandy asked, casually.

Suddenly on alert, Herandes answered, "I was born in Rochester but grew up in Houston. My dad was a petroleum engineer and took a job with Diamond Offshore there. I liked everything about the city except for the heat and humidity during the summer."

"How did you hear that Odyssey was hiring?" Sandy asked.

Deciding to carefully try to elicit some information, Vincendo said, "Believe it or not, I heard about the airlines from a friend who works for the *Miami Herald*. She was covering some murders there and some of the victims had flown in on Odyssey. I knew that Odyssey was based in Pittsburgh where I now live and decided to apply. It was sort of an odd way to find your employer."

"Yes, those murders were bizarre, for sure," Sandy said. "They were calling them the 'Swinging Sex Murders' or something like that. It made national news. Who's the friend you mentioned?"

"My friend?"

"The reporter at the Miami Herald."

"Her name is Andrea Torres, and she and I have been close friends for a while." Vincendo said quickly. "She and I met a few years ago on a Continental flight into Miami I was working. How did you hear about the murders in Miami? I heard that they took place at some kind of club?"

"I believe it was a sex club for people who swap partners," Sandy replied. Glancing at her watch, "Speaking of working, I'd better get to my workout," Sandy said changing the subject. "Maybe we can hook up for a drink later this evening. Just call my room. I'm in 247."

"Okay, I'll do that," Vincendo said, wrapping her towel around her neck.

In her room, Vincendo sent an email to the team, reporting on her conversation with Sandy Garland and offering the opinion that, as a senior flight attendant, she was asking questions because she felt responsible for people under her supervision. Molly's message was that Garland would serve as a good entry point for information, since she has been at the Odyssey for a time, seems to be in the know and is friendly, willing to share gossip. I can work her, she added.

Vincendo called Sandy later that afternoon, and they decided to meet up for a drink in the hotel bar at 7 pm. When she hung up, Sandy walked over to the mirror and stared at her image. "I think that bitch isn't who she says she is," she said, as she began removing her clothes. She pressed her naked breasts against the glass and began kissing the reflections of her nipples, while she masturbated.

"I think you and I are going to have to hurt Gloria Hernades, if that's who she is. We're going to have to hurt her badly," she said to the person staring back at her. "We will, count on it," it said back. Sandy's orgasm was intense and pleasurable.

Chapter Twenty Two

Miami

Gonzalez walked into the conference room and brusquely called the meeting to order. "Okay, gentleman, our task force and the FBI have been tracking Detective Vincendo every hour since she's been embedded at Odyssey. What has she learned?"

Cutrazulla reported first. "Sarge, Vincendo's floated a number of straw men theories and opinions of the murders and the type of individual who could be committing them among her fellow employees. So far, nada. No one has made a move or offered any opinions. Vincendo, as we all know, is a savvy investigator and if anyone can get the mole or killer to show his hand, it's her."

"Get to Vincendo and get her to push a little harder," Gonzalez directed. "This killer may strike at any time, either here in Miami or another city. The frustrating part of this is that we have no idea when or where."

"I'll call her tonight, Sarge," Cutrazulla said.

*   *   *

Vincendo's cell phone sprang to life with a salsa tune, its pulsing rhythm alerting her that she was receiving a call. It was nearly 10 pm and she was in her hotel room in Syracuse.

"Yes?" she said softly.

"It's me, Cut," said the voice on the other end of the line.

"Yea, what's up partner?"

"We had a squad meet this morning, and Sarge is getting a little antsy. He wants you to push harder. Try to come up with someone in the organization who might know someone who has been talking about the murders or has some involvement in any way. Anything at all you can learn will be more than we have now. It may just lead us to the killer."

Vincendo hesitated a moment. "It's been a week, and I'm just getting acquainted with other members of the flight crews. But I have to tell you, I'm hitting a brick wall. Either they have circled the wagons, or they actually don't know shit."

"Detective . . . ."

"I know, I know," Vincendo interrupted, fatigue clouding her voice. "Everyone's feeling the pressure, especially Gonzalez. His ass is directly on the line with the mayor and city council. All I can say is that I'm trying to finesse information from people who may or may not know anything."

Cutrazulla sighed. "Molly, stay cool. I understand and so do the other members of the squad. Things are just getting tense. None of us knows when this nut case is going to hit next, or even if he's going to hit. Gonzalez is not the only one getting heat. You know the trickle down theory, right?"

"Tell me about it," she said softly. "Alright, I'll try to speed things up a little, but not at the expense of exposing myself. Tell Gonzalez I'm ratcheting it up. I have a flight to Boston tomorrow, and I'm in Sandy Garland's crew. She seems willing to talk more than the other crew members, and I just think they don't know shit. I'll press Garland a little harder."

As they hung up, Sandy Garland lay on her bed, with her cell phone propped against her ear with a pillow. I'll be dammed, she thought. That Hispanic bitch is a cop, and John Gonzalez has assigned her to go undercover at Odyssey. I knew something wasn't ringing true about her. Sandy was grateful that she had the opportunity and time to grab Hernades' cell phone from her purse stashed in the galley during the flight into Syracuse last week. It wasn't difficult to upload cellular intercept encryption software on her phone from her laptop in the lavatory. This gave her the capability to pick up Vincendo's conversations within a reasonable distance, such as in the confines of a hotel. Sandy knew that giving that software techie geek back in Pittsburgh a couple of blowjobs would eventually pay off.

And speaking of payment, she owed Gloria Hernades or Detective Molly whatever her name is big time. And that would include Sergeant Gonzalez, that disloyal bastard. Sandy always paid her debts.

*   *   *

It was 8:45 am and flight 235 to Boston was nearly ready to pre-board. Vincendo was efficiently going through a pre-flight routine, checking to make sure the safety equipment was available and operational and that the galley was stocked with the correct drinks and snacks. Sandy Garland walked into the galley.

"We're full today and weather in the Boston area may stack us up as we approach," she said. "How's everything going with you, Gloria?"

"All is well. Safety check is complete, cabin has been inspected and commissary gave us more than enough supplies for the leg to Boston."

"Good. How about handling the departure and arrival announcements today," she said smiling. "Schilling and I will take care of safety instructions."

"No problem," Vincendo responded.

Garland nodded and called the gate. "We're ready," she said tersely to the attendant.

In a few minutes, pre-boarding passengers appeared at the cabin door and slowly made their way into the interior of the aircraft as Sandy's team smiled, welcomed them and assisted them with their luggage. Vincendo was busy helping an elderly woman into her seat, when a flood of passengers began filing their way into the aircraft, opening overhead bins and noisily stowing their luggage, as others behind them impatiently waited their turns to get to their seats. As this routine process continued, she noticed a rather diminutive, dark skinned young man, wearing sunglasses slowly stowing a small duffle bag in an overhead by his seat. He looked nervous as hell, and alarm bells sounded in her head. This guy is acting hinkey, she thought. She looked up the aisle and spotted Garland preparing for pre-flight safety instructions.

As the final seats were occupied and impatient passengers were placated with seats of their choosing, next to a loved one or a window, Vincendo drew close to Sandy.

"I want you to check out the guy in 26A," she said softly to her. "There's something about him I don't like. He's nervous as hell and if his facial twitches were any more pronounced, he'd look like Kramer on crack."

Sandy simply nodded and produced the passenger manifest from her blazer pocket, which provided a list of passengers and originally assigned seats. "Let's see who we have in 26A," she said, inspecting the document. "His name is Benjamin Jones."

"He doesn't look like anybody who would be named Jones, do you think?" Vincendo asked.

"I'd agree that it's certainly strange," she admitted. "He was pre-screened and checked, but that doesn't mean all that much. Some weapons or explosives can get through, no matter how diligent the screening process. There was that Nigerian kid who boarded a Northwest flight last Christmas with the high explosive PETN hidden in his underwear that the screeners didn't catch. Once the plane was airborne, he tried unsuccessfully to detonate it. Let's keep an eye on him."

Vincendo stationed herself by the intercom and made her initial boarding announcement. "Ladies and gentlemen, welcome aboard flight 235 nonstop to Boston. We have a full flight today, so please stow your personal items as quickly as possible so that we can close the door and push back from the gate. Our flight time into the Boston area today will be approximately 45 minutes. Once we have pushed back, our cabin crew will begin safety instructions."

The young man in 26A had his eyes averted and was studying a document that Vincendo would dearly liked to have seen. She decided to give it a try, as she nonchalantly walked toward the rear of the aircraft, checking each passenger to make sure his or her seat was upright, table locked and seat belt securely fastened. As she approached 26A, she bent down to speak to the passenger in 25A.

"Sir, please move your seat forward," she said. Quickly she looked over the seat to try and see the document he was holding. What she was able to see before he folded it up and stuffed into his jacket pocket was writing . . . in Arabic.

Vincendo continued her passenger check and then hurriedly walked down the aisle to where Sandy was standing.

"The document he's reading so carefully is written in Arabic. I have a bad feeling about this one."

As the aircraft taxied toward runway 09 for takeoff to Boston's Logan International Airport, Sandy was digesting this information. The tower gave clearance for takeoff, and the captain sounded the bell for the flight crew to take their jump seats.

"OA235, cleared for takeoff on 09, be advised a UAL heavy two mile final approach on 25R," the voice in the tower cautioned.

"Roger that, control," replied Captain John Williams. "Stand 'em up, Dan."

First Officer Dan Bates aligned the throttles to build maximum power. The pilots smoothly pushed the throttle levers forward simultaneously as Bates recited, "V1, Vx and rotate." At 170kts the Odyssey Airbus A380 lifted off the runway at the Rochester International Airport, the surface of its airfoils increasing with a whirling sound and its wheels retracting with a thump. The aircraft began its climb out to ten thousand feet. The bell sounded alerting the cabin crew that it was safe to begin moving about the cabin to prepare drink service.

Vincendo once again picked up the cabin intercom phone.

"Ladies and gentleman, shortly we will begin beverage service when the captain has reached a safe cruising altitude. We have an assortment . . . . ," she recited, letting the passengers know that alcohol and soft drinks were available to help get them through the flight, and please have exact change.

As she was addressing the passengers, Sandy was intently watching the passenger in 26A. She watched him nervously dig into the waistband of his pants. She sprung into action, moving swiftly down the aisle toward him. She was too late. The young man wearing sunglasses quickly rose from his seat and slid into the aisle.

"In the name of Allah, I have a bomb and am prepared to martyr myself in the jihad against Christians and Jews in your evil country to protect Islam, the one true faith," he shouted, in a heavy middle eastern accent. Everyone in the cabin looked around in horror at this unexpected outburst, some people shouting and others shrieking. Without a moment's hesitation, he grabbed Sandy around the neck and because of her height, had to bend her backwards.

"In the glory of Allah I declare myself in command of this aircraft," he cried. "Do this immediately or die. Allah Akbar!" As he shouted this, a second man across the aisle reached under the seat in front of him where a service worker, a Muslim sympathetic to the struggle, had hidden a handgun and rose from his seat, waving it menacingly at the passengers.

"No one moves or she dies," he yelled, training the gun on a little girl seated in the row in front of him. An audible gasp rushed from the nearby passengers, as they tried to assimilate the horrific events that were suddenly unfolding before their eyes. The little girl's mother clutched the child closely to her, but the terrorist never wavered, his gun pointed at her head. Dressed like a college student, the Muslim sympathizer wore a blue blazer, white shirt and sunglasses. His sandy blonde hair was curly and neatly cut, giving him an All-American look. But holding a gun to a frightened child's head dispelled any notion of a clean-cut kid. He was an American Mujahideen, who joined the struggle for global jihad, or the spiritual battle to enable the Muslim religion to be the last one standing . . . the one true faith. In short, their objective is the ultimate protection of the Islamic state. And Joseph Andato, from White Plains, New York, a kid who played Pee Wee football and rooted for the Mets, was one of the hundreds of foot soldiers recruited to die for Allah.

Sandy remained as calm as she possibly could, as the terrorist held her from behind in a pathetic head lock. She could break his grip and knee him savagely in the groin before he had a moment to react, but any such action on her part was tempered by the college boy training a pistol on the child. That's when she noticed Vincendo moving silently and quickly toward the boy. As Vincendo struck underneath the gunman's arm, guiding it quickly and carefully in the air, the pistol discharged a bullet through a cabin window, and immediately the cabin began to depressurize. Oxygen masks dropped from the overhead bulkheads as magazines, papers, cups, articles of clothing, purses, notebooks and general debris were violently sucked toward the broken window.

With the loud gunshot, and amid a sudden eruption of screams and shouts from the passengers, Vincendo struck college boy in the throat with her elbow, followed by a back fist into his anterior temporal artery and vein between his eyes. He was dead before he slumped between the seats.

As this was happening, Sandy simultaneously raised her knee and stamped her heel savagely into the terrorist's foot. He screamed in pain, his grip temporarily loosening. That's all the time Sandy Garland needed. She spun, unleashing a devastating spinning back kick to his head, followed by a front strike to his temple, which caused a massive hemorrhage in his brain and immediate death. He was now incapable of detonating the explosives he was carrying.

Chaos reigned as the plane lurched, precipitously losing altitude as the captain attempted to get to a level where the passengers could breathe without masks. The cabin lights inexplicably went out, the only visibility afforded by aisle floor lighting. Passengers were still in a state of panic, screaming and shouting, not sure what was happening. Sandy Garland decided it was the perfect time to repay her debt. Reaching into her pocket, she felt for the tanto knife, a six inch Japanese razor sharp dagger usually reserved for Samurai warriors but were useful for the ritual suicide called seppuku. She produced the knife and as the pilot and first officer struggled to get the plane level, Sandy spotted Vincendo in the dim light.

"Gloria," she yelled, "I need your help." Vincendo moved quickly toward her, offering to help subdue the Arab terrorist who she thought was still alive.

"Gloria, watch it, he has a knife!" Sandy screamed for all to hear. As Vincendo reached Sandy, without a moment's hesitation, she plunged the razor sharp dagger into the unsuspecting detective's stomach and expertly sliced left to right, causing a whooshing sound as her entrails began spilling out onto the floor. Vincendo was dead within seconds.

"Gloria, Gloria," Sandy shouted as she extracted the knife and thrust it into the already dead terrorist's throat. She began to sob, cradling Vincendo in her arms.

The cabin lights went back on and the panicked passengers aboard flight 235 to Boston were treated to a bloody tableau that would haunt many of them for years. Sandy Garland was holding her fallen Odyssey colleague, they and the young terrorist were covered in blood, which was quickly pooling around them and a string of Vincendo's intestines. Sandy was inconsolable, rocking back and forth, as the detective's body lay cradled in her arms.

The flight crew radioed for an emergency landing at T.F. Green Airport in Providence, Rhode Island, alerting airport personnel to have rescue equipment, fire trucks and flame retardants available. On the ground, the passengers were unanimous in their praise of the heroic actions of flight attendants Sandy Garland and Gloria Hernades, who saved their lives. They were only sorry that the Arab terrorist wasn't dead and in one final dying effort, took the life of the flight attendant named Gloria.

All realized that Sandy had done everything she could to thwart the attack but couldn't stop the killer in time.

For weeks, the story of the young terrorists' attempted takeover of flight 235 was on every news broadcast and the subject of theories and pontifications among talking heads around the world. How did one of the terrorists conceal explosives from security checks, and how did the American, who was trained in Afghanistan by the enemies of the United States, get a handgun on board without detection? Sandy Garland was a guest on Good Morning America and the Today Show and was asked by fawning news anchors what it was like facing certain death, and how did she and the deceased Gloria Hernades use what looked like martial arts to subdue the terrorists. Sandy, as was her style, downplayed any heroism on her part, and as for martial arts, she knew that Ms. Hernades was highly trained. As for her, she demurred by saying that she just got lucky. After all, she was trained to hold the safety of her passengers as her number one priority, and that she and Ms. Hernades were only doing their jobs. It was most unfortunate that the Arab terrorist she thought was dead was not. That was most unfortunate.

Odyssey subsequently awarded both attendants, one posthumously, its highest award for bravery, and their names were both read into the Congressional Record. Sandy Garland was uncomfortable with all the attention. Any other flight attendant would have done the same.

Chapter Twenty Three

New York City

George Stephanopoulos, hair immaculately coiffed, had his engaging smile firmly in place as he bade America a good morning. "Coming up, we will be talking to Odyssey Airlines senior flight attendant Sandy Garland, who will share her harrowing experience aboard flight 235 to Boston two days ago as two terrorists attempted to hijack the plane shortly after it left Rochester, New York." Quick camera cut to Sandy, serenely waiting in the green room for her interview to begin. Wearing a simple, yet elegant, tailored black suit with a cream colored ruffled blouse, she looked more like a movie star appearing to promote her newest movie.

"In the ensuing chaos and subsequent loss of cabin lights," Stephanopoulos continued reporting, "her fellow flight attendant Gloria Hernades was fatally stabbed by one of the dying terrorists, identified as Aalim Furman, who was in the United States illegally under the assumed name of Benjamin Jones. Both Mr. Furman and his accomplice, an American by the name of Joseph Andato who lived in White Plains, New York and was reportedly recruited by an al-Qaeda cell, were both killed. Ms. Garland, who received the Federal Aviation Administration's highest honor, the medal of valor, will join us right after this."

As GMA went to a break for commercial messages, Stephanopoulos joined Sandy at a small seating area adjacent to the main set, which had floor-to-ceiling windows overlooking 44th and Broadway in Times Square. Three robotic high definition cameras were slowly rolling into place for the interview, their cables snaking across the studio floor, resembling alien beings from *War of the Worlds*.

"Okay, Sandy, we'll be on in about three minutes," Stephanopoulos advised, placing his hand lightly on her shoulder. A woman was busily touching up his makeup as he spoke to Sandy. "Remember, just look at me as I ask questions and not into the cameras, just as if we were having a conversation in a restaurant."

"I understand," Sandy said. "I'm a little nervous, especially knowing that millions of people will be watching."

"Actually, last week we had more than five million viewers on average during the first week of January," he said, with a chuckle. "But, hey, who's counting? It's just you and me talking Sandy, and we just happen to be surrounded by a bunch of machines."

The segment producer suddenly appeared and gave Stephanopoulos the one minute to air time. As a camera dollied in, she raised her arm and counted down from five with her fingers. Smile reset, he said, "Today we have with us Sandy Garland, the senior flight attendant with Odyssey Airlines who, along with a fellow flight attendant, literally saved a plane filled with more than 120 passengers from a hijacking by using her wits and training. Unfortunately, flight attendant Gloria Hernades was tragically killed by one of the terrorists." He looked directly at Sandy. "Tell us what happened as Flight 235 lifted off in route to Logan Airport in Boston."

The second camera moved in for a full close up of Sandy Garland's face. "As we were conducting a routine safety check we noticed . . ."

John Gonzalez, sitting in his apartment back in Miami, watching GMA, carefully scrutinized Sandy's every movement and facial expression as she responded to Stephanopoulos' questions. He suddenly knew she was lying. He wasn't sure why he knew that, but given all that had transpired, his years on the force told him that she was being less than truthful. In his heart, he hoped his intuition was wrong.

"In the chaos, with no lights and the aircraft losing altitude, Gloria quickly moved to help me subdue the terrorist I thought was unconscious, but he was still functional and stabbed Gloria with . . . ," her voice trailed off and she hesitated, tears welling up. Time stood still on the GMA set, as a robotic camera focused in on a tight shot of Sandy, as she struggled to hold back her tears.

Gonzales grabbed his cell and called Wiggins. "You watching Good Morning America?"

"Hell Sarge, everyone is. We have it on here at the precinct."

"What do you think?"

Wiggins hesitated, silence on his end. "C'mon, Wigs, tell me what's in your gut."

"I think she's lying through her teeth. They may be gorgeous teeth, but she's fucking lying through 'em."

"I'm beginning to feel that way, too," Gonzalez said. "She's due to fly into Miami next Thursday, and she and I have a tentative date. I want you to put a four-man team together to tail Sandy when she gets into town. I'll let you know what time she is due to arrive and at what hotel Odyssey has booked the flight crew. Don't let her make you. She's highly intelligent, and I don't want her to even get a sniff that we think she's gone from advisor to a viable suspect. And if she is the killer, I don't want anyone engaging her. Understood?"

As his partner left his office, Gonzalez leaned back and closed his eyes. She couldn't have committed these horrible murders. Sandy is a beautiful woman who happens to be strong, fit and physically gifted, and I may just be falling for her. He suddenly opened his eyes and tried to snap out of his reverie. C'mon you dumb shit, if she's the murderer, it's your duty to bring her down.

*　　*　　*

Randall Miles contacted the FBI's Boston Division to get as much information as he could about the hijacking including the weapons used: a .38 cal Smith & Wesson with a 2 inch barrel, registration number filed off, and a knife, which was identified as some sort of Japanese ritual blade. He and Gonzalez met early the following Monday morning. As John entered Miles' office in North Miami Beach, he saw the frustration in his face.

"Hey John," Miles said as he grasped the detective's hand. "What the fuck do you make of this? We lose a first rate detective during a fucking hijacking and she's stabbed with a Japanese knife, which our guys identified as a tanto, a weapon traditionally used by Samurai in feudal Japan. What the hell were two Mujahideen terrorists attempting to hijack a commercial jet doing with a Japanese blade?"

Gonzalez took a seat and stared at the knife. "I don't know, Randy. I have an idea, but it's too thin to be honest."

"Let's hear it. At this point, no ideas are out of bounds."

"Sandy Garland is a student at the Isshin-Ryu Academy of Karate back in her hometown of Pittsburgh."

"So, thousands of people across the country study some form of martial art," Miles responded.

"True, but I have a suspicion that her devotion to karate has gone far beyond the average person. She has demonstrated an uncanny ability to protect herself from bad guys like drug dealers, and now armed terrorists. Although it was difficult to see in the darkened cabin, some of the passengers reported that Sandy broke the terrorist's grip with a savage blow to his foot, kicked him in the head with some fancy move and then knocked him unconscious with a blow to his head. Sandy Garland is highly trained, and that is of great concern."

Miles sat quietly, his fingers interlaced. "John, under most circumstances, I would disagree with you. But Sandy Garland has demonstrated a level of skill in the martial arts that I wouldn't have thought possible for a woman to achieve. If she's our killer, she is writing a new chapter in profiling."

"That's what I'm afraid of," admitted Gonzalez. "She and I have developed a relationship, and I believe it's pretty serious."

"She doesn't suspect that we may be looking at her for these murders," Miles replied. "Let's try to bring her in for questioning, without getting anyone injured or killed."

*   *   *

The cab pulled to the curb in response to Sandy Garland's hand signal. She opened the back door and got in. "West 50th and 17th Street," she said to the driver, her eyes averted. The cab lurched off into the stream of evening traffic. Sandy settled back, staring out of the back window at the collage of blurred colors as the driver sped past brightly illuminated store fronts and businesses. She was wearing her black wig and form fitting low rise jeans and a sleeveless vest that revealed her tanned, muscular stomach.

Since she was in the city for GMA, she was anxious to try the Splash Bar, one of New York's high energy gay bars. A 2,000 square foot dance floor and chest thumping sound system, surrounded by massive video screens depicting gorgeous men and women in various sensual embraces set this club apart from the hundreds of others in the Big Apple. The city's Chelsea district was a magnet for the city's denizens of the night, and Splash was the current center of the action.

Sandy entered the club and was greeted by a group of women who turned their collective heads to stare at her, appraising her body unabashedly, whispering to each other and smiling. She continued on into the massive club and took an empty seat at the bar, which was u-shaped and more than a city block long. She ordered a Cosmopolitan and swiveled in her stool to take in the action.

"Hey, haven't seen you in here," said the tall brunette, as she leaned in next to Sandy. "Than again, how in the hell could anyone remember seeing anyone in this fucking noisy cesspool," she said laughing. Sandy laughed as well.

"I'm Chandra," the brunette said. "And you are . . . don't tell me. Your name is Kirstin and you're from Indiana or Ohio. You're a receptionist at a Chevy dealership. Am I right?"

"Close but no cigar," Sandy said. "My name is Daisy, and I'm a shepherd on a Yak farm in North Dakota. I'm here in New York to attend a conference on do-it-yourself artificial insemination." She stared, smiling beatifically at Chandra. They both broke into laughter.

"Well, Daisy, what are you drinking? I think we're going to become fast friends before the night is over."

I don't think so, Chandra baby, Sandy thought. "I just ordered. How about you?"

"I'll have a dirty martini, thank you, Daisy."

"How dirty do you want it?"

Chandra moved close to Sandy, her right forefinger lightly tracing a patch across her belly. "As dirty as I can possibly get it," she whispered in her ear.

Late into the evening, Sandy and Chandra danced on Splash's illuminated floor, pressing tightly against each other's bodies, grinding into each other, occasionally exchanging deep, hungry kisses. Both women had a lot to drink and each felt a sexual desire building like the early tremors of a massive orgasm. But Sandy was inured to the effects of alcohol, having trained herself to always maintain control of her mind and body.

It was nearly 1 am when Chandra suggested they grab a cab and head to her apartment in the West 80s. Sandy initially reticent to leave the bar, finally acquiesced to the seemingly dominant Chandra.

Chandra's small one bedroom apartment overlooked Central Park and was located on the sixteenth floor of a pre-World War II building on 86th Street. The rent was $4,000 a month but was considered a "steal" given the outrageous prices of flats in Manhattan's high-rent upper West Side.

"Before we get naked," Chandra announced confidently, "how 'bout I whip us up my drink specialty . . . Sex on the Beach. It's a lethal combination of vodka, peach schnapps, cranberry juice and, instead of orange juice, I include a healthy jigger of brandy. If this doesn't get your clit stiff, nothing will."

They sat closely to each other on Chandra's day bed, sipping their drinks and listening to some soft jazz. Chandra was speaking quietly to Sandy, but her voice slowly receded as if it were morphing into a whisper. The Gerhard Richter impressionistic framed print above the fireplace, Merlin 1982, began to blur, colors swirling in a undulating pool of colors as Sandy was beginning to lose consciousness. The glass containing Chandra's special Sex on the Beach recipe, with a dash of Ketamine, a powerful anesthetic used by vets on animals, fell from Sandy's hand. She was faintly aware of her surroundings but was unable to move a muscle. She heard the front door of Chandra's apartment open and muffled male voices.

"Petr, dis won a fuckin' bebe," one of the men said to the other, as they hoisted Sandy's paralyzed body from the couch and out of Chandra's apartment.

*　　*　　*

Slowly Sandy began to become aware of her environment. She was naked and strapped face down to a flat table, legs splayed. Two men were setting up lights, cameras and sound equipment.

"Whaaa . . . ," Sandy mumbled, as she began to emerge from her dream state.

"Our princess awakes," mocked Chandra, as she stroked Sandy's bare ass, her fingers probing their way toward her anus. "Daisy . . . if that's your name . . . you are about to have a starring role in one of our hugely popular 'snuff' films," she said, slurring her words.

"Chanduh, ged hur reddy," ordered one of the men.

As Chandra began removing the wrist cuffs, a large naked man entered the room. Sandy began regaining consciousness but willed herself to remain perfectly still, as though she were still sedated. She carefully opened one eye and saw a large bed illuminated by two lights on stands. The naked man sat heavily on the edge of the bed as one of the other men focused a hand held video camera on him. He held a long serrated knife in his hand, as he spoke to the camera man in what sounded like Russian. He was demonstrating how sharp the lethal looking knife was. Chandra took off the final cuff on her leg and began to lift Sandy up, grabbing her lasciviously under her breasts.

"Hep hur to da bed, Chanduh," a man standing in the shadows instructed.

Chandra, much smaller than Sandy, was struggling with her dead weight, and Sandy wasn't offering any assistance, feigning unconsciousness. "Petr, for Christ's sake, give me a fuckin' hand. This bitch weighs a ton."

As Petr walked toward them, Sandy calculated that this would be her one opportunity, trusting that surprise would be her strongest ally. As Chandra was trying vainly to stand her up straight, Sandy broke free from her tenuous grasp and drove a side kick into Petr's throat and nearly at the same instant struck the naked man in the temple with a bottom fist. The knife flew from his hand, and Sandy grabbed it and drove it into the camera man's chest to the hilt. Within seconds the three men were lying dead or dying. Sandra turned to Chandra.

"Looks like it's just you and me, babe," Sandy said, smiling menacingly. "You're going to be my stand in for this film, and I don't think you'll be around to collect any residuals." She yanked the knife from the naked man's chest, with a sickening swoosh of air and spray of blood.

"Look, Daisy, you've got this all wrong," Chandra pleaded, backing toward the door. "We were just making an x-rated movie and you were going to get paid, once we brought you around from your drunken stupor. One of the scenes would have been you and me. You would have liked that . . . ." She never finished her sentence.

With a movement so quick that Chandra never saw Sandy move, she drew the long knife in one graceful arc across her throat. Sandy's years of working with a samurai's wakizashi blade had trained her for this moment. Chandra's head separated from her shoulders and dropped with a thud onto the floor. Her torso, its neck spurting a fountain of blood, slumped heavily to the floor.

Sandy quickly grabbed a nearby towel and wiped her prints off every surface she touched and gathered her clothes. When she was dressed, she stood for a moment and looked at the bloody tableau in front of her.

"Sorry I have to run, boys and girls. I don't think this movie making business is for me, but what the hell. Just being able to 'cut up' with you all was worth it," she said. Sandy began to laugh and she opened the door to leave. She suddenly opened it back up and looked back in at the gory scene.

"Oh, and by the way, please don't 'cut' my scene out of the movie, or I'll be really pissed." As she descended the staircase to the street, Sandy Garland whistled the tune, "You Oughta Be in Pictures."

Chapter Twenty Four

Gonzalez's cell rang early Monday morning. "Gonzalez."

"Hey handsome, Henderson here. And I have a 'this just in' for you, Sarge."

"Okay, Kathy, and what does my favorite IT geek have for me this fine morning, and I haven't even had my coffee yet?"

"Well, my dashing Latin caballero, I got a bulletin on NCIC this morning that four murders were committed yesterday in an apartment in New York City that fits some of our requisites."

"Go on, you have my rapt attention," Gonzalez replied.

"Here it is. It seems that three members of the Russian mafia from Brighton Beach were dispatched quite efficiently as they and a street hooker by the name of Chandra Wells were attempting to put together one of their specialties, a snuff film starring some poor woman they abducted from the street or a bar. It seems, though, that this woman and prospective snuffee wasn't as cooperative as they had hoped."

"Go on, Kathy."

"They found a 12-inch serrated knife at the scene that was used to literally decapitate Wells, but was probably used first to kill the naked guy they found with a stab wound in his chest that cut through his spine and nearly exited his back. NY homicide is surmising that he was probably cast to play opposite the reluctant star, whoever she was. The two other Russians were sent to their final rest by what looks like single blows delivered by a foot or hand."

"Sounds familiar," Gonzalez said. "Any prints?"

"The knife and the table which held the victim were wiped clean. Nada. Whomever did this, and I am guessing it's a woman, unless there's such a thing as gay snuff films, had the capability and strength to first, escape her captors, and the Russians aren't lax when it comes to capturing and securing their victims. Second, the woman had the skill to kill the three reportedly large men in what had to be rapid succession, or she would be history. Third, she had the presence of mind to wipe the place clean and make an escape, for whatever reason. You would have thought that she'd call the police immediately."

"Unless she didn't want to get mixed up in a crime scene that might shine a light on her penchant for killing, even in self defense," Gonzalez wondered aloud. "Hey, thanks, Kathy I owe you a big one for this."

"And I'll take it, lover. Just name the time and place."

"Get me the contact information for the lead detective in New York so that I can have a chat with him." Sandy Garland was in New York to appear on GMA, he thought, deeply troubled.

*   *   *

Odyssey Flight 365 landed Thursday night in Miami 35 minutes late because of storms in Pittsburgh. Sandy, who was given a couple of weeks vacation by a grateful airline, wanted to come spend some time with Gonzalez. They had a dinner date Saturday. John was tied up working a murder-suicide case in Miami Shores, and she told him she'd entertain herself until then.

Gonzalez had to try and bring Sandy peacefully into headquarters for further questioning and suggested that Sandy stay at the Palms Hotel and Spa on Collins. As her cab pulled up to the entrance, Wiggins sat in his car, balancing a cup of coffee on his knee. He watched Sandy emerge from the cab.

"She's in," he said tersely into his 2-way radio. "If anyone makes contact, be extremely cautious. Her karate training makes her very dangerous."

"Roger that," responded Cutrazulla. "Three, you copy?"

"Got it," said Simmons, sitting in the third unmarked around the block on 30th.

In a surveillance scheme like this, it's all about timing, the ability for each car to follow her tightly for a few blocks after she gets into a car and then 'hand her off' to one of the other cars.

"Let's keep our powder dry and see if she leaves the hotel," Wiggins advised the team. "This may take a while."

A little over two hours later, Sandy emerged from the hotel and got into a cab hailed by one of the hotel's doormen. Wiggins alerted his team and started his unmarked. The cab pulled away from the entrance with Wiggins following at a safe distance. After three blocks he handed the cab off to Cutrazulla, who followed it for another few blocks, who then turned the tail over to Simmons. This pattern continued until the cab pulled to the curb in front of the Cameo Club on Washington in South Beach. Sandy paid the driver, skirted the line waiting to get in and was admitted immediately by one of the burly security team checking to see if she was on the 'V.I.P. list.' It didn't matter. He looked up, smirked and admitted her. The Cameo was a Miami mainstay for those who wanted to dance or listen to live music and always had a long line of people waiting to be 'blessed' with entry. Most of them hoped to be a part of the in-crowd, if only for one expensive night.

Wiggins' team took positions on surrounding streets.

"Man, they didn't waste any time checking to see if our girl was on the list," he said into the two-way.

"Shit, you kidding me, bro," responded Cutrazulla. "A chick like that gets a free pass anywhere she goes in life. She's got the 'gold' that every dude wants and ain't never gonna get."

"And I'd like to be a 'gold digger' for a few minutes for that treasure," added Simmons. "You feel me boys?"

"Okay, let's clear this line and run quiet just in case someone has this frequency on a scanner," Wiggins ordered.

When it was nearly midnight, he dismissed the other detectives and said he would simply try to locate Garland and report back to Gonzalez. He planned on doing that from a safe distance. After Cutrazulla and Simmons left, Wiggins decided to check out the club himself to see what Ms. Garland might be up to. He approached the club's security guards who immediately stopped him until he flashed his shield.

"Have a very pleasant evening, detective," one of them said with a smile, as he unlatched the velvet rope barring entrance to the club. Wiggins paid the twenty dollar cover charge and entered the club. Every one of his senses was assaulted with sound, motion and color. It was like walking into a giant pinball machine only ten times louder. The dance floor was writhing with sweaty, half-clothed bodies. A sound system that only could have been designed by Boeing was pumping out an old Gloria Estefan hit, "The Rhythm is Going to Get You." The place was pulsating.

It took Wiggins a few minutes for his eyes to get adjusted to the multi-colored strobe lights, flashes of brilliant white light and deep dives into abject darkness. The club was massive with multiple bars and a number of private rooms on the mezzanine level available for a couple hundred dollars a pop. That included a bottle of champagne. With a crowd he estimated at in excess of a couple thousand people it was going to be tricky spotting Sandy Garland. He slowly, in an orderly fashion, began searching the cavernous innards of the Cameo Club, surreptitiously scanning faces to locate Sandy Garland.

Completing his exploration of the first floor, Wiggins took a massive marble staircase to the upper level and the line of twenty private rooms. As he walked along a series of closed heavy oak doors he could smell the acrid scent of marijuana and hear moaning coming from a few of the private rooms. As he passed one room, he noticed that the door was slightly ajar and could hear voices rising in anger. Suddenly, the door was flung open and a naked woman carrying her clothes bolted toward the staircase. A naked man, save for a dress shirt and loosened tie, was in hot pursuit.

Wiggins followed the two. "Stop, Miami police," he commanded. He held up his shield as he ran after them. The woman stopped abruptly at the top of the staircase, and her pursuer slammed into her. Both bodies tumbled down the stairs, landing with a loud thud on the first landing. Wiggins walked down the stairs, as the woman tried to dress while extricating herself from beneath his inert body of her dazed companion. Couples on their way to the mezzanine level pointed and laughed as they skirted the two.

Displaying his shield, Wiggins said, "What the hell are you two doing running around naked, disturbing the sanctity of this fine entertainment venue? Have you no decorum? No sense of propriety?" he asked a smile beginning to crack his stern countenance.

The woman was crying, as she struggled to pull her skirt over her panties. "That bastard tried to get me into a threesome with his girlfriend," she sputtered, her mascara beginning to run down her cheeks. She was beginning to resemble Alice Cooper, Wiggins thought.

Wiggins pulled the man to his feet. "Go put your pants on and get your fat ass back here," he ordered. He immediately did as ordered and retrieved his pants, returning to the landing.

"Look, if I wasn't on an assignment I'd book you both for indecent exposure, disturbing the peace and smoking marijuana. Judging by the gaseous smoke plume that followed you from the room, you were both doing more toking and less stroking. This is your lucky day. Go get your clothes and checkout of your hotel menage a trois and keep it down while you are doing it." Both thanked him and began to walk up the staircase.

"Oh, and hey stud muffin, when a woman says 'no,' that means no. Stop, cease and desist. Next time you could be facing attempted rape charges," Wiggins warned. The man nodded his head and continued up the stairs.

Wiggins looked at his watch. It was a little after 1:30 am, and he decided that Garland must have slipped out of the club and to call it a night. It was probably a waste of time anyway. He left the Cameo and headed for his car parked in a vacant lot around the corner. It was a clear, warm night in Miami and the silence enveloped him like a shroud after having spent over an hour and a half in the ear-splitting club. As he pressed the unlock button on his key ring, there was a sudden rustling sound behind him. Before he could react, something slammed into his lower back with the force of a sledge hammer. He dropped to one knee and nearly blacked out. When his faculties returned, he pulled his Glock and got to his feet but saw or heard nothing. Silence once again. There was a faint soreness in his back, but that was all. Wiggins looked everywhere in the lot but was only greeted with stillness. He wasn't sure what transpired, but whatever it was, it was no more. He started up his car and headed for home.

Sandy emerged from the shadows, smiling faintly. She knew that the dim mak 'delayed strike' to his kidney would cause sepsis and hemorrhage in a few days. Wiggins was a dead man walking, and John Gonzalez was next.

Chapter Twenty Five

Sandy watched Wiggins gather himself up, look around and then slowly, painfully fold himself into his vehicle and drive away. She waited in the shadows for another thirty minutes, drawing upon the discipline honed by years of studying martial arts. She never moved a muscle as she stood perfectly still, her breathing so shallow as to be nearly imperceptible, her heart rate at 44 bpm. By all measures she was a statue. Finally, she moved stealthfully along the dark recesses of the buildings until she was in the next block. Sandy hailed a cab and ordered the driver to take her to the Palace on Ocean Drive, a bar she had visited occasionally over the past few years when in Miami.

She had a yearning that was consuming her, causing her to begin to lose control, an unacceptable condition for someone like her. She was invincible and knew that Gonzalez and the rest of his trained monkeys couldn't grab their own asses, let alone catch her. She was power and strength, speed and force, cunning and intelligence, beauty and grace. She was death.

Sandy entered the Palace, carefully avoiding light and, instead, choosing shadows. She was stalking prey. The bar was three deep with men and women, pressed together in loud conversation, punctuated with peals of laughter. How she hated these hypocrites, smiling and nodding their heads as they spoke to you and talking about you behind your back. No loyalty, no discipline, overweight, lazy and worthless.

Nicky Bonesso looked up from his martini and was stunned when he saw Sandy Garland standing quietly at the perimeter of the bar crowd. She was tall, drop dead gorgeous and built like the proverbial 'brick house.' The seventies hit "She's a Brick House" by the Commodores clicked and dropped to play in his cerebral juke box. He raised his glass and waved her over to the bar. She noticed the short, balding man as he lifted his pathetic little arm. The audacity of a worm like him to actually think that he could attract someone like her. He had no idea what was in store for him.

Sandy walked slowly toward Nicky, her smile masking the anger that was building in her. He was wearing a rumpled dark sports coat and jeans, with ostrich skin cowboy boots. His thinning black hair was slicked back, ending in a small pony tail. He reminded Sandy of Dustin Hoffman's character, Ratso Rizzo, in *Midnight Cowboy*.

"Hey there, foxy lady, can I buy you a drink?" Nicky asked as he pushed a stool out for her to sit down. Sandy, her smile fading, stared at him. He returned her gaze, but there was something behind the pale blue eyes that disturbed him. Breaking the spell, he swiveled his head and motioned to the bartender.

"What can I get you . . . uh?" he asked, returning his gaze directly into her chest.

"I'm up here, lover, and the name's Jen." Sandy said, pulling his chin up to her eye level with her forefinger. "I'll have a glass of Chardonnay. Make that Iron Horse, if they have it." She made certain that she kept her face away from the bartender, providing only a view of her back.

Nicky ordered for Sandy and then launched into small talk. His harangue about life in Miami, his job as a political consultant, difficulty in meeting quality people, crime in the city and his philosophies of life bored Sandy until she was ready to erupt.

"Look, you're an interesting guy, who seems pretty cool," she said, interrupting his monologue. "How about we go to your place? I am just passing through the city and have a flight to catch tomorrow afternoon."

Nicky reacted as though he just discovered that his five numbers matched the lottery. "Well, hell, babe, let's go. I'm parked right around the corner."

She stayed well into shadows as they walked to his car, a beat down 1995 Subaru with so many scratches and dents that it looked like a fifth place finisher at the Dade County Demolition Derby. The back seat was littered with magazines, hats and empty cans, and he had to move a stack of papers and books to provide her access to the passenger seat.

"Sorry about the mess. I am on the road a lot with my clients during their campaigns, which requires a great deal of travel in Florida."

Sandy was quiet as she stared out the front window. "You know, you fat bitch, that this little bastard spread rumors about you in Edgewood," the soft voice whispered in her mind. "You have to kill him, but make the pain last. You hear me, Glob?"

"I hear you," she said aloud.

"What did you say, babe?" Nicky asked, keeping his eyes glued on the road. With two DWIs on his record, a third one wasn't on his to-do list tonight. Sandy didn't answer and continued her vacant stare.

"I want this fat shit in pieces, just like your fucking drunk of a father who paid the price for sticking his dick in you when he should have been reading you a book. You didn't cut him a break, did you, Glob?" The voice laughed at its own stab at humor. "He deserved it, didn't he?"

"He did, that son of a bitch," Sandy said, her voice beginning to rise. Nicky was now staring at Sandy, clearly alarmed.

"You okay, babe?"

Sandy suddenly trained her eyes on him. "Hurry up and get us to your place, lover boy. I'm going to take you to places you have never been."

Nicky Bonesso, whose life on this planet was going to come to a painful end in a few hours, redoubled his efforts to get to his home in Lauderdale Lakes. As he turned onto West Oakland

Park, Sandy was rubbing her hand lightly over his crotch. He nearly missed his own driveway.

"We're home, Lucy!" Nicky cried, trying to bring a smile to Sandy's face. She was robotic, almost trance-like. "Are you feeling okay?" he said, hoping that now that he was so close to Nirvana, she wasn't going to do something stupid like die on him or slide into a catatonic state.

Nicky guided Sandy through the foyer of his modest house into his living room, which mirrored the interior of his car. Empty pizza boxes, beer cans, newspapers and candy wrappers were strewn about. The place smelled of body odor, sweat and stale beer.

"Nice house . . . what did you say your name was again?" Sandy asked, looking around, disgust souring her expression.

"It's Nick. Most people call me Nicky."

"Well, Jimmy, why don't you and I go somewhere in this place where it's a little less, shall we say, crowded and get comfortable?" Nick wanted to correct her, but decided he didn't give a shit if he was about to bang this fine lady. Call me anything, just don't call me late for pussy, he thought wryly.

"Glob, get a fucking move on with this little prick," the voice said, a little louder. "It's going to be daylight soon, and he's still breathing."

"Alright, okay, give me a few minutes," Sandy replied.

"What did you say, Jen?" Nicky asked, looking at her as they ascended the stairs to his bedroom. Sandy's eyes were glazed, and she looked as though she was drugged, but he hadn't seen her take anything since he had been with her. Christ, he thought, just as I am going to score the piece of ass of a lifetime, she's got to go space cadet on me.

Quicker than Nick Bonesso's addel-pated brain could comprehend, Sandy struck him in the nape of the neck with a knife hand. Darkness instantly enveloped Nicky like a shroud.

*   *   *

Florida morning sunlight illuminated Nicky's bedroom, as he began to regain consciousness. A painfully stiff neck was trumped by a roaring headache, and he twisted his head slightly and saw Sandy Garland sitting across the room, naked. He was stunned by her physical perfection and voluptuous body and tried to rise. He couldn't. To his bewilderment, his hands and feet were tied to the bed. He was struck by the thought that maybe they had played some sort of sexual game and, dumb shit that he was, somehow missed the action because he passed out. But he hadn't had that much to drink at the club, he thought.

Jen looked almost comatose, but she was staring at him. It was then that he noticed the kitchen knife in her hand. It was the razor sharp twelve inch Iron Chef carving knife his mother gave him last Christmas.

"Jen, what's going on?" Nicky asked, his voice quivering. "Untie me, and we can make passionate love," he said, his words ringing hollow.

Sandy rose slowly from the chair. "I've been waiting for you to wake up, Jimmy," she said, her eyes unfocused but burning with intensity. She was perspiring heavily, the droplets shimmering down between her pendulous breasts. Nicky, scared shitless, couldn't believe it. He was getting an erection. Sandy noticed it as well.

"Well, well, sunshine, are we getting a little morning wood?" In one slashing motion she drew the knife across the surface of his penis, cutting only a fraction of an inch into its surface, drawing a small fountain of blood and eliciting a howl from Bonesso.

Sandy reached down by the bed and picked up a roll of duct tape that she had found in his garage and quickly tore a strip, slamming it across Nick's mouth. "You and I are going to have a little fun, and we wouldn't want to be disturbed now would we?"

"Will you get to it, Globo?" the voice screamed in frustration. "Quit fucking around!"

Sandy crawled up onto the bed and straddled Nick's naked body. The blood from his penis was beginning to slow. He was crying now, only emitting a series of soft gasping squeaks beneath the tape. His eye bulged in horror as Sandy leaned in close to him and drew the sharp stainless steel blade up to his face, slowly caressing his cheek with it.

"You were the pig who told those gossiping bastards in Edgewood that I screwed Tom Stanion and that slut cheerleader in the club's pool," she said evenly, without a trace of rancor. "What am I going to do with you, Jimmy? Tsk, tsk."

Nicky yelled, "Whose Jimmy? Where in the hell is Edgewood? Lady, I don't even know you. What the fuck is going on? Are you nuts?" But only muffled gibberish came from behind the tape.

"It's too late now, Jimmy," Sandy said sadly. "The damage has been done and your malicious gossip stripped away my dignity and made me the laughing stock of that fucking little town. And now I am going to strip much more than your dignity from you in repayment. With that, Sandy began to slice into Nick Bonesso's throat to begin the painful flaying of his skin from his body. His agonizing, muted screams couldn't be heard beyond the bedroom, as the delightful sounds of children playing and laughing outside in the courtyard resonated during this warm Saturday morning. It would be hours before Nicky died, as Sandy worked slowly and methodically.

*　　*　　*

Gonzalez pulled up to the front of the Palms Hotel and phoned Sandy's cell to let her know he was outside. Miami was jumping this Saturday night, and the long line of lowriders and customized rods, many with hydraulic suspensions that allowed the drivers to change their cars' height with the flip of a switch, cruised slowly along Ocean Drive. Spectators urged them to let their vehicles 'dance' and many obliged, adding a preprogrammed song played by the horn. Some had colorful rotating lights underneath their chassis, providing a circus-like effect, to the delight of the crowds promenading the strip.

Sandy's cell phone rang five times and her voice said, "You've reached the phone of Sandy Garland. Please leave a message, and I will return your call as soon as possible."

Gonzalez clicked his phone shut and headed for the hotel lobby. The young, attractive woman at the front desk said, "May I help you sir?"

"Yes, would you please ring Ms. Garland's room . . . 560 . . . and tell her John is in the lobby waiting for her."

The young woman walked over to the mail slots and removed an envelope and handed it to Gonzalez. "She checked out this afternoon and instructed me to give this to you when you arrived."

Perplexed, the first thing he thought was that she might have had to return home for a family emergency, but given that she had no family, that didn't make any sense. Possibly Odyssey needed her for a crew out of Miami. He sat down in a leather couch in the lobby's seating area, opened the envelope and unfolded the letter.

> John—I can't believe that you assigned your detectives to follow me last night. Your suspicions are misdirected, and given the relationship we are trying to develop, I am literally shocked that you could stoop that low. I am angry and have decided the best course of action was to fly back to Pittsburgh. I need some time to think, and you need time to examine your heart. If I am a real suspect in those horrible murders you have been investigating, then I will be available for questioning when needed. Nothing more.
>
> Sandy

Gonzalez stared at the letter, trying to organize his thoughts. How in the hell did she know that she was being tailed? Professionals wouldn't have been able to 'make' Wiggins' team, as good as they are at remaining invisible during a tail. He drove home, his mind whirling, his thoughts torn between his growing affection for Sandy Garland and his suspicions that she may somehow be involved in murders that not only have been perpetrated in Miami but in other cities as well.

* * *

Monday morning Wiggins entered Gonzalez's office holding a tablet. He walked slightly hunched forward. "I just got a call from Plantation homicide," he said, wincing slightly.

"What happened to you?" Gonzalez asked, smiling. "Finally got a date with someone who could out-screw you?"

"I wish," Wiggins said. "I got hit from behind by some drunk or druggie as I was getting into my car during the night we tailed Sandy Garland. Never saw the sonofabitch. Took off before I could get up. I'm alright. Listen, there's been a murder over at house in Lauderdale Lakes that you and I had better check out. A political consultant named Nick Bonesso was discovered dead in his bedroom by his sister, who had been trying to reach him for a couple of days."

"Okay, so? Gonzalez responded.

"The guy's entire skin was peeled from his body, and it was hanging above his bed. The homicide guys said they have never in their careers seen anything so horrific. There was blood everywhere in the bedroom, and the kitchen knife that was obviously the murder weapon was wiped clean. There wasn't a trace of anything in the room, except for Bonesso's own prints, his blood and his skin. No footprints, no hair, nada. Whoever did this was one crazy, but careful, mother."

"Ay dios mio," said Gonzalez, crossing himself. "What a way to die, but how does it have a connection to our investigation?"

"The words 'Gonzalez and his squad are next' was written on one of the bedroom walls in his blood," Wiggins said.

Chapter Twenty Six

The crime scene at Nicky Bonesso's Lauderdale Lakes home was in chaos. In addition to Miami PD, homicide detectives and the ME's office, the news media was swarming behind the yellow crime scene tape like a disturbed nest of hornets, buzzing and holding out microphones as officers went by, pleading for a quote. Wiggins and Gonzalez pulled up, stirring up the media who recognized him as the lead in the 'Swinging Sex Murders.'

Beth Adams, an investigative reporter for WTVJ, the NBC affiliate in Miami and a royal pain in Gonzalez's ass since she first joined the station from a small news operation somewhere in East Bum Fuck, Texas. She dogged him on every crime he investigated, none bigger than this string of serial murders.

"Sergeant Gonzalez, is this murder related to the 'Swinging Sex' investigation?" she asked imploringly, stabbing the microphone over the tape into his face.

Gonzalez hesitated for a moment, giving the rest of the swarm time to attack, holding out microphones and tape recorders, like pulsating stingers, trying to hit any target within teach. Camera flashes illuminated the early morning mist, while TV reporters solemnly spoke into their station's cameras, using Nicky's house as a backdrop.

"At this point, we have no information or evidence that this murder is related, but this is an ongoing investigation, and that may change," Gonzalez said, trying to move away from the assembled media.

"Detective Gonzalez, there's a rumor that your name was written on the wall in the victim's blood," shouted Kathy Shields of the Miami Herald. "Was it a threat, Detective?"

"I can't comment on any part of this investigation," he said quickly. "But I will tell you that I am threatened constantly by criminals. It comes with the territory." He joined Wiggins, and together they walked back to the car, while shouted questions rained down upon their backs as they made their exit.

"Detective, the people have a right to know . . . . Can you tell us where . . . What about Nick Bonesso . . ." Their voices faded into the amalgam of ambient noise of police shouting orders, distant sirens and technicians from the Medical Examiner's office scurrying back and forth with forensic equipment.

"You okay, Wigs?" Gonzalez asked, noticing the perspiration dripping down his partner's face, his features distorted in pain as they walked.

"Man, I feel like shit. Vomited my guts out early this morning."

Gonzalez stopped and looked his partner over. "Let's go, I'm taking you to the hospital now."

"No, I'll be okay. This will pass. Probably a stone or something I ate."

"Bullshit, something you ate. I'm taking you over to Florida Medical Center right away, to be safe. Get in, Wigs."

Wiggins slowly and painfully got into the car, as Gonzalez radioed ahead for emergency personnel to be ready. Within ten minutes he pulled into emergency department parking, and they were met by a male and female nurse who helped his partner out of the car and into the ER. A fast track triage system got Wiggins immediately into an examination room, while Gonzalez took a seat in the waiting room. An hour later, a doctor walked into the room and called John's name.

"Right here," Gonzalez said, as he rose to meet the physician.

"I am Doctor Raphael Serebreny," the doctor stated, shaking hands with Gonzalez. "Let's go into the small conference room over there," he said, pointing beyond the administrative desk.

As they entered the room, Gonzalez said, "How's Detective Wiggins? He looked like he was in a lot of pain."

"We have him stabilized, but I'm afraid it doesn't look good." Serebreny said, quietly. "He's suffering from acute renal failure, and from what I can see at this point, it was caused by some sort of traumatic blunt force. His entire system is beginning to shut down. For that reason, I have called a nephrologist, a specialist in kidney disease and injury, to consult. He should be here in twenty minutes."

"Blunt force trauma?" Gonzalez said. "He hasn't been in an accident that I'm aware of . . . . ," his voice trailing off. He recalled his description of being hit from behind in the parking lot near the Cameo Club, after tailing Sandy Garland there. But he described it as no big deal; it just knocked him down. When he quickly got back to his feet, there was no one there.

"Can I see him?" Gonzalez asked the doctor.

"Just for two minutes. We are getting ready to move him to ICU, for continuous monitoring." Serebreny led him to the exam bay, in which Wiggins lay hooked to a monitor and other devices. Wiggins looked groggy.

"Wigs, you'll do anything to get out of work," Gonzalez said lightly, as he grabbed his partner's hand.

"I have no clue as to what the fuck's going on," Wiggins said softly. "All I know is that I feel like I was rode hard and put away wet," he said, smiling weakly. He began to nod off.

Gonzalez left the hospital with a heavy heart. Not only was his long-time partner struggling with life-threatening kidney failure, he had no idea where Sandy was or what state of mind she was in, given the letter she left him. And there was still a serial killer loose in Miami. Could things get any worse? Unfortunately, his years on the force told him that, indeed, they could.

*   *   *

Sandy woke with a start, disoriented. She then realized where she was. She had checked into the seedy Studio 6 Motel in West Palm Beach, in the belief that Gonzalez and his band of incompetents would never guess she would stay at a place like this. Under ordinary circumstances, they would be right. But what she had in mind was nothing that could be remotely described as ordinary.

"Hey, Glob," the voice in the bathroom said sternly. "You've got work to do, so get moving. We're going to throw Gonzalez and his bunch a party they won't forget. Those fuckers are just like the rest of them in Edgewood, a bunch of lying back stabbers, who made your life miserable with their gossip and rumors. It's payback time, and we're going to have some fun."

Sandy stared at her reflection in the cramped bathroom's mirror. She had been neglecting her training, and the junk food she was eating wasn't doing her any good. She looked like shit, she thought. She looked at her watch and saw that it was nearly 6 pm. Time to get moving.

She opened her overnight bag and withdrew the man's wig and clothes. Detective Cutrazulla, I can't wait to get to know you. It didn't take long to find out where you hang out at night, she thought. His favorite watering hole was simply called The Bar, in Coral Gables, not far from where he lived. He would never expect to have become the quarry, and now it's time he atoned for his transgressions.

"You got that right, Glob," the voice said soothingly. "He's way overdue, from that night in the pool when that arrogant bastard and his slut violated you. Now you're going to violate him."

When she was finished dressing, Sandy regarded the man staring at her in the mirror. "I'm a good looking guy," he said, to Sandy's surprise.

"You are a hunk," she replied. "You're me."

"And I'm you," the image said smiling. "Together, we are going to extract payment from these fucks who made our lives a living hell. Now let's get on with it."

Sandy began to gather her keys and wallet. "Come back in here for a second," the voice from the bathroom commanded. She returned to face the image in the mirror.

"What?" she asked the slim, dark haired man facing her.

"You haven't forgotten to pack the 'stars' of our little show that's about to begin have you?" he asked mischievously.

Sandy held up the razor-sharp shurikens, killing stars, and waved them.

"There you go, girl," he said, grinning. "Those will help you make your points with these assholes," he said. As she left the shabby motel room to get into her Ford Focus rental, she could still hear him laughing in the bathroom.

*   *   *

Detective Vincent Cutrazulla, called 'Cut' by his fellow officers, lived alone in a condominium complex on Edgewater Drive in Coral Gables. Divorced for nearly a decade, and with no children, Cut's life revolved around work and his evenings at The Bar, where he and the other locals shared in each other's conviviality, gossip and dirty jokes. This evening was no different, except that he would be making the acquaintance of a fellow named Randy Starr, a good looking but rather effeminate chap who was visiting family in the area. This gentleman would be the last person Cut would ever see in this life.

As Cut approached The Bar's entrance at 8 pm, he heard someone calling to him. "Excuse me, excuse me, sir. Can you give me a quick hand here?"

The hood on Sandy's Ford was up, parked in an alley across from The Bar. Sensing that it was probably broken down, Cut decided to walk across the street to see what he could do to help. As he approached the man leaning over the fender looking into the engine, he said, "You need some help? I am pretty good with . . . ." He never completed his sentence. The man stood up and produced some sort of metal star from his sleeve and with a speed that was nearly imperceptible, threw it underhand at his head. In the fraction of a second it took to bury its sharp points into his forehead, he noticed something remarkably familiar about the man. He had the most pale, crystal blue eyes he had ever seen.

Chapter Twenty Seven

As Gonzalez pulled into the hospital's indoor parking garage, his cell rang.

"Yea,' he said, trying to talk and look for an empty parking spot.

"Sarge, it's Simmons. Cut's dead! He was found in an alley across from The Bar, his local hangout in Coral Gables."

Gonzalez jammed on his brakes, nearly causing an elderly woman in the car behind him to slam into his rear end. "What? How'd it happen . . . . when?" he yelled into the phone.

"A guy walking his dog found him this morning, lying behind some garbage cans. Preliminary examination by the ME said that it looked like he was stabbed with some sort of sharp metal object in the forehead. He estimated the time of death around 8 pm. Hopefully, he'll be able to give us more after the autopsy."

"Christ, first Wigs is attacked, and we have no fucking idea if his illness is related to the murders we're investigating and now Cut. Listen, I'm going into the hospital now. Call the rest of the team. I want a meeting at the precinct in an hour." He snapped his cell shut and thought, is this open season on my squad? Are the hunters now the hunted?

When Gonzalez got up to the ICU, he noticed an inordinate level of activity, nurses rushing through the hallway with a crash cart, a doctor following, When he got to the nurses station, he asked the duty RN what room Detective Wiggins was in. She looked surprised by his question.

"Ah . . . detective, wait right here. Doctors Serebreny and Shevchik are in with him."

"Is he okay?" Gonzalez asked, alarmed.

"One of the doctors will be right with you. Please have a seat in that small waiting area across the hall," she said ignoring his question.

Reluctantly, he did as he was asked. Within twenty minutes, Serebreny entered the room.

"Detective, I have bad news. Detective Wiggins went into cardiac arrest about an hour ago. We did everything we could, but his system shut down completely, and the strain on his heart killed him. I am truly sorry."

Dazed, Gonzalez was having great difficulty processing all the information that he had received this morning. He stood up and thanked the doctor, mumbling, "I'm sure you did everything you could. Thank you."

He took the elevator to the parking garage, trying to make some sense out of everything that had transpired over the previous couple months. He sat in his car and thought. Sandy has disappeared, and that alone is causing him great anguish. Finally admitting it to himself, he realizes that he's deeply in love with her and wants to be with her at this very moment. She would be his anchor in the shit storm that is hitting him and his squad. He needs to tell her that he's sorry that he ever doubted her veracity and just wants her with him.

When he arrived at the precinct, his team was assembled in the large conference room. Simmons was glumly talking to Russo and Keller. Gonzalez couldn't help but think, two down, four to go. The white boards still had photos of the victims adhered to them, notes in black marker scrawled underneath. Gonzalez was struck by the fact that they weren't any closer to catching the killer than they were three months ago.

"Guys, I have bad news. Wigs is dead . . . ."

The assembled detectives began firing questions at once. Gonzalez raised his hands. "Hold on a minute. I don't know shit at this point. I just came from the hospital and was told his heart gave out because his kidneys had shut down. The doctors have no idea what caused it. The only diagnosis one of the docs gave me is that Wigs looked like he had suffered some sort of blunt trauma to one of his kidneys. But as far as Wigs could tell, he didn't have any exterior contusions or evidence of a blow," his voice rising as he completed the sentence.

"Where's Sandy Garland?" Simmons asked.

"She checked out of her hotel and presumably caught a flight out of Miami," Gonzalez explained. "She was pissed at me for assigning a tail on her last week and left me a note indicating her disappointment. But that's my problem. Our problem is that we still have a killer loose in Miami, and we gotta get this carbón now. Okay, Russo and Simmons, I want you to canvas the Cameo in Sobe. Someone had to have seen or heard something. Wigs was hit from behind, but we are not sure at all if that was a contributing factor in his death. Keller and I are paying a visit to The Bar, to question the regulars as to what they might have seen. Cut was a well-known guy there. I can't imagine someone getting to him without being seen. It just doesn't make sense.

"I want you all to watch each other's back. Stay in hourly contact with me and one another. The killer is now stalking us."

*   *   *

The figure staring back at Sandy was pleased. "Glob, you outdid yourself with Cutrazulla. It was a thing of beauty. He didn't have a clue who you were, until he had a shuriken lodged deep in his tiny brain. It was, shall we say, a 'heady experience' for our dearly departed detective." He laughed and leaned closer to her reflection.

"Listen to me carefully. We only have three to go, and then we get to the pièce de résistance . . . . Detective John Gonzalez. Are you ready to do this?"

Sandy stared at the image speaking to her. "I have been preparing for this all my life. It's payback time for all those bastards who made my childhood a living hell. Oh, they will pay."

"That's what I want to hear, dear Glob. I hope you have something extra special in mind for Gonzalez."

"I thought that unfaithful, disloyal prick was in love with me. How in the hell could he suspect me, of all people. I have a special treat in store for him."

"I get hot when you talk like that," said the image. He began caressing Sandy's heaving breasts and her now erect nipples. She pressed tightly against it and felt the initial stirrings of an orgasm.

* * *

Russo and Simmons flashed their shields to the Cameo's burly security guy and were admitted immediately. It was 10 pm and the denizens of the Miami night were just beginning to gather and howl.

"Holy shit, how in the hell can you hear yourself think in this place?" Simmons yelled into Russo's ear. The sound system was roaring like an A 380 Air Bus taking off.

What?" Russo said, bending close to Simmons.

"Forget it. Let's get going." The two detectives began bracing patrons, showing them photos of Wiggins and asking them if they recall seeing him at the club last week. They hit pay dirt on the mezzanine level.

"Yea, I remember dis guy," said a thin, scraggily young man in a nasally New England accent. He began to chuckle, tilting his head toward the photo. "He cat dese two numb nuts running dan dis hallway stakers . . . nayked as jay bads, the guy chasing de broad with his weeny wagging like a windsheld wipa."

"Was he alone?" Russo asked.

"Yea, just him and dose two fuzz balls. Geez. Ya neva seen nuting like it. The guy runs into de broad, and de bath go asses ova tits dawn dem stairs ovea dere." He shook his head and said, "What a caple of fuck wads!'

"Did you see the detective meet anyone here? Simmons asked.

"Nah, I watched him leave abat an hour ago or so. No one with him."

"If you think of anything else, please call us right away," Russo said, proffering his card.

As the two detectives headed for their car, Russo's cell phone buzzed. "Just got a text message," he said, stopping to read it. His face contorted in anger.

"What's up?" asked Simmons.

"Read this," he ordered, handing his cell to him.

Simmons read the words, "Russo and Simmons. Dead Men Walking."

"What the fuck is this?" he asked, staring at Russo.

"Got me, partner. I see the phone number where it came from, but I would bet the phone is stolen. Somebody's being cute. Let's go."

They entered the parking garage on Southwest 22nd Street, and Russo pressed the button for the fourth floor. Both men were silent as the doors opened. Their car was among only two left on the floor. It was nearly midnight.

Suddenly there was a rustling sound behind them, and both detectives reached for their weapons. It was too late. Sandy Garland, wielding a razor sharp samurai sword, decapitated Russo in one swooping arc. Simmons tried to pull his Beretta from his shoulder holster, but her second thrust was pure Kissaki, with overhead power driving down and through his shoulder, which separated from his body. His scream was brief, as Sandy's final cut was Hasuji, a left to right arc that decapitated him as well.

All was quiet once again in the parking garage, the only sound a gurgling as blood spurted and pooled around the bodies. Sandy calmly wiped the blood off her weapon. She returned the two-foot blade to the Koikuchi of its sheath and walked down four flights to street level and around the corner where her rental was parked. It was a lovely, warm Miami evening.

Chapter Twenty Eight

Keller and Gonzalez walked into the dimly lit pub aptly named The Bar. There were a half dozen patrons gathered along the deep cherry wood bar and a few full tables of people having dinner. It was a friendly, local watering hole that reminded Gonzalez of the bar in the series *Cheers*. But there wasn't anything cheerful about their official visit, investigating the circumstances surrounding Detective Cutrazulla's death.

He called the bartender over and showed his shield. "I'm John Gonzalez and this is Detective Keller."

"We were shocked to hear of Cut's murder," the bartender said. 'Everyone loved him."

"Well, somebody didn't love him," Keller said. "We'd like to question your regulars as to what they might have seen or heard."

"No problem. We'll do what we can to help."

As the detectives questioned the patrons, one elderly man recalled seeing a tall, thin man trying to get his car started across the street.

"Did you speak to him?" Gonzalez asked.

"Sure did. I asked him if he needed any help. He looked up from under his hood and said that he didn't. Looked kinda gay to me."

"Did he say anything else?"

"No, but I'll tell you one thing. I remember that he had the palest blue eyes I've ever seen, and there was something about him. It was like he was looking at me, but then again, he really wasn't. It's hard to explain, but you've heard the expression, 'The lights are on, but nobody's home.' That describes what it was like looking into his eyes. Gave me the creepers that one did," he added with a shudder.

Keller jotted notes into his small pocket pad and flipped the lid shut. "Thanks, folks. If anyone recalls any other details of that day, please call the number on the cards we just gave you." As they left The Bar, Keller stopped on the corner to talk.

"Sarge, what do you make of the description of the guy who was broken down? The ice blue eyes?"

"It sounds like a description of Sandy Garland, but this was a guy."

"Think about it," Keller persisted, "the guy was tall and thin, and the man from The Bar he spoke to described him as looking gay. It could have been Garland dressed like a man. Christ, don't tell me we've been chasing our tails, and we should have been zeroing in on her."

"I don't know," Gonzalez hesitated for a moment. "We tailed her and turned up empty. Maybe she isn't the killer we're after. I have to say, there have been a series of coincidences that have cast some suspicion on her."

"Coincidences?" Keller exclaimed. "Sarge, everyone knows you have a thing for her, but with all due respect, we have a job to do, and that's to get this killer off the street and behind bars. If the evidence points in her direction, so be it."

"Okay, I've been trying to reach her, but she's pissed off at me. I would bet the ranch that she's back at work on an Odyssey flight somewhere as we speak." He grabbed his cell and called Avanides' office in Odyssey's human resources department. He wasn't in, but his assistant fielded the call.

"Maybe you can help me. I am detective John Gonzalez here in Miami, Badge number 1662. I am trying to reach one of your senior flight attendants, Sandy Garland. Could you help me locate her?"

"I might ask you the same thing, since you are a detective," said Avanides' administrative assistant wryly. "She hasn't reported for work in several days, and we have had no luck in reaching her. She has never not contacted us if she's ill or taking some time off."

Troubled at this news, Gonzalez asked, "Has anyone gone to her house to check on her?"

"Yes, we contacted the Edgewood Police Department, and two officers were dispatched to her residence, but there was no one there. They looked in the windows, but saw nothing amiss. We have asked the department to get a warrant to enter the house."

"Thanks for the information," Gonzales said. "Here's my cell number to contact me when she's located." Gonzalez shut his cell phone and looked at Keller.

"It looks like she hasn't returned to Pittsburgh," Gonzalez admitted. He opened his phone and began pressing the keyboard.

"What are you doing, Sarge?"

"I am directing communications to issue an ATL on her here in Miami. If she's still in the city, we'll locate her."

* * *

Gonzalez had a restive night, his concerns about Sandy and where she might be was running a continuous loop through his mind. He got up at 5 am and made some coffee. His phone rang. Jesus, he thought, who in the hell's calling at this hour?

"Gonzalez."

"Sarge, it's Keller." He sounded horrible.

"What's wrong, Kels?"

"Sarge, get over to Coral Gables right away! We're in the public parking garage on Southwest 22nd !" He sounded panicky.

"Slow down, Kels. What's wrong?"

"It's a bloodbath here. Russo and Simmons . . . both murdered. Sliced up horribly."

"I'm on my way."

Dashboard light flashing, Gonzalez slammed on his brakes in front of the parking garage and was greeted by a phalanx of emergency vehicles, their lights spraying red glowing gashes across the buildings, as well as over police and ME personnel. Gonzalez ducked under the tape and walked up to Keller.

"Where are they?"

"Fourth floor. I was up there. I've seen about everything over twenty two years and nothing makes me ill. This one did." The two detectives grabbed an elevator, and when the doors opened, Gonzalez was greeted by a scene that only could have been scripted by Quentin Tarantino. It looked like someone had soaked the floor and walls in red paint. There were lengthy blood splatters on the walls, from arterial spurting and high velocity impact. A grim-faced Patricia Solez and her team were still examining body parts. She looked up and saw Gonzalez.

"This is the worst crime scene I've ever seen, and it had to be our guys. I'm sorry, John," she said, shaking her head.

"What do you have so far?" he asked.

"Well, it looks like they were hacked to pieces with a sword. If I had to guess from the precision of the cuts, I'd say it was a samurai sword, made of an extremely sharp carbon steel of some sort. They were clean, and whoever wielded the blade knew what he was doing."

Or knew what *she* was doing, Gonzalez thought. He saw that the various body parts were being photographed and catalogued, trajectories of blood splatter and distances measured and recorded. Some of the parts were being zipped carefully into small vinyl bags for transport to the morgue. He had enough.

When they were back on the street, Gonzalez turned to Keller and said, "For the first time, I think our killer is Sandy Garland. Maybe I didn't want to believe it because I have very deep feelings for her. But her years of martial arts training, her physical conditioning, the freedom of movement her job affords her and her psychological profile combine to possibly paint a portrait of one of the few female serial killers on record who seems to murder for sheer gratification."

"Sarge, we won't have to look for her," Keller said. "She's hunting us."

*   *   *

Sandy unlocked the door to the Studio Six Motel and immediately saw her reflection in the mirror over the dresser. She was covered in blood. She was reminded of the movie *Carrie*, when a bunch of bastards poured a bucket of pig's blood over her at the prom. That dance could have been held at the fucking Edgewood hell hole I attended, she thought.

"Glob, get your perfect ass in here right now," it summoned from the bathroom. She walked in and faced the image. "Holy shit, Glob, it looks like you hit another home run for our team. Either that, or you've been in a food fight at a Heinz Ketchup plant." It laughed uproariously.

Sandy, fatigued, said, "Let's just say that Detectives Simmons and Russo, as others before them, completely lost their heads over me." They both laughed and embraced, ignoring the blood.

Chapter Twenty Nine

Keller was sick to his stomach and completely drained as he made his way up the stairs to his second floor condo on West Broward in Ft. Lauderdale. But no matter how tired he might be, he was on full alert, knowing that Sandy Garland was out there somewhere. For some reason known only to her, she was trying to exterminate the Miami detective unit assigned to the 'Swinging Sex Murders', and she was doing an efficient job. He wasn't about to become her next victim on the list.

As he was unlocking his door, which was dimly illuminated by an overhead yellow bulb, he heard a scrapping noise to his left. Quickly pulling his .45-caliber handgun from his waist holster, he spun and leveled the weapon at a child pushing a buggy containing her baby doll. Unconcerned, she stared up at him.

"Hello," she said. "Would you like to meet my new baby, Molly Megan Sarah?"

Keller slowly raised his weapon in the air and slowly uncocked it, breathing heavily. Holy fuck, he thought. Easy, man, easy!

"I sure would, sweetheart," he said, bending down to see her baby. As he adjusted the blanket to better see the doll, something hard and cold was pressed into the side of his neck.

"Don't move a muscle," the female voice pleasantly. "You wouldn't want your little friend to become covered in your blood, would we? Keep looking at her and begin backing into your apartment, ever so slowly." Looking at the child, she said, "We have to go now, dear, but it was lovely meeting Molly," Sandy Garland said. The little girl regarded them quizzically as they both slowly backed into Keller's apartment.

"Now, carefully pull that handgun of yours from its holster, your hand on the barrel, and drop it in front of you . . . slowly," she instructed. "Before you try anything, let me describe what I am holding up to your throat. It's a nine-inch Tanto blade made of hand forged steel, tempered, oiled and sharpened by a master craftsman in Okinawa. It can literally slice through an ox's spine with a single, effortless Hasuji overhead strike. Imagine what it could do your neck." She was calm and spoke softly as she described the weapon's potential, as if she were giving a demonstration to a class.

Not moving a muscle, Keller said, "Sandy, what are you trying to accomplish by murdering members of our task force? No one has done anything to you."

"That's where you're wrong, Dirk. You lured me to that shitty studio and tried to take advantage of my desire to get a good grade in your class. You actually got me to take my clothes off, you fucking letch. Her voice was rising in anger, and the sharp blade of the Tanto pressed deeper into his throat, drawing a stream of blood.

"Now, we're going to have a little fun, Dirkster. I want you to slowly take those handcuffs you carry on your holster and put them on and lock them," she instructed. Keller began to object, turning his head slightly to look at her. With blinding speed and power, she leg-swept the detective, and he found himself prone with her knees in his back, the Tanto positioned in front of his throat.

"Move again, Dirk, and I'll give you a show that you'll simply 'lose your head' over," she warned. She reached under his sport coat, removed the cuffs and tossed them on the floor. She dragged him by his jacket lapel into an upright position, never allowing the Tanto to stray from its position at his throat.

"Now, put them on one wrist and lock it." He did as instructed. Sandy grabbed the free end of the cuffs and dragged Keller into his bedroom.

"I love your bed, Dirk. You don't see these metal posters every day." She yanked his arm over to the headboard and locked the free handcuff onto a post.

"Why do you keep calling me Dirk? You know who I am. I'm detective Ben Keller, and I work with John Gonzalez . . . ."

She thrust the Tanto deeper into his neck. "Dirk, I would appreciate it greatly if you wouldn't mention that bastard's name in my presence. There is no telling how I might react the next time."

Keller was watching her as she spoke. She didn't look anything like the Sandy Garland he saw in the precinct. Her hair was uncombed, and she wore no makeup. She was wearing a stained men's suit, and her eyes were unfocused and twitching. She looked disoriented, and she had lost weight but still exuded power and speed. What struck Keller most was her sereneness broken only by occasional bursts of temper. Sandy Garland was clearly psychopathic and in no hurry to complete whatever task she had created in her mind.

"Dirk, you had a lot of fun taking photos of me in the nude. I think it's only befitting that I return the favor. Only we're both going to be naked," she said, as she began to remove her clothes. Even though she looked thinner to him, he was astonished at the voluptuousness and sexuality of her body. She was perfect. Save for her mind, he thought.

"Now it's your turn," she said, grinning mischievously. He closed his eyes as she raised the long, sharp blade and began easily slicing through his clothes. Although he now stood stark naked before her, he counted himself fortunate to be alive. At least so far.

"Sandy, you don't have to do this," he said. "I'm not this 'Dirk' you're referring to, and it clearly seems as though you might have a problem."

That stopped her. Drawing up close to him, her large breasts pressed against his bare chest, her lips nearly on his, she whispered, "Problem? What kind of problem do I have, Dirkster? It seems to me as if you're the one with the problem. You think you can talk young girls out of their clothes, just because you teach at a modeling school and have power over them. Well, you fucking creep, I got you out of yours now, and we're going to play a little game."

Sandy pushed Keller flat onto the bed and produced a roll of duct tape from her overnight bag. "This tape is great for a multitude of uses," she said brightly. "Plumbing, construction, packaging, kidnapping, restraint and murder." Humming quietly she taped Keller's free arm to the bed post, then his legs, the gleaming Tanto pressed tightly against his throat, blood continuing to trickle down his chest.

"Have you ever heard of the ancient Asian game called Lingchi?" Keller began to respond, but Sandy slapped a large piece of duct tape across his mouth.

"See, Dirk, it's even useful for stifling bullshit, which is what you are full of!" She looked closely at his eyes. "I knew it," she exclaimed. "Your eyes are brown!"

Keller tried to remain calm, not responding to her threats and insults. She was suffering from a serious psychosis, and anything could set her off.

"Lingchi, my dear Dirkster, is known as 'death by a thousand cuts.' It's very simple. I begin cutting small pieces of your flesh from your arms, then your legs and finally your chest. But that's only the overture to this symphony of pain, Dirk. You, unfortunately, will be conscious as I literally cut you to pieces. Just wait until I get to your groin area. The pain will be exquisite."

Keller displayed no reaction to her ramblings. "Oh, my sweet Dirk, I can't allow you to actually *see* the horrors that are in store for you." She drew the Tanto up to his nose, and before he could even process this information, she cut both of his eyes out of his sockets and flicked them onto the floor. She was correct. Duct tape was a wonder at stifling screams of agony.

*   *   *

Gonzalez got the news that Keller's body was discovered by his girlfriend, who couldn't reach him all day Saturday. Worried, she let herself into his condo with a key that he provided. The scene that greeted her in his bedroom sent her into hysterics, which alerted neighbors, who called paramedics for her. She was sedated and hospitalized and had morphed into a catatonic state. No one from the homicide bureau has been able to question her.

The entire Miami police force was looking for Sandy Garland, including Gonzalez, who was personally checking area hotels and clubs. Not knowing where to turn to get some help, he decided to call Bill Deardon, her karate instructor back in Pittsburgh for some advice.

Deardon picked up on the second ring. "Academy of Isshin-Ryu Karate."

Mr. Deardon, this is Detective John Gonzalez here in Miami. We haven't met, but you spoke to two of my detectives, Cutrazulla and Simmons, a month or so ago."

"Yes, how are those two gentlemen? I enjoyed our conversation."

"Unfortunately, sir, they are both dead, murdered by a serial killer who has been killing people connected to a case we've been investigating. That is, until now. It seems as though this killer is now targeting the homicide task force assigned to the case, and we need to find this individual before there is another murder."

"My God," Deardon said, "that is terrible. But how can I help you?"

"We strongly believe that one of your students, Sandy Garland, is the killer."

There was silence on Deardon's end. "Are you certain, detective?"

"No, I am not . . . . we're not. No one on the force, including an FBI profiler, believed the killings were being perpetrated by a woman. They were too violent, and the killer was using his bare hands, until recently."

"What is he using now?"

"Our ME believes he . . . or she . . . is killing with ceremonial swords and knives. And these murders have been as gruesome as any of us in law enforcement has seen during our collective years on the job, and that's experience tempered by dealing with drug cartels, gang bangers, addicts and other flotsam that wash up onto Miami shores."

"What can I tell you about Sandy Garland that will help you capture her, if she is indeed the killer?"

"Give me a feel for exactly how skilled she is, her approach to the martial arts, interactions with other students, her mental make up? Anything you can give us will be more than we have now."

"Detective, you are dealing with one of the most gifted karateka I've ever had the privilege to train. She has been with me for over a decade and has achieved the rank of Roku Dan, or sixth degree black belt. She is the first woman in the world to ever have reached that level. Her dedication and discipline are beyond that of any student ever at the school, and we have had thousands go through our doors over the years."

"What about her mental approach, and in your estimation does she have the capacity to commit these types of murders?" Gonzalez asked.

"Reluctantly, I must respond in the affirmative to the latter part of your question. Although I was in denial as to her mental stability, she could emphatically have committed those crimes. Although she was aloof and quiet, there was a rage within her that, frankly, scared the other students, including her fellow black belts. No one wanted to spar with her; she was too fast, too powerful and very determined."

"Can you offer an opinion on her psychological makeup?"

"What you may not know, detective, is that Sandy and I traveled together to Okinawa, where our master, Tatsuo Shimabuku, resides, so that we would have the opportunity to learn from the master who created the style. He was very elderly and has since passed away. We spent a few months learning what we could from him, beyond what the Isshin-Ryu books and documents contained. Sandy's behavior during that period and over the subsequent years has become, shall I say, erratic. In my opinion, she seems to be losing the struggle against her inner demons. Taunted and bullied as a child, Sandy, in her mind, is getting even."

"Could Sandy have the capability to strike someone with a delayed punch to the kidneys, which would not kill him immediately, but result in organ failure within a week?"

"You are referring to dim mak," Deardon said. "Considered a myth by Westerners, I can assure you it is not. Sandy spent days working on nothing but this deadly technique when we were in Japan. I am afraid to tell you that she likely has perfected it. A student never knows until the situation would arise to demonstrate it on another human being, but that is out of the question in our society. Hence, it remains a myth."

"Can you offer any advice on how we may capture her?"

"Detective, if Sandy Garland is indeed the killer you seek, you are dealing with a deadly dichotomy. She is a beautiful woman who has the persona to immediately captivate and charm, combined with the physical ability of a highly trained killer. She probably doesn't fully understand these reasons herself. I've suspected some of these qualities in her for years, but hearing what you have to say now confirms my worst fears. The only advice I have to offer is that she has demonstrated a special aptitude for weapons; swords and knives. There has been no one faster or more precise wielding a sword than Sandy Garland. That will create a problem for you."

"Does she have any weaknesses we can exploit, in your opinion, Mr. Deardon?"

There was silence as Deardon considered the question. "The only weakness, and I wouldn't even call it that, is that it is best to agree with her and show her understanding and genuine respect. She seems to react more favorably to people who treat her in that regard. If she is angry or feels as though you have betrayed, embarrassed or harassed her in any way, you will pay a very high price."

Chapter Thirty

Sandy switched to another rental car and cheap motel using a false identity she created with the help of a girlfriend back in Pittsburgh, who when she wasn't developing fake identities for people willing to pay large sums of money, was a master counterfeiter. She was a favorite of the mob, who used her 'funny' money for laundering drug revenues and various other crimes. She was considered the 'Botticelli of bogus bucks.' Sandy got her identity papers by trading sex, a remuneration the gay young lady gladly accepted.

She had one more assignment from the image in the mirror, before she could rest. As she was unpacking her small overnight bag, she heard it.

"Glob, front and center, soldier. We have a lot to talk about."

Sandy walked into the bathroom and looked into the mirror above the sink. It was staring at her.

"You've been a busy girl. And I must commend you on some outstanding work."

"Thank you, I . . ."

"Don't get carried away, Glob," he interrupted. "The tough job is ahead, and that's going to require all the stamina and guile you can muster. Are you with me, soldier?"

She drew herself up to attention. "I am with you. You are me, and I am you."

The image looked closely at her. "God damn, we're one. Ain't that a pisser? We are strength, we are cunning, we are beauty. We are death."

Sandy pressed her lips against the image. "I love you," she said.

"We love us," the image said. "Now get moving. Every fucking police force in South Florida is looking for you. You don't have a lot of time."

Sandy began preparing, checking her weapons, making sure they were oiled and sheathed properly for transport. She carefully opened the ivory box Master Shimabuku gave her nearly a decade ago and withdrew the black cloth garment, mask, cowl and boots, known as the shinobi shōzoku. This was worn by the shinobi no mono, or silent warrior—the Ninja.

Sandy had trained secretly with the Master deep in the jungles of the small island of Okinawa. Unbeknownst to even Sensei Deardon, she learned the secret techniques of Ninjitsu, the unseen assassin. Deep into the night they would discuss the art of silent stealth, climbing and rappelling, hiding, keeping to shadows and other ways of the black warrior. Killing silently. Her training in this style of the martial arts was the most rigorous she ever experienced—conditioning her body to endure cold and heat, sleep deprivation, staying concealed in a small, cramped space, insects crawling over her body, muscles aching, the silence deafening. The only sound, the beating of her heart.

*   *   *

Randall Miles stared across the desk at Gonzalez. "John, Sandy Garland is breaking new ground in the empirical evidence we have on serial killers. At no time in the history of crime has any female killed with the ferocity she has demonstrated, and the sadistic murders are getting worse. She's also taking more chances, as a result of her thinking. I would suggest that her thinking is becoming disorganized, and she may be hearing voices or responding to some demons in her own mind."

"My conversation with her karate instructor, Bill Deardon, did not paint a hopeful picture. In his estimation, she was the most dedicated and committed student he ever had. Her years of training coupled with her possibly worsening psychosis and a sick distortion of her personal reality, makes her extremely dangerous," Gonzalez said.

"That's what's most troubling," said Miles. "If she's responding to hallucinations or voices, she is justifying her actions and believes what she is doing is just and necessary."

"Like Son of Sam," Gonzalez added.

"Precisely, but this woman is not only highly intelligent but as physically trained as any decathlon champion. I would think she's on auto pilot, being driven by her demons and killing for reasons known only to her. Her erratic behavior and willingness to take risks are going to make her difficult to capture without injuring her or those who come into contact with her."

"Every police bureau in South Florida is on the lookout for her. We need a break, a small mistake on her part." Gonzalez stood. "I had better get moving. It looks like she's saving me for her last victim, and I don't want to be a stationary target."

Miles consulted his notebook. "The FBI is monitoring you 24/7, John. We have a surveillance truck stationed near your apartment. I have agents you can't even see tracking you. We even have coordinated air surveillance from helicopters with the latest electronic technology. An agent in the cockpit can hear a conversation on the ground. There is no way she'll get through the layers of defense we've established."

"Thanks, Randy, but I'll feel a whole lot better when we catch Sandy. In her state of mind, there's no way to predict her next move."

Gonzalez left the precinct and drove his unmarked north, keeping in contact with other divisions as he cruised through the City of Miami. It was nearly 9 pm and the streets were thronged with tourists enjoying the warm, pleasant evening and visiting the many restaurants and bars the city had to offer. His emotions were confusing him. On the one hand he was driven to catch

Sandy Garland, and on the other, he was deeply in love with her. These opposing feelings were conflicting, and he only wanted to hold her in his arms once again.

His cell phone vibrated, alerting him that he was receiving a text message. He pulled over to the curb and flipped open the phone.

> John, I love u very much. I only want us to be together.
> Meet me at 11 pm at the Harbor Terminal on Port Blvd.
> Come alone. Will watch for u. Love Sandy

Gonzalez stared at the text. His spirits suddenly were buoyed by the prospect of being with the only woman he really loved, no matter the dire circumstances surrounding a possible reunion. However, he was suspect of her real motives and decided to develop a strategy that protected not only him, but Sandy as well. He placed a call to Joe Handly, a Miami vice detective and a good friend. Handly was a tough cop, a throwback to a time when there were more 'Dirty Harrys' on the force than there were politically correct graduates of the 'Miami Academy of Pussy Police' that was churning out cadets by the hundreds.

Handly served in special ops in Vietnam and was awarded a Silver Star for diverting machine gun fire from a well concealed bunker in a hillside to protect his fellow Marines. As he drew fire, Handly scaled the rocky hillside and got himself above the entrenched enemy nest. As one of the Viet Cong climbed out of the cave, Handly slit his throat and followed that up with a well placed grenade. Gonzalez took a measure of comfort knowing that 'Dirty Harry' Handly had his back.

John Gonzalez was familiar with the Harbor Terminal, a large international operation that imported and exported goods around the world, some of them illegal. Customs and Narcotics were always busy busting Arab, Asian and South American companies trying to smuggle heroin, cocaine and other drugs into the port in containers marked 'Spices' or 'Flour.' The Terminal complex consisted of four large concrete buildings that included expansive warehouses, storage facilities, container facilities and a labyrinth of smaller buildings. It was a perfect place to hide, and Gonzalez knew he needed a guy like Handly to watch his back.

Handly picked up on the second ring. "Hey, Joe. Gonzalez here. I need your help, and I need it quick."

"Hell, John, you don't even need to ask. I assume this concerns the woman that every man, woman and canine officer on the force have been looking for?"

"That's right, Sandy Garland. If what we believe is true, she's killed a dozen people here in Miami and probably more in other cities. She's also murdered the members of my task force, including Cutrazulla, Simmons, Keller, Russo and my partner, Wiggins. And the way she killed them makes the Marquis de Sade look like Mother Teresa."

"Yea, I've heard. I also understand that's she's highly skilled in the martial arts."

"That's correct, Joe. I spoke to her instructor in Pittsburgh, and he divulged some information about her that's going to make catching her extremely difficult, not to mention dangerous. That's why I'd like to have you with me."

"No problem, John. You know I love a good search and capture mission. What else can you tell me?"

"She just sent me a text message telling me to meet her at the Harbor Terminal international shipping complex at the Port of Miami. She's hiding there."

Handly whistled. "She texted you? Why in the hell would she do that?"

"Because we're in love," Gonzalez confessed. "At least I know that I love her and don't want to see any harm come to her. She's sick and needs treatment. I am asking you to use only the force necessary to capture her so that we can get her to a hospital."

"And if I have to protect my own life?" Handly asked.

"Than do what you have to do, of course. I am going to try to talk her into surrendering. I believe she will listen to me. Meet me at the Harbor Terminal at 10:45 pm. We have to make this a covert operation. I don't want her to know that I brought a backup."

"I'll be there, John."

"Oh, and Joe, she's a sixth degree black belt and an expert in the use of swords knives and other Japanese weapons. Be very cautious."

"I think it was the beloved philosopher, Malcom X, who said, 'It's not called 'violence when one kills in self-defense, it's called intelligence.' Don't worry, caution is my middle name."

"Here's a quote for you," Gonzalez countered. "Killing is like changing a tire. The first time you are cautious, the 30th time you forget where you laid the lug wrench."

"Who said that?" Handly asked.

"Ted Bundy."

Chapter Thirty One

Gonzalez arrived at the secluded parking lot across from the Harbor Terminal at 10:25 pm. He came with conflicted thoughts. He and Sandy Garland were in love. He wanted nothing more than to spend the rest of his life with her. But if she was the monster she was being made out to be, he had to protect his men and the community from her. He was bound by his oath to bring her to justice.

Handly was already there. He was dressed in camo, his face blackened and armed with an AK-47, in addition to an S&W 50 caliber handgun on a sling over his shoulder.

"You have some fire power there," Gonzalez remarked as he approached the detective, grabbing his hand. "Thank you my friend, for joining me on this dicey little mission. Looks like you're cocked and locked."

Handly nodded to the massive handgun hanging over his shoulder. "This baby can blow a hole in a tank from over two hundred yards." He opened his utility belt to reveal an assortment of other weapons. "It's that 'caution' thing we were talking about."

"Hands, let me remind you that Sandy Garland and I have been having a relationship," Gonzalez said. "That's a fact that's pretty well known throughout the bureau. My main concern for this meeting tonight is to try and talk her into surrendering and getting the medical help that she needs. She's a beautiful, intelligent woman, but possibly a sick, dangerous woman. She has allegedly killed more than a dozen people here in Miami, including five of our fellow officers. I don't want either of us to take any extraordinary risks while we try to talk her to giving up."

"John, what's your take on why she wants this meeting?" Handly asked. "Do you think you're the final target on her list?"

"I don't know what's in her mind at this point. I do know that's she's a highly skilled hand-to-hand fighter, fast, accurate and deadly. And now the fact that she may be using weapons, Japanese swords and knives, significantly changes the complexion of what we're dealing with."

"Okay, what's the plan?"

"First, I'm going to text her that I'm here alone to meet her. I want her to give me a location in this complex to do that. I will pass that information onto you. I want you to slowly and carefully make your way to that area, but you must stay well hidden. If I would need help, you'll know it." As he was taking, Gonzalez was writing a text message. "Here we go, Hands. God be with all of us tonight." He pressed 'send.'

Both officers stood quietly and waited. Suddenly his phone vibrated with her response.

> John, building number four has a side door that I left open for u. This warehouse is used for storage. I am at the lowest level, where this company stores what looks like chemicals. Take the second bank of elevators. I'll be waiting for u. Sandy

Gonzalez looked up at Handly and then showed him the message. "I'm on my way," he said, checking his Glock's ammo. It was a warm, balmy night in Miami, the full moon illuminating the empty parking lot of the terminal. The winds off the harbor were calm and the silence was palpable. It was at least a mile walk through the complex to building four.

"Give me a two minute start," Gonzalez said. He began walking. Within twenty minutes he was facing a side door that had been jimmied open and left slightly ajar. He could sense Handly's presence out in the shadows as he slowly opened the door, his Glock out and at his side, a bullet loaded into the chamber of his automatic weapon.

Handly, deep in the dark recesses of building three, watched Gonzalez intently with night vision binoculars as he entered four, his AK-47 trained on the doorway. He was preparing to move to stay in visual contact and proximity to him, when he heard a faint rustling behind him. He froze. He began to pivot with his weapon in the direction of the sound, when Sandy silently appeared behind him. With the speed and ferocity only achievable from years of training, she grabbed his hair, yanked his head backward and slit his throat in a single motion. Handly went down, his gurgling death throes and convulsions undetectable from more than a few yards away. Sandy moved silently on toward building four.

Gonzalez found himself in a hallway with windows along each wall looking into offices, which were most likely for accounting, dispatching and other administrative activities. Desks were cluttered with papers and desktop computers. All was silent and dark, a tiny bit of illumination filtering through a few small windows facing out into the parking lot.

Sandy watched Gonzalez tentatively walk through the entrance hall to building four. She was kneeling atop stacked cartons in the first storage facility and was completely undetectable in the dark shadows. Her breathing was shallow and not a muscle quivered. She held a tanto blade, her sword sheathed behind her. Completely in black, the cowl on her head was drawn tight, allowing only a slit for her ice blue eyes. As Gonzalez moved through a small patch of light from an outside window she saw the Glock in his hand.

Soundlessly, Sandy climbed down from her vantage point atop the cartons and moved toward Gonzalez. The door to the first warehouse opened and he slowly entered, Glock first. The warehouse, with no outside windows, was completely dark. He produced a flashlight, its narrow beam penetrating the blackness.

He slowly began moving the shaft of light over different quadrants of the warehouse to get a sense of his surroundings. Sandy made her move, emitting a deep guttural yell that shattered the silence, causing Gonzalez to freeze for a split second. That's all the time she needed.

"Hi-yah," she screamed and struck Gonzalez from behind with a sai, a truncheon used in feudal times by farmers in Okinawa, which subsequently became weapons of self-defense against marauding rogue samurai. Gonzalez dropped his Glock and went to his knees, but a man as large and powerful as he was doesn't go down easily. He quickly stood with his weapon moving in a circle, but all was silent once again. Like a wisp of smoke, she had evaporated. His neck ached from the blow, and he wondered why she didn't use a sword.

"Sandy, I have come for you. I know you are watching me," he said as he rubbed the back of his neck with his free hand. "Please, drop your weapons and walk toward me. I want to get you the help you need. I love you and don't want to see you injured."

There was no response. Gonzalez had lost the flashlight and in the darkness, couldn't locate it. He tried moving his foot slowly to try and touch it, to no avail. He was alone with Sandy Garland. He reached into his pocket for his cell and reluctantly called Handly. He could hear a cell phone ringing faintly in the darkness of the warehouse. Suddenly, the phone came crashing down in pieces at his feet.

"John, are you by any chance looking for your friend?" Sandy yelled from the shadows. "He's permanently indisposed. He called in sick with a sore throat."

Gonzalez grabbed for his cell phone and dialed 911. "This is Detective John Gonzalez. There is an officer down, and I'm in the first warehouse in building four of the Harbor Terminal. I need an ambulance and a SWAT unit back up stat. Suspected serial killer Sandy Garland is cornered in this building. Detective Handly is probably severely wounded and outside the building." Wounded or worse, he thought.

"Sandy, I didn't want to do it, but I've called for the cavalry," he yelled into the darkness. "They'll be here any minute. Please give yourself up now." As he took a step forward, his toe bumped the flashlight. Grabbing it, he turned it on and managed to illuminate a black clad figure running into the next warehouse. He followed.

He shined his light on the sign above the doorway, which read, 'Industrial Chemicals. Danger—Highly Explosive' He saw stored barrels and tanks of chemicals with names like Acetone Peroxide, Nitrogen Triiodide and Sodium Azide printed on the sides. He had no idea what they were used for, but figured from the sign that they were highly flammable.

"Sandy, this is not a good place for either of us to be," he yelled. "The signs indicate that these chemicals are volatile and highly flammable. For your sake . . . and mine . . . . please drop your weapons and come down to me. Sandy, I love you very much. Let's go back together."

He heard the wail of sirens in the distance and knew she didn't have much longer until a SWAT unit would descend. He continued walking deeper into the chemical storage facility.

"Sandy, a SWAT team with snipers will be here in minutes. Please come to me and let me hold you." That's when he heard the door to the office area where he had entered the building burst open and running feet. He bolted deeper into the darkness, following only a slim beam of light. He had to reach her before it was too late. The footsteps became louder, and he heard someone softly giving orders, as they approached the chemicals storage facility where they were.

"Spread along the perimeter and stay in visual contact." The were equipped with night vision goggles and automatic weapons. They, too, were clad in black with 'MIAMI PD SWAT UNIT' in large gold letters on their backs.

"Johnson, you and Hicks come with me. I want you each to take a side of this warehouse up on that catwalk," he motioned with his light, "and then report when you're in position," he said quietly to the two snipers.

Gonzalez kept moving toward where he believed Sandy was retreating. As he lifted his flashlight, he suddenly saw her. She was standing, waiting for him, the weapons lay on the ground around her. She was crying.

"John, oh John, I can't harm you. I love you," she cried as she moved toward him. They embraced and kissed.

The directive from the officer leading the SWAT unit echoed off the walls loud and clear as he spoke through a bullhorn. "Sandy Garland, this is Captain Hugh Burson of the Miami Police. Our SWAT unit has this terminal completely surrounded. You have nowhere to go. Drop your weapons, put your hands behind your head, fingers interlaced, and walk backward slowly toward the light I am holding."

Captain Burson's large spotlight illuminated a path for her to follow, as she was ordered to walk toward them. Red dots from the laser scopes that surrounded her were jumping back and forth across her chest and forehead, like a video game.

The sniper named Johnson was uncharacteristically nervous, having heard rumors of some of the atrocities the suspect performed on his fellow officers. He was perched on a metal grated catwalk above the warehouse, the night scope on his Remington 700 rifle aimed at the end of the captain's beam of light, his scope training one of the red dots across her body. Perspiration was beading on his forehead and dripping into his eyes, creating a burning sensation. He kept trying to keep it out of his eyes, while maintaining his aim.

Suddenly Johnson thought he saw Sandy reach behind her, his reflex reaction jerking the trigger, which was set for very slight pressure. His movement pulled the rifle off target and it fired. The errant bullet missed the target and pierced a tank container of Carbon Disulfide. The explosion caused a chain reaction detonating other chemicals in the warehouse, generating a blinding fireball hundreds of feet in the air. The giant fireball could be seen for miles, illuminating the Miami skyline in its orange light, the thunderous explosion shaking houses and buildings in a fifteen mile radius like a magnitude five earthquake.

*   *   *

The printed title below the woman staring somberly into the camera read "Beth Adams, Investigative Reporter." The WTVJ TV Miami logo was displayed prominently in the corner of the screen.

"A horrendous explosion at the Harbor Terminal complex late last night claimed the lives of more than two dozen members of a Miami Police Department SWAT team. Among those thought to have perished in the explosion were Captain Hugh Burson and Detective John Gonzalez," she read from the teleprompter. "Another detective, Joseph Handly, was found murdered outside of the complex. Also presumed dead is alleged murder suspect Sandy Garland, the object of an investigation into the so-called 'Swinging Sex Murders.' Garland, a flight attendant for Odyssey Airlines, was wanted for questioning.

"It is speculated that an errant bullet from one of the SWAT members ignited the highly explosive industrial chemicals stored there, and the massive chain reaction completely incinerated the building and all of those in it, making the identification of the bodies impossible.

"Sandy Garland was the prime suspect in the series of violent murders committed here in Miami as well as in Philadelphia and Chicago. Highly trained in karate, Garland is suspected of killing five Miami detectives assigned to a task force to locate the killer."

"Hey, Gary," yelled medical examiner Patricia Solez to the bartender at the Transit Lounge. "Turn off the TV will you. It's fucking depressing enough to have to slice and dice stiffs everyday, but to sit there and listen to how your colleagues and friends were incinerated is beyond the call of duty."

The bartender pointed the remote at the flat screen hanging above the bar and changed the channel to ESPN.

"That's much better." She said, rolling her eyes. "Now we can watch hockey players crush each other's skulls with sticks," Solez said to no one in particular. Her assistant Bobby Fong, nursing a beer next to her, laughed at the remark. It was accompanied by a snort.

EPILOGUE

Okinawa Prefecture
Japan
2010

The heavy, oak door to the dojo slowly opened and the tall American brunette named Susan Srellik entered, carrying her gi with a black belt wrapped around it. The Isshin school of martial arts, nestled in Yomitan Village, in a remote jungle setting on Okinawa's mainland, was one of four traditional styles taught in this modest setting. Thousands of devout karateka from around the world regarded Yomitan as the mecca of Japanese karate and visited Okinawa for months at a time to study traditional systems of Uechi, Goju, Isshin and Shorin taught by descendents of the masters.

The small class was stretching as the students prepared for what they knew would be a bruising workout. The tropical heat index was beginning to soar as the sun rose like a glowing ball of fire, slowly lifting off the horizon of the Pacific Ocean. It would reach one hundred and five degrees in an hour, and the class would find it difficult to breath in the dojo. Their white gis would quickly be soaked in perspiration, and their quads and glutes would scream in protest as they were led through hundreds of kicks, punches and blocks. But the American woman leading the class this day looked unaffected by temperature, pain or fatigue, perfectly comfortable, totally aerobic. She was a machine.

After thirty minutes of warm up exercises, the class broke into groups. The American, who towered above the diminutive Japanese students, went off by herself to an empty mirrored room to perform her advanced kata followed by heavy bag work. Master Kichero Shimabuku, the son of the founder of Isshin-Ryu, entered. The American immediately stopped her exercise and bowed deeply and respectfully to the Master.

"You honor me, Sensei, with your presence," she said, keeping her eyes down, staring at the ground in front of her. Although Kichero had never met this deeply dedicated student until she located permanently to the island, her unwavering dedication to Isshin-Ryu was unmatched by any other student, past or present. Gloria quickly became his favored black belt, the one he designated most often to lead the class, considered a great honor. The other Japanese students were angry at her intrusion into their world, but their sense of honor and decorum would never allow them to exhibit any outward signs of discontent. Master Kichero cared little for petty jealousies and internal intrigue in his dojo, and he regarded their idle chatter as envy by those who couldn't match her speed, power and commitment to the art.

"Ohayou, Missa Srellik," Kichero said politely in his accented English, bowing. His voice was deep and his speech guttural. He had been living in the United States until his father, Tatsuo, died. He returned to Okinawa to assume leadership of the Worldwide Isshin-Ryu Confederation and was pleasantly surprised at the number of karateka from around the world who made the pilgrimage to Yomitan. And the most outstanding student was this American who moved permanently to the island with her husband, a very tall, handsome olive skinned man with black curly hair and dark brown eyes. This muscular man was quiet and kept his own counsel. He had taken a post in security at a large Chevron refinery outside of Naha. The Srelliks purchased a traditional Japanese residence in Kurihara, in the northern prefecture of Okinawa, which afforded a breathtaking view of the ocean.

"Hai, haf you hea'd abod all duh mudders in Naha?"

"No, I haven't, Sensei. My husband, Bill, and I try to avoid reading or seeing anything violent. This island is heaven and we believe its serenity . . . its *wa* . . . should not under any circumstances be disturbed by violence."

"Hai," Kichero agreed, emphasized by short nod of his head. The city had been experiencing a series of horrible murders that were being perpetrated by someone using his bare hands, frightening residents and baffling police. These crimes were distinct from the usual shootings and stabbings committed by a few of the forty thousand American military personnel still living on the island. These atrocities were committed by someone who was clearly psychotic.

Kichero bowed once again. "Onegai, solay to disturb training . . . and wa. Prease continue," he said with a slight wave of his arm. The Master left the tiny bag room to speak to some of the other students. But the attractive brunette stayed in his mind. She has an athlete's toned body, with the voluptuous curves and looks of a super model. But her most striking feature are her eyes. They are the palest, light blue eyes he has ever seen. Like ice.

Edwards Brothers, Inc.
Thorofare, NJ USA
November 22, 2011